MANNY SOS

Manny SOS: Book One
By Andi Lee

ROGUE FIREBIRD
PRESS

Dedication

To The Five, you know who you are. Love you all heaps.

Acknowledgements

To Tammy, for knowing when to give a gentle nudge or a swift kick up the arse. I admit, I generally need a swift kick more often than a gentle nudge! Thanks for all your help!

CHAPTER ONE

AIDEN

THE CLUB WAS now called Sparkle. Aiden remembered when it used to be Thrust, and he'd spent every weekend there dancing and picking up hot guys. He didn't know why he'd come here of all places tonight. Perhaps he was trying to relive his glory days.

Once upon a time, this kind of place was Aiden's stomping ground. He'd felt powerful, happy—on top of the world from the moment he entered through the double doors to the moment he left. His good looks had gone a long way, and he'd used them. It hadn't mattered that he'd had no money or was in a dead-end job. No one cared about that when they were only after one thing.

But the feeling of invincibility he used to have was long gone. The flashing lights highlighted tanned and glittery skin all around him, and instead of admiring how it accentuated the best part of a man's form, it gave him a headache. He was too old for this. Was forty-two old? When he'd been twenty, he'd thought so.

How long had it been since he'd come to a club? Once with his ex when the kids had been babies? A few times with his friend Nio, but that had been years ago.

His hair was threaded with grey now, the scruff he could never be bothered to shave properly more silver than brown, and there were more lines at the corners of his eyes that made it impossible for him to look younger than his years. He didn't want to be one of those creepy old guys who drooled over twinks barely old enough to drink, yet that was what he felt like.

His jaw cracked as he tried to swallow a yawn. He was exhausted. The boys were having a sleepover at Nio's, so he could, as Nio put it, "have grown-up time." He'd much rather have a nap than be in a club blaring out music he didn't recognize and where the clientele only looked ten years older than his own kids, but there was no dissuading Nio when he had an idea.

Aiden had been blocking the doorway, and a man bumped into him from behind. His apology was automatic, but the stranger had already danced around him and been swallowed up by the crowd.

Aiden straightened his spine and walked to the bar to order a drink. Something strong to dull the voice that told him he wasn't supposed to be there, and then something he could hold in his hand and give him something to do while he tried not to seem out of place.

He knocked the shot back, hoping it would help him relax, and then propped himself up next to a rickety table overlooking the dance floor as he nursed his beer.

He used to be fearless. Now he was a little older, not a lot wiser, not as toned as he used to be, and couldn't even remember if he'd brushed his hair that day. That was the life of a single parent. Sometimes he cursed his ex for leaving and making him do this alone. It wasn't as if he was qualified to parent either. They'd read the same books, gone to the same classes, but Wyatt had left and only came back long enough to confuse the kids and leave a sour taste in Aiden's mouth.

Enough of that! He was here to have fun, not be maudlin and think about the past. He took a deep breath and rolled his shoulders, attempting to relax and at least appear as though he was having a good time. Mostly, he tried not to look old—or creepy—as the club filled with people.

Once he'd finished his beer, he'd dance. Then he could tell Nio he'd partied without lying—because Nio would ask for details, and Aiden wouldn't be able to lie to him—and if he didn't at least dance, he'd never hear the end of it. When Nio got an idea in his head, it was just easier to go along with it because he was like a dog with a bone.

When Aiden reached the bottom of his glass, he still didn't want to dance. Perhaps another drink would help? After all, he hadn't danced to anything but The Wiggles in years. He'd undoubtedly lost his moves.

The area around the bar was packed now, so he found a section that looked the least busy and got in line to wait his turn. At least it gave him something to do. A man stopped beside him and smiled at him in solidarity; Aiden felt his heart skip a beat as their eyes met.

He was gorgeous—cute. Not like the show-offs on the dance floor wearing skimpy clothing and thrusting their hips to the beat. He was real. Lithe, a little taller and younger than Aiden, but not young enough to be child bait. His thick brown hair was longer on top and brushed back off his forehead. There were faint laughter lines around his clear blue eyes, and his lips were full and bow-shaped.

Aiden looked back towards the front of the queue, but he couldn't stop glancing at him from the corner of his eye. He wore a simple slim-fitted grey shirt that showed a hint of the firm body beneath, and his dark blue jeans were so tight they left little to the imagination.

Should he smile? Say hello? Damn, he was rusty. Aiden groaned, thankful that the music was so loud no one could hear him. It had been too long since he'd looked at another man. Not because he was still pining after his ex—God, no. Because he was busy with work and trying to wrangle his kids, there simply hadn't been time to date, hook up, or do anything NC-17

The queue at the bar moved. People jostled against each other as those loaded with drinks pushed their way out and others joined the back of the queue. Aiden couldn't help but glance at him again.

He was staring blatantly right at Aiden. His eyes crinkled as he smiled, and Aiden stopped pretending he wasn't looking back and turned to face him, awareness crackling between them. A hand briefly touched his arm, and he shivered as the cutie leaned toward him.

His breath tickled the shell of Aiden's ear moments before he heard the confident drawl of his voice. "Shall we make a deal? If I get to the bar first, I'll buy us a drink. If you do, you buy."

His words blocked out the music and the chatter around them, and Aiden forgot how to speak. He frowned when the cutie straightened up and moved a fraction away from him. He used to be smoother than this.

"Deal." Aiden held out his hand, and the cutie took it, the shake firm, his thumb caressing the back of Aiden's hand before pulling away and looking back towards the bar. Aiden did the same, body hyper-aware of the man next to him as his eyes scanned for a gap in the crowd.

"What are you drinking?" Aiden said loudly, realizing they'd never exchanged drink preferences.

"Jack Daniels and Coke. You?"

"A pint of lager," Aiden replied.

CHAPTER TWO

CARTER

CARTER STOOD CLOSE to his hot new queue-mate as they closed in on the bar. For once, he wasn't in any real hurry to get a drink. Each time they were jostled, it was an excuse to stumble into him, and Carter used it to his advantage.

He didn't go clubbing often, he was busy with work and family, but sometimes he needed to let his hair down, especially when they finished shooting. Tonight was one of those nights. Dance, have a few drinks, and hit on an attractive man. Check.

He sent the guy—correction, the *hot* guy—a wide grin when a spot opened and went for it. Twisting his body like a gymnast, Carter skirted around torsos and elbows to get to the front, triumphant when his hand grasped the edge of the sticky bar. The barman gave him a thumbs-up as he took their drink order, but Carter didn't flirt with him like he would have in the past. He had someone he was much more interested in waiting for him.

Someone who was right behind him now, so close the heat radiated off him. He twisted around with both drinks and almost tipped Hot Guy's beer down his shirt—which wouldn't have been entirely terrible. The wet fabric would probably cling to his firm chest in the best possible way.

"Here you go." As he passed the glass over, their hands

brushed, and Carter swallowed, mouth becoming dry when Hot Guy leaned in so close that his mouth brushed the shell of his ear. "I'm impressed at your ability to sidle into the tightest of gaps."

"It's a talent of mine," Carter replied.

People shoved them in their hurry to get to the bar, and Hot Guy stumbled into him. Carter grabbed hold of his upper arm, but not quickly enough to prevent the delicious scrape of stubble against his cheek.

"Sorry," Hot Guy said.

"Don't be," Carter replied, his hand running up and down Hot Guy's arm, feeling the flex of muscle beneath. "Come on, let's get away from the bar."

He scanned the club for a quieter spot, his grip tightening on Hot Guy's arm as he steered them out of the sea of people waiting for drinks and into a darkened corner where they'd have a little privacy.

The music was a touch quieter, and they weren't getting bumped into quite so often. Carter lounged back against the wall, and Hot Guy leaned in next to him. It would be so easy to close the gap between them and capture those lips with his own, but Carter didn't want to rush this.

They talked for a while, but Carter didn't take much notice of the words. No one paid attention to the chit-chat that came before making out at a club—it was pre-foreplay, everyone knew that— but he really enjoyed watching Hot Guy's mouth move as he spoke.

"This is my first time here. It's interesting," Carter said and glanced up at the hundreds of disco balls above them, then down at the floor that glittered under their feet.

"I remember when it used to be called Thrust—does that make me old?" Hot Guy's eyes sparkled when he smiled— though it could just be the amount of glitter everywhere.

Carter laughed but shook his head. If Hot Guy was considered old, then he aged like fine wine. "Not. At. All." Carter shifted closer with each word. He was getting bored of just talking. He slipped his arm around Hot Guy's waist and rolled his hips against his thigh, driving home his point. "Although Thrust is a much better name."

Hot Guy groaned and gripped Carter's thighs, urging him on. Heat pooled low in his belly. The song playing in the background changed, and the beat turned to something fast and sexy, making his heart skip in time to it.

"Dance with me?" Carter asked.

"Over there?"

He looked over his shoulder at the dance floor and all the men on it. Some were wrapped around each other, ignoring the music. Others were dancing crazily, going from one man to the next. Carter shuddered as he imagined being out there, how men would try to join in, to pull them away from each other, and how he would ignore them all in favor of the guy in front of him.

Carter took his hand, the calluses on his palm pooling heat deep in his stomach, and pulled him away from the wall. "Yes, over there." He took Aiden's bottle from him and abandoned their drinks on a table as they passed by.

When they reached the dance floor, Carter threw his arms around Hot Guy's neck. His hips rocked with the rhythm of the music, dancing closer with each beat until he felt Hot Guy's erection brush against his own with each teasing movement.

Hot Guy groaned, a low rumble in his chest that vibrated through Carter's body and made his knees weak. As if he knew Carter was having trouble standing, Hot Guy's hands slipped around his waist, fingers spreading out over his back until their chests were pressed tightly together.

As predicted, gorgeous men danced around them. Some tried to sidle between them, another grabbed Hot Guy's shoulders and tried to peel him away, but neither of them was having it. The work-roughened hands on his back locked in place around him, and Carter smirked at every man who tried to take his place until they eventually faded into the background. They could look but not touch.

He pressed his cheek to Hot Guy's and caressed the soft hairs on the back of his neck as they swayed in the sea of people. Those strong hands roamed his back, followed his spine down to his ass, and massaged each globe. Their erections pressed together, the friction making him harder with each thrust of hips against his. Carter gasped at the small movement, fire shooting through his veins.

He tipped his head back enough to look into Hot Guy's eyes. What he saw there made him forget how to breathe. He wet his lips with his tongue, teasing his bottom lip with his teeth, enjoying how Hot Guy's eyes were drawn to the movement. The hand he had on Carter's ass slid up his back, tangled in his hair, and pulled him into a kiss that showed no hesitation.

Finally.

The air crackled around them as Hot Guy nipped at his lips and licked a pathway into his mouth. Carter's eyes fluttered closed as their tongues tangled. He tasted of beer and mint— Carter couldn't get enough of it, and within seconds he'd taken over the kiss.

He swallowed Hot Guy's groan, and the hand still in his hair tilted his head to the side to deepen the kiss and give him better access. Carter's heart hammered in his chest, and his cock was painfully hard in the confines of his jeans.

He could hear the electronic beat of the music, the jeers of men surrounding them, and feel the occasional bump as others danced too close, but nothing could tear him away from those lips and that tongue as it teased his.

Jesus, if he kissed like this, what did he fuck like?

Carter's body was wound tight. He needed more. A kiss, no matter how amazing, wasn't enough. He'd known that from the moment he'd set eyes on him, but he'd fooled himself into thinking a sexy dance and make-out session would do.

But no matter how tempting it was to find an empty stall and do more than kiss, Carter was too old for trysts in the bathroom— and his job was much too public.

When they both had to pull away to breathe, he placed a hand on Hot Guy's cheek, thumb pressed into the corner of his swollen mouth. "Come back to my hotel room."

The need to see him completely naked and map every inch of skin with his tongue was so strong he felt like a coiled spring ready to shoot as Hot Guy's eyes roamed over his face. Butterflies danced in Carter's stomach, nerves and excitement bumping together until he wasn't sure what he was feeling. He just knew he'd have a serious case of blue balls if the guy said no. He hadn't wanted a man as much as this in years.

"If we go now, we won't even have to wait for a taxi." *Please say yes*, Carter added silently. His heartbeat sped up as he waited for an answer.

"Let's go."

He let out a breath of relief. Carter slid his hand down his arm, caressing his firm biceps, and then clasped his hand loosely as they weaved in and out of people mingling on their way to the exit.

MANNY SOS

CHAPTER THREE

AIDEN

HE WAS NERVOUS. How ridiculous was that? He was so rusty when it came to picking up men that he didn't know what the hell he was doing. Though technically, the cutie had picked him up and not the other way around.

Said cutie turned on the lamp next to the bed, a soft glow surrounding him like a halo. He raked his hands through his hair, messing up his perfect quiff. Aiden's fingers itched to touch those soft strands again, but his feet were glued to the generic hotel carpet. He was on edge—he just wasn't sure what edge.

As if he could see the indecision play over his face, Cutie walked over and clasped Aiden's cheeks with both hands and, without a word, steered their mouths into a surprisingly tender kiss that quelled the butterflies in his belly. While they kissed, his clever hands skimmed over Aiden's jaw, down his neck, arms, and finally gripped the waistband of his jeans, pulling their groins together.

Aiden gasped into his mouth, and his whole body relaxed into the kiss, tension dissipating with each stroke of his tongue. He cupped the cutie's jaw, then slid his hand upwards, fingers threading through his thick, soft hair. He'd wanted to do that desperately, and now Aiden couldn't get enough of it. He tangled his fingers in the silky locks and held on tight.

As the kiss deepened, the cutie unbuttoned his own shirt and yanked it down his arms, letting it fall to the floor at their feet. Aiden's hands slid out of his hair, skimmed down his neck, and explored the expanse of his bare back.

Cutie whimpered into Aiden's mouth and clutched the hem of Aiden's T-shirt, trying to yank it up and over his head without breaking from the kiss. The fabric lay tangled around his neck while they kissed and explored each other.

When they finally broke for air, Aiden pulled his T-shirt the rest of the way off. Cutie was lean—lithe like a swimmer, with only a spattering of hair over his chest and a happy trail beneath his belly button that led to his denim-covered erection. Aiden was stockier, muscled from working construction, but they fit perfectly together.

Aiden's heart hammered in his chest, and his cock strained against his jeans as he slid his arms around him and brought their bare chests together. Then he smiled, a wicked curve of his mouth that went right to Aiden's cock, and wrapped his arms around Aiden's shoulders. Before he knew what was happening, they were tumbling backward onto the bed.

A breathless laugh fell out of Aiden's mouth, and he settled back against the pillows as the cutie threw a leg over his hips and settled on top of him, grinding his ass purposefully against Aiden's erection.

Aiden hissed and bucked up into it, his hands grabbing the cutie's thighs to control his movements. It didn't work. He continued to tease him until Aiden couldn't see straight, exploring his chest with light touches and the scrape of nails that sent goosebumps down his arms and even made his toes curl.

Aiden's back arched with each touch, but it wasn't enough. Desperate for friction, he thrust up against the ass nestled into his groin. He wished they'd taken the time to remove their jeans. That was easily remedied, though. Threading an arm around Cutie's waist, Aiden pushed himself up on one hand, rolled them over, and pressed him to the bed with his whole body.

Cutie practically purred and wrapped his legs around Aiden's waist. Heart hammering against his ribcage as they kissed and rubbed against each other, Aiden slipped a hand between them and managed to undo the zipper enough for him to shove his hand inside and finally feel the hard flesh that had teased him on the dancefloor.

The cutie tipped his head back with a gasp, breaking their kiss, and Aiden watched the lust play over his face as he gripped his erection. There wasn't enough room to do more than explore the hot, hard flesh, but he did his best, watching that handsome face, learning what drove him mad.

Aiden swiped a callused finger over his tip, and he writhed, heels digging into the mattress. His pupils were blown, his lips wet and kissable. Aiden leaned over him and did just that. It was an awkward position, his hand still in Cutie's open jeans, so with one last lick of his lips, he pulled away, eliciting a whine from the man beneath him, then started to push his own jeans down over his hips. Realizing what he was doing, Cutie pushed his hips up and shoved his jeans and underwear down, his cock springing free.

Aiden practically fell on top of him, pressing their bodies together until their cocks nestled so close that they both gasped as they touched. He shuddered, closed his eyes, and pressed his face into Cutie's neck, the scent of his spicy cologne and sweat tingling his senses. It had been so long since he'd had sex, since he'd been attracted to someone enough to act on it.

He heard the slide of a drawer, felt the body beneath his shift, and he turned his head sideways and watched the cutie fumble for a condom out of the bedside cabinet.

"Fuck me," he whispered into Aiden's ear, making his cock jump. He pressed a kiss to the cutie's shoulder, nipping the sensitive skin, and swiped the condom as he sat up, holding it in his palm as he took in his fill of the man beneath him.

"Lube?" he asked, and Cutie muttered under his breath and

dragged open the drawer again, practically throwing a packet of lube at his head. It bounced off Aiden's chest and made him smirk. "Eager, are we?" He pressed Cutie's legs further apart, hands skimming his thighs and cupping his balls, feeling their weight in his hands before he pressed a finger further behind.

He used his teeth to rip the foil open and spat the section of the wrapper onto the bed. He almost had the condom out of the wrapper when the sound of *Hot Stuff* filled the air. Aiden frowned. Cutie really was hot stuff, but still... the song didn't exactly fit the mood.

Cutie's brow furrowed, looking as confused as Aiden felt. Where was the music coming from? Next door, perhaps? No. It sounded too close.

Aiden craned his head to look behind him. His jeans were crumpled at the end of the bed. His heart skipped a beat, and his stomach dropped when he realized why he recognized the song—the ringtone Nio had programmed into Aiden's phone earlier that night.

"Shit, fuck, sorry," Aiden said as he scrambled for the end of the bed, desperately patting his jeans until he found the phone.

The cutie sat up, watching him with a frown. "Everything okay?"

He ignored the question.

"Sorry, I have to take this." Nio would only ring if the boys were in trouble. A cold sweat broke out over him, and sickness churned in his stomach as he turned away from his bed partner for a touch of privacy. "Nio, is everything okay? The boys?"

"Aiden, you need to come home and save me," Nio's voice was so quiet Aiden strained to hear him.

"Why are you whispering? Just tell me they're okay."

"I'm whispering so they don't hear me through the door and scent my fear."

Aiden's gaze flickered to the cutie, who had pulled a sheet over his naked body. He was looking at the creases in the fabric as if he were trying not to listen to the phone call. Aiden appreciated the effort, even if he knew it wouldn't stop him from hearing one side of this crazy conversation. "Scent your fear? Just tell me they aren't hurt."

"They're not hurt, Aiden. Of course they aren't. They're criminal masterminds in the making."

"What's happened?" His heartbeat slowed. The kids couldn't have been hurt or Nio would have said something by now. He was dramatic, sure, but Nio wouldn't beat around the bush.

"They've locked me in the toilet, and I can't get out."It would be funny if Nio hadn't interrupted what was about to be the best sex he'd had in a very long time. If only he'd waited fifteen— maybe twenty—minutes longer before calling. Aiden glanced sideways again. Okay, that probably wouldn't have been enough time either, but now the mood was well and truly broken.

"They're five, not fifteen—how on earth did they manage that?"

"They're like Dennis the Menace—if Dennis the Menace had a twin and was extra...mischievous. How do you think? They stole the fucking key when one of them went to the toilet earlier in the day. That's what I get for having old-fashioned doors with old-fashioned locks and keys. It's my own fault. I said they'd add character. Who needs character? Not me if your children kill me. They've also packed the keyhole with slime and jammed crayons under the door. I don't think I'd get out even with a key."

Yeah, Nio was never going to offer to look after his boys again.

"You'll be okay. They're just being—"

"Don't say it. It won't help. Boys will be boys. Well, serial killers will be serial killers."

"This couldn't have waited for ten more minutes?" Cutie raised an eyebrow, and Aiden felt his cheeks start to flush. He stood up from the bed, holding his phone between his cheek and shoulder while he yanked on his jeans. Even if Nio told him everything was fine, he wouldn't be able to relax until he was sure the boys were safe. Plus, the magic was gone. It was disappointing, but he should have known this wouldn't work out.

The harsh light of reality was a boner killer, and he didn't even know how to start explaining his life. It wasn't like they could go back to sucking on each other's faces after this interruption. And it wasn't as if he could explain what was happening. This was a one-night stand. You didn't explain your family dynamics to someone you were never going to see again.

"I can smell murder. My murder. You need to get here before I'm dead. If you're late, I'm going to haunt your ass so hard you'll never be able to walk straight. Aiden, I'm your best friend. Don't make me bang on the wall and ask Nanny Biscuit to rescue me. No one wants that."

Nanny Biscuit—if she had a real name, Aiden had never heard it—was Nio's ninety-year-old neighbor. She might be old, but she had the hearing of an elephant, and she'd taken a liking to Nio when he'd moved into the apartment next to hers four years before.

Nio was a little scared of her.

"I'm on my way," Aiden said reluctantly.

"Come on, why are you so annoyed? I can't hear any music, so I know you're not in the bar. I probably woke you from a nap, you old codger. Now, get here before your errant sons take over my apartment, and then the world, dammit." He hung up, and Aiden turned back to the cutie, who was doing his best not to look interested in the phone conversation.

"I, er… have to go. Sorry." Aiden shoved the phone into his pocket and yanked on his T-shirt. He wondered if he should ask for his name and number, but the words stuck in his throat, and the cutie didn't offer the information up, just watched him with what looked like regret. Aiden understood regret.

CHAPTER FOUR

CARTER

THE CONDOM, ITS wrapper torn at the corner, lay on the edge of the bed, mocking him. Carter glanced at his phone. 23:59 blinked back at him.

"It's not even midnight, Cinderella," he said mournfully into the empty room as he reached for the condom. "And I didn't even get to see if it would fit." He shivered as he imagined how explosive the sex between them would have been. The foreplay was out of this world, and now he was unsatisfied and feeling like he'd possibly been used by someone to cheat on their partner.

He'd tried his hardest not to listen to the conversation, but it was impossible not to hear. He groaned, threw the condom in the direction of the wastepaper bin, and flopped back down on the bed.

Was it wrong of him to wish the phone call hadn't happened? They could have had sex and parted ways in the morning, and Carter would never have known if Hot Guy had a family waiting at home for him.

Carter's skin smelled of sweat and sex, despite not getting to the good part, and he couldn't relax, never mind sleep. He wasn't hard anymore, but he was antsy, unable to stay still, so he threw off the covers and padded into the bathroom. He turned the shower on and stepped under the spray, washing away all evidence of what might have been.

It wasn't that late, not for clubbing. He could always go out again, dance, flirt. But he didn't want anyone else. If he couldn't have Hot Guy, he'd rather stay in and pout about it. Plus, he'd lost all enthusiasm for dancing as he watched Hot Guy run out of his room, T-shirt on inside out.

Carter gave a little smirk as he tipped his head back and let the water beat down over his face. Did Hot Guy have a family at home? A husband, kids? A boyfriend? Or worse—a wife? Carter shook his head and wrinkled his nose. Was he a closet case? He tried not to judge. Hot Guy might be divorced, have an open relationship—Carter didn't exactly have a nuclear family himself. He'd just wanted him, dammit.

From the moment they'd met, it had been foreplay, and Carter knew sex with him would have been mind blowing His cock gave a tiny twitch of interest, but he was too drained from being left unsatisfied. If he couldn't have actual sex, then he wasn't interested in using his right hand either.

He spent a long time in the shower, just letting the water pound over him until the tension drained out of his limbs and he couldn't smell sex on his skin anymore. He dried off fast, towel-dried his hair, and rifled through his suitcase for pajamas.

Then he remade the bed while trying not to picture what had been happening less than an hour ago.

He lay down and channel surfed until he found some random 1980s movie and settled back on the cushions to watch.

His mobile started to ring, and he jumped, eyes flying open. He hadn't even realized he'd closed them. He fumbled for his phone and saw it was his best friend—his very pregnant best friend—and also the mother of his son. See? Unusual family dynamics.

"Nora? Is everything okay?" He pulled himself up and leaned against the headboard.

"Hi, Carter, it's Dennis," Nora's husband added, as if Carter wouldn't recognize his very male voice on the end of the line.

"Is it time?"

Dennis chuckled, and he heard Nora shouting in the background. "Nora says it's time. We're just taking her to the hospital. We wanted to let you know."

"Shit, I'm still out of town for work, and I've had a few drinks tonight. No way I can drive. Tell her she sure picks her moments."

Dennis laughed. "Don't worry about it. We know you're just wrapping up filming, but we wanted you to be the first to know. Also, Kyle wants to speak to you." The phone changed hands.

"Hey, Dad? Mom and Dennis said I could have the day off school if Mom went into labor in the middle of the night."

"Hey, kid, so I take it you're more excited about a day off school than having a baby sister?"

"Of course! I have an English test tomorrow!"

"Well, make sure you look after your mom, and do everything she and Dennis tell you to. And call me if you need me. I can be there tomorrow morning if you need anything."

"I know, I know. I'll text you updates, okay?"

"That would be great, buddy. Love you guys."

Kyle screamed, "Dad said he loves you all!" loud enough that Dennis and Nora could hear, and they all shouted it back. They ended the call, and Carter slipped back down the bed, a smile on his face.

He had an awesome family. He and Nora had Kyle as teenagers, when he'd been figuring out if he was gay or not. They'd never been a couple, but they'd brought Kyle up together, and when she met Dennis four years ago, he'd become part of the family. Now there was going to be a new baby. Not his, but she was Kyle's sister, and he would love her the same.

MANNY SOS

CHAPTER FIVE

AIDEN

BY THE TIME Aiden got to Nio's, the damage was done. Nanny Biscuit was already in the kitchen, and she and the boys were mixing cookie dough. They were all covered in flour.

"Daddy! Are you having a sleepover with us?" Ryan said as he stirred vigorously. Luke ran over to him and gave him a quick hug that smeared batter all over his jeans. Aiden ruffled his hair, and he was off again, back to the cookies.

The boys looked perfectly fine. There was no scent of burning in the air, and the apartment was still in one piece. The only thing missing was Nio.

"Hi, Nanny Biscuit. Where's Nio?"

"Uncle Nio is still in the toilet. He's doing a number two," Ryan interrupted, a large innocent smile on his small cherubic face.

"A number two is a poo," Luke said with a loud whisper and a nod of the head.

Aiden bit the inside of his cheek to stop himself from laughing. If he laughed at their antics, it only made them goofier.

"The poor man has locked himself in. He's not too good at DIY, bless his heart. I heard him banging on the door and calling for the boys from my place, so I came around to see what the commotion was. I couldn't get him out, but he did say you were on your way back, so the boys and I decided to bake." Nanny

Biscuit rifled through Nio's kitchen cabinets until she found a baking tray.

"At..." Aiden looked at his watch. "Twelve-thirty in the evening?" He raised an eyebrow.

"It's never too late—or early—for cookies. Isn't that right, boys?" They agreed with her wholeheartedly.

"Luke, Ryan, aren't you tired?"

They glared at him as if he'd asked them a trick question.

"You don't sleep on a sleepover, Daddy," Ryan said.

"But isn't it in the name?" Aiden asked.

"You have fun at a sleepover," Luke said as he grabbed the spoon Nanny Biscuit gave him and started to scoop out some of the dough.

"Then wouldn't it be called a fun-over?"

"Excuse me, excuse me!" a voice bellowed from the direction of the bathroom. Nio. He'd almost forgotten. "Instead of chit-chatting, do you want to get me out of here?"

"On my way," Aiden said, and with a wink at the boys and a kiss on Nanny Biscuit's cheek, he went to see exactly what his children had done to lock their uncle Nio in the bathroom.

Bright yellow slime dripped out of the keyhole, a puddle of it drying on the carpet. Aiden winced. He knew how difficult it was to get slime out of fabric. In the tiny gap beneath the door, an array of different colored crayons were all wedged in tight. It must have taken some time and concentration to do that—concentration he was sure the boys didn't have. So, on the one hand, he knew it was bad for them to do this, but on the other hand—he was impressed. They'd worked together without fighting and got the job done.

He'd been working on that with them for weeks. Okay, that was regarding tidying their room and not fighting about whose toy belonged to who, but it was the same thing. Almost.

"Well?" Nio asked from behind the door.

Aiden bit his lip. "They've done a good job."

Nio sighed, and Aiden could hear him bang his head against

the door. "I was afraid of that."

"I'll get you out. Where's your toolbox?"

Nio went quiet.

"You can borrow my toolbox," Nanny Biscuit called out. "It's under my kitchen sink. If you'll be a dear and nip next door to get it. I've got my hands full. It's not locked."

He thumped the bathroom door and leaned in. "I'm getting you a toolkit for your birthday."

"You know that sounds sexier than you meant it to, right?"

"He's right, dear, it did," Nanny Biscuit said as she turned on the oven. Jesus, did that woman have supersonic hearing?

Nanny Biscuit's toolbox was exactly where she said it would be and was full of surprisingly good-quality tools. "Hey, boys? You should come and help remove some of these crayons from under the door."

They both looked at him with identical expressions on their identical faces. "Can't. Nanny Biscuit got us to try," Ryan said.

"They're wedged in tight," Luke said with a nod in agreement.

Aiden sighed, got to his knees, and tried to pull the crayons out. They were stuck right in there. He rooted around Nanny Biscuit's tools until he found a flathead screwdriver and slowly picked pieces of crayons away from the gap beneath the door.

"Right, now I'm going to take the door handle off," he told Nio through the eye-wateringly expensive paneled door. He undid the tiny screws on the ornate handle and pulled it away from the door. Drying slime had run down the door and was stuck to the inner workings of the handle. It would be a complete mess to clean up if it dried in all the nooks and crannies.

When Nio pulled away his side of the handle, Aiden spotted screwed-up paper and crayon shavings in the small gap where the key would slot. The boys certainly hadn't wanted Nio to get out anytime soon.

With the door handle removed completely, Nio was able to

yank open the door. His eyes showed a little too much white, and there was sweat on his forehead.

"Thank God. I thought I was a goner for sure. Tell me, when did your kids turn into little terrors? It was only yesterday that they were just eating-and-pooping machines. I miss that stage." He yanked Aiden into a hug. "Nanny Biscuit has invited herself to stay for the rest of the sleepover. You and the boys won't get away leaving me alone with her," he whispered into Aiden's ear as he gave him an almost-friendly thump on the back.

"What's this?" Nio said and yanked on something that drew the neckline of his T-shirt tight around his throat.

Crap. His T-shirt was on inside out. Heat flooded Aiden's cheeks as he brushed Nio off and hurried back to the boys.

"While your cookies are baking, you should put the crayons in the bin and tell Uncle Nio you're sorry you locked him in the bathroom. That wasn't nice, was it?"

"We're sorry, Uncle Nio. We didn't think it would work," Ryan said.

"But we really wanted to find out. Just in case." Luke sat on the floor next to the pile of broken crayons, but he didn't pick up any of the pieces.

Aiden didn't want to know what the 'just in case' was about, but he was definitely going to throw away every pot of slime they had at home. He placed a plastic bag in front of them. "Put them in there. Then we're going to look up how to get slime out of keyholes... and carpets."

Nio was still staring pointedly at him, a smirk on his face. "I won't make you pay to clean the carpet if you tell me why your T-shirt is on backward."

"I was napping," Aiden said quickly—too quickly.

Nio raised an eyebrow. "Is that a white mark on your jeans?"

Aiden's eyes widened, and his gaze shot to his jeans. He was ready to wipe off the remnants of whatever he'd been doing with the cutie and then... lie, deny, whatever. Instead, he only needed to brush away the evidence of Luke's exuberant hug. But apparently, his short-lived panic had told Nio whatever he needed to know.

"It's flour, smart-ass," Aiden whispered so the boys wouldn't hear.

Nanny Biscuit tutted. "Language, boys." She tottered over to the sofa and made herself comfortable. "Can you turn the TV on? They have the best movies on at this time of night."

Nio rolled his eyes but did as she asked. "We are going to talk later. For now, we're going to watch TV, eat cookies and make sure the boys don't take over the universe."

"I'll fix your door tomorrow," Aiden promised as he took the parts to the kitchen sink and attempted to get as much slime off as possible so it wouldn't have dried like glue when he put them back together.

The boys had given up clearing away their mess and were having a thumb war instead. When Luke almost won, Ryan's grip tightened, pulling their fists close to his mouth so he could bite Luke's thumb.

"No biting," Aiden said, tired suddenly. He leaned down, scooped the crayons into the bag, and put them in the bin. "Come on, let's see what Nanny Biscuit is watching." They stood up and scrambled to sit next to her.

"Why's it that color?" they asked when they saw the black-and-white movie on the TV.

"This is what color movies were in my day," she said. "This film is called *The Birds*. It's a little scary, so you boys will have to protect me, okay?" They nodded and settled down to watch.

It was almost one in the morning. He was ready for bed, and they were still going strong. Aiden sighed and slumped down onto the two-seater sofa beside Nio.

"Were you at a club? Did I interrupt you getting it on?"

"I'm watching the movie," Aiden said, pointedly not looking at his best friend and definitely not thinking about the cutie he'd abandoned at the hotel room. He should have gotten his name and number.

MANNY SOS

CHAPTER SIX

CARTER

NORA'S NEW BABY was ugly in the way that all newborns were. A scrunched-up face with blotchy red skin and a swirl of black hair. Carter fell in love the moment he held Bobby. Despite there being no shared blood between them, he would die for her. He'd probably have to get in line behind her actual mother and father, but he looked forward to there being a new baby in the family.

He gently stroked the hair on the top of her head, marveling at how soft it was. Kyle hadn't had any hair as a newborn, but there was something in the way Bobby stuck out her bottom lip that reminded Carter of him as a baby.

"She looks like you," he said, glancing over at Nora.

He stood in the middle of the living room, gently swaying because he'd learned a long time ago that babies liked motion. Nora laughed, a loud, full belly laugh that made him wince, but Bobby carried on sleeping. She'd been in the world almost a week and was already used to how loud her mother was.

"You're such a bullshitter," Nora said. "She could have been swapped at birth and none of us would know. She still has that alien baby look. You know, like her huge head got squeezed out of much too small a hole."

"Please, I don't need the visuals. I lived it, remember? I've tried to repress that." Bobby made a soft mewling sound, and he rocked gently.

"You always were a baby whisperer, damn you."

He didn't remember being this good with Kyle, but they'd both managed to figure it out. Not without many sleepless nights, though.

"Now, as much as you love me, Kyle, and especially your new goddaughter-to-be"—Nora lifted her eyebrow at him—"I know you're not just here for snuggles."

How could she be so damned perceptive?

Sprawled on the sofa in jogging bottoms and a ratty old T-shirt Carter was sure Kyle stole from him months ago, there was sick over one shoulder, her hair was scraped back haphazardly, and there were bags under her eyes, yet Nora had never looked so happy or content. This is what parenthood should look like, not the blind panic they'd gone through together as teenagers.

"Shouldn't you be too sidetracked by this gorgeous girl to be able to read my mind?"

"Can't help it, babe. I know you too well."

She did, damn it.

"I want what you have."

She frowned at him, head cocked to one side. "Dennis? Because he's totally straight... and my husband. I don't think you could sway him— *Oh*! You mean the baby? Well, you can't have her either, not unless we die. And don't go getting ideas." She jabbed a finger in his direction.

Carter rolled his eyes at her and nudged her leg with his foot. She couldn't retaliate because he was holding the baby.

"Don't be ridiculous. You do need more sleep. I want to settle down... have a meaningful relationship. Like you and Dennis." An image of the man from the club filled his mind for a second. If only he'd gotten a name or a number—or a glass slipper—before he'd run off at midnight.

"*Oooh.* I understand. Good, because I'd have a thing or two to say about you going after Dennis or trying to kill us to get custody of Bobby. We share a son already. I'm not giving you Dennis or Bobby." She nodded firmly.

"I'm sick of one-night stands, quick gropes in clubs, and guys either wanting to fuck Carter the reality TV Manny for their five minutes of fame, or for them to run in the opposite direction when they realize I have a kid."

He thought of Cinders again: their dance at the club, the scorching almost-sex they'd had before he'd run off with only an open condom left to show he'd ever been there. Now he was left wondering and trying his hardest not to think about him—which he was failing at miserably.

Carter shivered. He put Cinders at least eight years older than himself—closer to forty than thirty, with a little grey in his hair mixed with the light brown. Fuck, some people paid good money to get hair that color, and he came by it naturally. He hadn't seemed like one of the older guys who were only there to pick up twinks. Carter snorted at that thought. Good thing, too, because he wasn't what you'd consider a twink—not even when he'd been twink age.

"What has you thinking so hard?" Nora asked.

Carter looked at the baby, and she pushed her bottom lip out again. "See? She's doing that lip thing Kyle used to do. Pretty sure that means he got the magical pout from you."

"Oh please, every baby does that. You should know that *Mr. Manny SOS.*"

He'd give her the finger if he could, but his arms were still full of baby, so Carter stuck his tongue out instead.

"Tell me what you're thinking," Nora pressed.

"There was this guy at a club. He was nice. We kissed, danced." *Groped, almost had sex.* "But he had a phone call and had to leave. I guess it just has me wallowing."

Dennis came through the doorway, balancing three large cups of coffee on a tray. He placed one in Nora's hands, and she groaned, smiling as she sniffed the cup. "What? I can take a sniff if I want. I'm not going to drink it." She was breastfeeding, so not drinking caffeine at all, but her love of coffee knew no bounds.

"I didn't say anything," He wouldn't dare. Nora shot him a death glare anyway. Luckily, she was sidetracked by her wonderful husband.

"Carter is trying to steal you away from me, Dennis," Nora said, laughter now in her voice. His eyes widened comically, and he patted Nora's leg as she cackled.

"Now, now, you could be a bit more concerned about that," he said.

She swung around on the sofa and draped her legs over his lap—all without spilling the coffee. "I am. I told him you wouldn't be swayed, and he couldn't have you. We need to find him a man. What about your strait-laced brother? He'd at least be related to you, so he'd have a bit of your DNA."

Carter didn't like where this conversation was heading.

"Mikhail?" Dennis asked.

"You have another strait-laced brother I don't know about?" She took a sniff of her coffee.

"He's straight, as opposed to strait-laced."

Nora's shoulders slumped. "That's a shame. He could do with something besides a stick up his ass, and we have to find Carter a man. It could have been a win-win."

"I can find my own man." Carter regretted saying anything. He couldn't imagine Dennis having a strait-laced brother, plus he was pretty sure it was much too incestuous to go there. It sounded creepy.

Nora stood abruptly and pointed at him. "Are you doing a good job all by yourself?"

Carter thought back to the man in the club. He'd been doing okay there until Cinders had run off. He sighed and shook his head. "I'm sure your brother isn't as awesome as you, anyway, Denny. If I can't have you, I'd rather go without," he said with a wink.

"I could ask Mikhail... If anyone could sway him, I'm sure it could be you?" Dennis didn't sound too sure about that. It was probably for the best.

"No, no. I've changed my mind. Single is good. It means hook-ups and sexy dancing." Even that made him think of his Cinderella. He couldn't win.

Maybe he was doomed to be single.

Kyle burst through the door and threw his rucksack on the floor next to the TV. "Dad! I didn't know you were coming over tonight. Are you staying for dinner?" He gave Carter a one-armed hug and then stole the baby from his arms. Carter felt weirdly incomplete without her.

MANNY SOS

CHAPTER SEVEN

AIDEN

THE BOYS SCREAMED like an enraged herd of velociraptors as they raced around the garden as fast as their legs could carry them. Luke crashed into the back of Aiden's legs as Ryan chased him, and Aiden flailed comically before falling to the ground with a thud.

The air left his lungs, and he blinked up at the sky while Nio cackled from the sidelines, and Ryan jumped over his knees as he carried on chasing Luke. They alternated between screams and giggles. At least they were having fun together, and they weren't arguing. Perhaps if they used up all their excess energy, they might even go to bed and sleep.

Aiden just wished he could turn down the volume or put them on mute. Just for fifteen minutes. He'd turn the subtitles on. His head pounded, and he massaged his temples as he sat up.

It had been a shit few weeks. The boys' childminder, the person they went to for the holidays, couldn't have them this year because she had a family emergency. All the other local childminders were full, the holiday clubs were fully booked, and Aiden was trying to convince himself that he could take the boys to work with him. Renovating a house. With machinery and tools all around. Nothing unsafe about that. His two tiny terrors—who made enough noise and chaos that Nio's elderly neighbor had to save him—were angels.

Head pounding at the thought, Aiden watched the boys, hoping inspiration would strike. Luke dove stomach first onto one of the swings, propelling himself into the air like Superman. Aiden was sure Ryan would try and yank him off using one of his legs, but he jumped onto the swing next to him and scrambled into a standing position, bending his legs to get the swing moving.

"I'm higher than you!" he shouted.

"I'm swinging faster, though! Aren't I, Uncle Nio?"

Uncle Nio shot them both a thumbs-up, not committing to anything, but it appeased them, and they went back to swinging.

With no sign of a fight about to start, Aiden let out a slow breath and turned toward Nio.

"Want a hand there, old man?" Nio smirked and held out a hand, yanking yanked him onto his feet.

"Thanks." Aiden brushed the grass from his butt.

"So, the boys are entertaining themselves. We have a few moments spare. It's time to fess up. Tell me what I interrupted when the boys sent me to bathroom prison."

"Nothing much." It felt like such a long time ago, and Aiden had barely had a chance to think about that night. Well, only on the few occasions he hadn't fallen into bed exhausted and passed out. Those nights, he thought about the hot cutie with the talented tongue and a body to die for.

He sighed.

"What was the sigh for? *Was* there a guy? Was he hot? Did you F.U.C.K.? I *did* interrupt you, didn't I? Fuck, I'm sorry. If I'd known, I would have happily stayed in the bathroom longer."

"You know you spelled out fuck and said it out loud in the same breath, right?"

"Yes, but one was for the physical act, and the other was a swear word. Totally different reasons. The boys shouldn't hear about their father's love life."

"Thanks…"

"Anything to get you laid, man."

Aiden snorted. "It's okay. It was just a hook-up in a club, no big deal. I went back to his hotel room, you called, I left," he admitted, glancing over at the kids to make sure they weren't getting into mischief.

"What?" Nio was loud enough that Ryan and Luke looked their way.

"Sshhh!" Aiden hissed, "if you get all excited, then they'll be over here, and you'll never get any details out of me."

Nio tried to school his face and gave a quick nod. "You went to his hotel room?" he whispered.

The whole story spilled out, and Nio did his best not to be excited about Aiden's almost hook-up, and he was genuinely sorry he'd interrupted him. Aiden was too. He'd liked the cutie a lot.

"I'm bored," Ryan said as he jumped from the swing into the flower beds. Aiden winced as petals went flying.

"There go my flowers," he said to Nio, then called out to Ryan. "Get out of the flowers, please!"

"I want to play in the treehouse," Luke said.

"Treehouse?" Nio asked and looked around the large garden, not seeing anything that looked like a house up a tree.

"There's an old, derelict treehouse and rope swing in the woods that belong to the farm over there." Aiden pointed towards the small woods at the bottom of the garden. "Clive built it for his kids twenty-odd years ago. It's mostly rotten and unsafe now, but he said I could fix it up for the boys."

"Please, Daddy," they chimed together.

"We can't yet. I've got to make it safe first, and we've not had a chance." More like, he didn't want to saw wood, climb trees, and rebuild a treehouse while the boys ran riot below. Still… "Soon, I promise. Why don't you show Uncle Nio how fast you can go on your scooters?" That sidetracked them enough they forgot about the treehouse, grabbed their scooters off the patio, and raced along the path in front of them.

"Good job, guys!" Nio said with a clap.

"I'm considering asking Wyatt to have the kids during the summer holiday," Aiden burst out. Nio's mouth was wide open, and he stared at Aiden, completely forgetting to clap as the boys zoomed back and forth. He'd known that would be Nio's reaction—which was why he'd just come out with it. "What? He's their dad too. He should take them, help with childcare."

"But he's been a complete dick since you split up, and I can't even remember the last visit he showed up for. Are you feeling all right?" Nio leaned forward and pressed his palm to Aiden's forehead. Aiden brushed him off with a laugh.

"He's my last—and only—hope. Ironic, I know. Literally no one else can have them over the holidays. He's their father too. He should be the first person I ask, not the last."

Nio's eyes widened, then narrowed thoughtfully. "Shit. Well, you know I would if I wasn't working—and they hadn't already tried to kill me. Oh, what about the treehouse couple from the farm? Clive and Barb?"

"They did babysit once. And only once. Barb found the boys digging a hole in her vegetable garden. They were trying to get to Australia." Nio raised an eyebrow, and Aiden shook his head. "Don't ask. They'd watched something on TV. I had to buy her a shed load of new onion bulbs. Apparently they were very committed to a new life down under."

"The weather would be better. But the spiders?" Nio shuddered. "I couldn't cope with them. Not that I'm great at coping with kids either. I mean, two five-year-old boys managed to lock me in the toilet. They're evil masterminds, aren't they? When they take over the world, do you think they'll look after me or feed me to their fluffy white cats while they laugh maniacally and twirl in their chairs?"

"Nah, you'd end up dead within the first five minutes," Aiden joked, but his smile faded. "Marriage. Kids. Surrogacy. They were all Wyatt's idea. Did you know that? A way to form the family neither of us had. I didn't expect to be doing this alone. Any experience I have with healthy families comes from Hallmark," Aiden said, trying to lighten the mood again.

Nio burst out laughing. "Hallmark? Please. It's full of angst and broken families."

"But they always get their happily ever after."

Nio bit his bottom lip, and his eyes flittered away from Aiden's face as if he was nervous about something. "I might not be able to get you your Hallmark Happy Ever After, but I do have a happy-for-now option..."

Aiden raised an eyebrow and stared at Nio. "Are you coming on to me?"

Nio half spluttered, half snorted. "As if. I mean, I can help you with the whole childcare thing..." Nio said hesitantly.

Aiden frowned. "What? How? Not your mother? Because I know she's not the maternal type—as much as I love her."

"No, not her. I would have said it earlier, but you threw me for a loop with your crazy talk about that dickhead ex of yours looking after *my* nephews. And you have to understand I did this for you... while I was in the bowels of hell. Literally. Sitting on the toilet while the boys took over my apartment. You get it, don't you?"

Aiden didn't get it at all.

"What do you mean? A holiday club? I've already asked all the local ones."

Nio patted him on the shoulder and took a deep breath. "Sort of? Remember, I have your best interests at heart. You're like a brother to me. And I was locked all night in the bathroom with only my phone for company, and your wonderful, clever serial killers in the making were plotting to cook me for dinner until Nanny Biscuit brought cookie mix. Remember that, all right?"

"You've already said that. I remember..."

"Have you ever heard of *Manny SOS*?"

"The TV show?" Aiden vaguely recalled it, though he'd never watched an episode. He didn't get to watch much grown-up TV, and when he did, he wasn't going to watch some fake male nannies pretend to fix fake families like Mary Poppins.

"Yes, the TV show…" Nio kicked a clump of grass with his toe as he squirmed in his seat. He looked everywhere but at Aiden. "It's a great TV show. You should watch it. Hot, gay, male nannies looking after sweet, adorable, rambunctious children."

"I might not have watched an episode, but I know what it's about. I don't get why you do or why you're telling me about it now." Aiden had a sinking feeling, and he lowered himself to the bench behind Nio. The boys were now sitting properly on the swing set, their little legs pushing high into the air. "What did you do, Nio?"

Nio blushed, and he fidgeted. He turned to look at Ryan and Luke. "Boys, let me push you!" he called out to them, jogging over to the swings.

"Nio, what the hell did you do?"

"What the hell, what the hell!" The boys screamed as Nio pushed them higher. *Crap.* He and Nio ignored the boys chattering, and they quickly got distracted.

"Don't be mad. I was just thinking of you. And the boys. The show was asking for submissions, so I sent one in for you. I got a reply. Well, technically, *you* got a reply."

"What? You *actually* signed us up for a TV show?"

"I submitted a reel on your behalf. While I was imprisoned in the bathroom, scared for my *life*."

"Are you crazy?" Aiden demanded. Nio had a screw loose. Was it acceptable to strangle your best friend? No, not in front of the boys, but he couldn't promise Nio's safety once they went to bed. He could totally get away with it. Nanny Biscuit would help him bury the body.

He must know someone… or someone who knows someone who would be able to have the kids during the holiday…

"You should be thanking me. I did this before I realized you were going to ask W.Y.A.T.T. to babysit. If I'd known that was what you'd come up with, I would have made a professional reel to send in."

"You are insufferable. I am not making a spectacle of us on TV. Wy—W.Y.A.T.T."—his eyes flickered to the boys, but they were oblivious as to who they were talking about—"is a perfectly fine choice." He didn't want the whole world to see how bad he was at looking after his kids. He didn't want strangers watching him and judging him. Especially not when he always felt like he was catching up, like he didn't know what he was doing.

"As if. He's a terrible choice. And the whole world will fall in love with you. You've got that strong, silent single dad vibe going on. Plus, the boys will get some practice for when they try taking over the world in a year or two. They'll have the nanny wrapped around their fingers."

"Absolutely not." Aiden didn't want to air his dirty laundry in public. "You're insane. Your time in the bathroom has sent you around the bend."

"Not even if it helped? Just watch a few episodes. Go on, what can it hurt? Plus, you need a nanny ASAP. No, in fact, you need a *Manny SOS*."

MANNY SOS

CHAPTER EIGHT

CARTER

HE WAS NEVER late. Not *ever*. Except this once.

Damn commuter traffic, and damn whoever decided it was a good idea to situate the *Manny SOS* headquarters on the outskirts of London.

Carter shoved the glass double doors open and waved his pass at the receptionist. Not that he needed to, she recognized him. Since its conception, he'd worked as one of the male nannies for reality TV show *Manny SOS*. He'd even been in the pilot episode they'd pitched to the TV studio. But before that, he'd worked at an LGBTQ+ friendly nursery. It wasn't as glitzy or glamorous, but the hours and holidays had fit around his son.

Yes, now he worked in TV, there were weeks, sometimes months, when he was away. But there were also months in between where he had time off or only had to do preproduction marketing, so it evened itself out. It wasn't what Carter thought he'd be doing with his life, but he enjoyed it. Before Kyle came along, he never even thought about going into childcare. Life worked in mysterious ways.

Carter's coffee sloshed out of his reusable cup as he bounded up the stairs to the conference room, where six nannies, a gaggle of TV producers, editors, and production crew were already in the room for the annual reel review party.

"Good of you to join us," Joe, their director, said pointedly, even though it didn't look like they'd started yet. Everyone was still mingling and catching up, and the TV screen that took up the front wall was black.

Carter took a deep breath and collapsed into a chair. "Sorry, Kyle's mom was up all night with the baby, so I took Kyle to school, then got stuck in traffic."

Russ, one of the other nannies, nodded in sympathy and reached over to pat his arm. He shot Joe a playful scowl, then grinned at Carter. "Ignore Joe. He's in a mood today. You've not missed anything, apart from us stuffing our faces and trading stories."

"I was just telling everyone about the last kid I looked after. She kept stealing rocks from the playground. She'd fill her coat pockets until they were so full she could hardly walk. When I tried to put them back, she cried. I ended up carrying them home and washing each one so she could display them on her bookcase," Frey said as he filled his plate from the buffet set up against the back wall. His auburn hair was longer than the last time Carter had seen him, and he had it scraped back into a messy ponytail—definitely not a man bun—and a new tattoo peeked from beneath his sleeve. Out of all the mannies, Frey was the one that looked like he was in the wrong profession. He should be a rock star or working in a tattoo studio. He was awesome with the kids, though, and viewers went crazy for his bad-boy good looks.

"Did she want to paint them? Rock pets are all the rage now, aren't they?"

Frey pointed his butter knife at him. "That's what I thought, but it's much simpler than that. Her favorite color is grey."

"That simple, huh?" Carter laughed and pushed himself out of the chair when his belly rumbled. He placed a few croissants from the buffet on a plate and refilled his coffee cup.

"Yep. I bought her a grey plush elephant, hoping she'd get rid of the rocks, but Mr. Ellie Phant just became the Rock Overlord instead."

"I wish the kids I looked after collected rocks," Sebastian said, looking up from the book he was reading at the end of the table. "I'm still covered in Sharpie from the four children I looked after." He moved the book away from his face, revealing faded black lips and a drawn-on mustache. His blond hair was so short he couldn't even try to hide behind it.

Frey and Russ cackled, but Carter did his best to keep a straight face. He'd had marker on his face courtesy of Kyle when he'd been a toddler. Luckily, there were no cameras following him back then, so only he and the nursery where he worked knew about it.

"Come on, guys, let's get this party started," Joe shouted. Everyone broke away from their conversations, and Carter gave a quick nod to Richard and Isaac, the other two nannies who'd been talking on the other side of the room when he'd burst in.

"You're all going to love these reels," Ronnie, their producer, said with a large smile as he settled down to stare at the TV. He patted his shirt pocket for his glasses and frowned when he couldn't find them. Carter watched him for a few seconds before leaning over and hooking the glasses from where they were seated on top of his head and handing them to him.

"Oh. Thanks," Ronnie said as he pressed play.

Carter raised an eyebrow in question towards Frey, who shrugged his shoulders and gave a shake of the head. He didn't have a clue why Ronnie thought these reels were so important either.

The lights were lowered, and the first reel showed a baby sleeping in a Moses basket and a toddler trying to catch a hyperactive puppy before the image jumped to the parents sitting stiffly on the sofa.

"Hi, *Manny SOS*..." the woman said over the child's

laughter.

The reels went on, all similar; nothing out of the ordinary, just typical families all needing a little help, a lot of routine, and a manny to assist them.

Carter was in a reel daze, wondering which family he'd end up with, when an image of a handsome dark-haired man sitting in what looked like the bathroom filled the screen. "Hi, I mean, hello. I need your help," the man whispered, and his eyes kept shooting around the room. He was using his phone, and he kept moving the camera in so close all they got was a good view of his eyeball or nose.

"Technically, it's not me who needs your help. Well, I need help right now, but I doubt you'll get here in time, so… I'm doing my future self a favor. And my best friend."

It was difficult to keep up with what the guy was talking about, but it was so different from the other reels that Carter was riveted. He frowned and leaned closer to the TV as if that would help.

"Sorry, where are my manners? I'm Antonio—Nio to my friends—I hope we can be friends, yes? Currently, I am sitting on the toilet in my small but perfectly formed bathroom. It's so small." He stood up and did a little twirl so they could see where he was. "I'm here because I'm looking after my best friend's kids. I'm their prisoner now. They've locked me in the bathroom, I can't get out, and Aiden—that's my friend—needs help." He walked over to the door and showed them the door handle with a weird substance leaking out of the keyhole. "That's slime. I've been slimed. Aiden has two boys. They're five, almost six. He's a single gay dad in want of a husband, but failing that, a manny who can help him with the boys would do."

Antonio—Nio—swung the camera back up to his face. "Look, I love the kids—my nephews—and Aiden's a great dad, but we are all clueless. Three men and a baby? That's us, minus the extra set of hands, which we could really do with. We're making it up as we go along and need help. Aiden doesn't have any 'dad' friends, he's terrified of the moms at the school gates, and the kids are too clever for the likes of us.

"It's the summer holiday soon, and I know he's lost his only childminder, and he's having trouble finding anyone to take them. He needs you guys, so I'm begging on his behalf. He'd hate me for doing this, but let's face it, he's not the one locked in the bathroom. On behalf of humanity, come help a poor single dad out. Did I mention he's hot? That the kids are cute as buttons, and they'd pull in the ratings? Just in case you didn't think me pleading my case was enough.

"*Manny SOS*—come help my friend before I end up locked in a room without water next time. I don't do well in prisons." His eyes flickered around the room, and he pulled at the neck of his T-shirt. "Peace out," he said, and the TV screen faded to black.

"Did he say peace out?" Frey asked.

Everyone else was quiet for a few seconds; then the talking and laughing began. "He did. He said peace out. Who is this guy?" Richard said, looking at Ronnie.

"We don't know much more than you at this point," Joe said.

"I'm presuming that because you've shown us the reel, you've accepted the submission?" Carter asked.

"Sort of. We need the permission of the family, not the man on the reel. Once we have that, then we've got them."

"I'll be the manny if Nio's there," Russ said, fanning himself with his hand.

"He won't even be the client," Isaac said.

"But he's the best friend, so he'll be over a lot, right?" Russ waggled his eyebrows when Isaac rolled his eyes at him. Russ was a born flirt.

"We're trying our hardest to get dad on board, but without his consent, this could be another one for the 'one that got away' pile. But we agree, this could possibly make a very interesting story, especially if we include Nio's reel and why he called us."

"He's got to say yes. I'm sure Nio will persuade him. He seems persuasive."

"Russ, stop drooling," Frey said. Russ scowled back, though he did dab at his mouth.

"Carter, if we get this family on board, you'll be working with them." Joe slid a slim file across the table, and Russ cursed under his breath. Carter opened it, but there weren't any photos of the actual family, just a few selfies of Nio pulling a face, another photo of the toilet, which was at least spotless, and the names and ages of the potential clients. It didn't give him a lot to go on.

"Thanks?" He glanced towards the other mannies, who all looked like they wanted to be in his shoes, but he wasn't too sure he wanted the assignment. He liked to have more information about the family he was helping. This didn't give him much more than a hapless father, a clueless best friend, and two kids who knew how to run rings around them.

CHAPTER NINE

AIDEN

WAS IT WRONG to imagine his ex-husband drowning under two spit-soaked Peppa Pig plushies or dying from spider bites? No? He didn't think so. It was the only thing getting him through the day.

It should have been a joyous occasion. It *was* a joyous occasion. But Wyatt had promised to be there, and Aiden was sick of making excuses for him. It wasn't like Aiden had given his ex any responsibility. He hadn't even needed to bring a gift—the kids would be excited enough just to see him. He didn't even have to do any of the parenting. All he'd had to do was turn up for an hour to celebrate his children's birthday.

Aiden's sons sat opposite him on the well-worn picnic bench, a large blue cake between them. Twelve candles—six on the left, six on the right. One set for each boy, one candle for each year of their life. How could they be six already?

Ryan and Luke wore innocent expressions on their identical faces. Those faces filled Aiden with so much love and joy—he didn't understand how Wyatt didn't feel the same. However, over the last six years, he'd learned that those expressions weren't as sweet as they'd have you believe. Whenever the boys looked like that, something was going to happen. He never knew what, but it would always be memorable. Life with his sons was never dull. Nio could attest to that.

There were no other children around—it terrified Aiden to even think of two, five, ten—however many—other kids racing around his garden with only him in charge. Wrangling Ryan and Luke was tough enough. Still, they were old enough now to want friends their own age at their birthday party. Instead, they got Aiden's rag-tag group, who had somehow become his family and pseudo-uncles to the boys over the years.

Next year would be different. Ryan and Luke would be older, less likely to persuade those friends to sneak out of gardens and climb onto shed roofs with wings made from expensive duvet covers—which they'd done at their last childminders.

It might not have been quite as daunting if he knew other people with children. But not one of his friends had kids, and the women at the school gates scared the living daylights out of him, so he stayed clear when he dropped the boys off at school.

Ryan took a deep breath, and before Aiden got the last 'Happy Birthday to You' out, he let out a lungful of air and blew out all the candles—including his brother's.

It was the calm before the storm, a full six seconds before disaster struck. Aiden was experienced enough to know it wouldn't be good, though he wasn't experienced enough to stop the escalation. Luke's eyes grew wider, his bottom lip started to tremble, and the storm broke.

The wail that finally fell from Luke's mouth did not sound human, and large tears rolled over his cheeks and dripped down his chin.

"It's all right, buddy." Aiden leaned over to console him and tried to think of something meaningful to say, but his mind was white noise. Birthdays and birthday parties were beyond him—- until the boys, he'd never been to one in his life—if this could even be called a birthday party. When they'd been little, presents and cake were enough to keep them entertained, but now they were getting older, he needed to plan actual activities.

His hand missed Luke's shoulder because Luke lunged at Ryan, and they both tumbled off the bench to the ground. Aiden's breath caught in his throat as they wrestled until he realized neither of them was hurt. Yet.

Shit, shit, double shit.

Aiden raced around the table and paused. It was hard to decide where to pull them apart. It looked like a cartoon fight— all he could see was dust, swirly lines, and the odd arm and leg. His friends had stepped back to give them room. They'd seen the boys fight like cats and dogs before, so they didn't look overly worried.

"That's enough, boys." He sounded confident and in charge. Didn't he? He looked at his friends and wasn't so sure, but there wasn't any time to try again.

"He blew out my candles," Luke said as he sat on top of Ryan and twisted around to look up at Aiden. His sadness was rapidly turning to anger. Aiden lifted him off and helped Ryan stand. Ryan stuck out his tongue, and if Aiden hadn't held them away from each other, they would have started again.

"Look, I'm lighting the candles again. Luke, you can take a turn blowing out *all* the candles by yourself," Nio interrupted, stretching his arms out in emphasis.

Relief flooded over Aiden as his best friend and savior pulled a lighter from his pocket and lit the candles. Distracted from each other, the boys went back to the cake. Why hadn't he thought of that? He was their dad, after all. He should know how to stop fights or bad behavior by now. Perhaps he did need *Manny SOS* to come and help him out. He was as clueless now as he had been when they were babies. As soon as he thought he'd got the parenting lark under control, they grew into the next phase and he'd be back to square one.

Would a TV manny be any worse than asking Wyatt to look after the boys? Wyatt, who hadn't seen them in months, who couldn't be bothered to come to their birthday party? Which was worse? He was screwed either way.

"What a great idea!" John said with a big smile. "Perhaps we could all take turns. When I blow my candles out, will you both help me?" The boys nodded their heads vigorously. They loved Aiden's work friend, who was nearing sixty, had no children of his own but always made time for the boys, and was so kind to them—kind enough to come to a kids' birthday party on his day off.

Ryan was now grinning and sliding mischievous glances at Luke as they sang *Happy Birthday* and took turns to blow out the candles. It was no surprise when Luke cackled and slammed his hand into the cake, then picked up a handful of splattered sponge and threw it at Ryan.

Ryan's eyes widened comically in surprise, but he didn't cry or get mad. He laughed, scooped icing off the cake, and smeared it over Luke's face.

No fighting ensued, just both boys shrieking in delight as they scraped icing off their cheeks and stuffed it into their mouths. If Aiden had tried to stop it, he knew they'd be fighting now. Sometimes he had to pick his battles, and it was better for all of them if he let this one go.

It was their birthday, his friends were all laughing, and Aiden felt his lips twitch. He took out his phone and snapped a few photos. They would be good blackmail material when the boys turned eighteen.

"Perhaps next year I should get two cakes."

The kids were playing with their remote-control cars, showing John in intricate detail how they worked and who could do the best tricks, when Nio sidled up next to Aiden. There was no cake, dirt, or mess on his perfectly tailored suit.

Aiden ran a hand through his hair in case there was any leftover cake in it—the stuff had gotten everywhere.

"If I'd known we were dressing up..." Aiden gestured at Nio's suit and tie. His friend was always smart, but today he was... business sharp.

Nio snorted. "Work stuff after the party."

"You're either incredibly brave or stupid to wear that here."

Nio grinned and smoothed out the wrinkles in his tie. "Maybe a bit of both. It's not going too badly, is it? You averted one disaster and let another happen. All in a day's work, I'd say."

Aiden took a bite out of his smushed cake. "So, I've just thought of a few options for the boys."

"Oh?" Nio raised an eyebrow.

"The house I'm renovating? The front room has mostly been completed. They'll be safe there while I'm working. I'll take toys to entertain them. It'll be fine."

Nio laughed, and Aiden frowned at him. "Those two imps? In a house that's basically a building site? Yeah, I'm not sure that's a good idea. Did you watch any episodes of *Manny SOS*?"

"I'm not going to get some fake TV Manny to look after my kids while I go to work." Aiden's heart thumped against his chest. That could not be the only option.

"Because taking them to work is a much better idea."

"It could be." He didn't know who he was trying to persuade, himself or Nio. "I also put their names down on a cancellation list for a summer club."

"Sure, it could work," Nio drawled, "Do you think there will be any cancellations?"

"Maybe a kid will get sick or break a leg and there will be a spot?"

"One spot? I know they're twins, but it's easy to tell there are two of them. Plus, you know you just wished sickness and broken bones on innocent kids, right?"

Aiden groaned and closed his eyes. "I am a terrible, terrible person."

"You know my mama would have them, but she just doesn't like kids that much. No offense. She didn't like me when I was a child, either."

"None taken. I love your mother, but I don't know who would kill who in that situation. I don't want to come home to a bloodbath... or an uneven patio."

"I get you. So what *are* you going to do?" Nio asked. "Because kids on a building site? Not a good idea. Your kids on a building site? A catastrophe."

Aiden wracked his brain for every person who had ever looked after the boys since they'd been born. "Chrissy? Her mom works at the supermarket. She said she's looking for a babysitting job."

"Sixteen-year-old Chrissy? I'm not sure that's such a good idea. Is sixteen even old enough?"

Aiden knew he was right. The thought of letting a sixteen-year-old look after his kids full time for the entire holiday was a little scary. "Or Nanny Biscuit. The boys loved her."

"My wonderful eccentric dear of a neighbor? You want to ask her? Is that wise? She slept on my sofa for two days after the boys locked me in the bathroom. She was afraid of PTSD. Plus, she's a hundred years old."

"She's ninety. And she was a teacher. She told me all about it when you, Ryan, and Luke fell asleep." The boys had loved her. Why hadn't he thought of her before?

"Fifty years ago. She hasn't got the stamina to chase after those two at her advanced age. Just think about *Manny SOS*. Come on, Aiden. Pretty please. For their sake and yours, and for all those poor kids who don't want to break a leg or get chicken pox. But mostly, do it for me. Your best friend. The person who still has nightmares about being locked in the toilet. Perhaps Nanny Biscuit is right—maybe I do have PTSD."

"I smell bullshit. I could kill you for submitting me to a bloody TV show. We aren't a spectacle, you know." Aiden folded his arms and watched the boys as they chased John with their cars.

"Stop pouting. You need help." Nio poked him in the ribs. "You need someone who can chase after them if they run off at the park. Nanny Biscuit can't do that, and Chrissy would probably be too busy sexting her boyfriend. Watch a few episodes tonight. It's not all B-list celebrities looking for a bit of fame by using their kids. Most families do need help."

"I'm not that desperate." Only, Aiden was beginning to suspect he really was that desperate.

"All right, if you don't want to watch it for the childcare, watch it for the nannies. The very gay, very hot nannies."

MANNY SOS

CHAPTER TEN

CARTER

HOME, SWEET, GLORIOUS *home.*

Carter abandoned his bag in the hallway and yawned so hard his jaw clicked. The lights were already on. Not just one, but all of them, which meant Kyle was there. He couldn't walk past a light switch without turning it on.

"Hey, kid, you trying to outdo Blackpool Illuminations?" Carter shouted as he made his way into the living room.

Kyle was lying on the floor; textbooks and papers surrounded him as he highlighted passages and wrote notes in a tattered notebook. Carter couldn't stop the smile spreading over his face at seeing his son in his house. It always felt more like home when he was there.

"Wha'?" Kyle said, around the pen top he was chewing.

"Our house looks like Blackpool Illuminations," he said.

Kyle pushed himself into a sitting position. "God, aren't you too young for dad jokes?"

Carter laughed and walked towards him, bending over to press a kiss to the top of his head. "Perhaps this means I'm getting old? I thought you were at your mom's tonight."

Kyle rolled his eyes but didn't get up. "Bobby's turned into a vampire." Carter looked at him, one eyebrow arched, waiting for an explanation. "You know. Sleeps all day, parties all night. Or in her case, cries all night."

Ah, that explained it. Newborns were never as fun as their parents remembered. As cute as Kyle's half-sister was, having a screaming baby around wouldn't help him study for his exams.

"I remember how that is. You never stopped screaming." Carter reached down and ruffled his hair. "Still, too late to be up studying. Does your mom know you're here?"

"Of course, it was her idea. She knew I was struggling to concentrate, and we knew you'd be back sometime tonight." He stifled a yawn, and Carter bit back a grin.

"I'll make you a cuppa, then bed. I don't care if it's Saturday tomorrow. It doesn't mean you can stay up all night and then sleep in until midday. Leave vampirism to your little sister."

"Yes, Dad. You know, other parents would be happy I was up studying and not drinking or doing drugs," he said in a sing-song voice that made Carter chuckle.

"Yeah, well, I happen to know that you like the freedom of coming and going from your mom's and here. If you did any of that crazy teen stuff, you'd be stuck with a screaming sister one week on, one week off."

That had been Kyle's schedule when he was younger, but now he was a teenager, he liked to make his own choices, especially as he wanted to be out with friends more than he wanted to be with his parents. Carter and Nora had given him more freedom, and he hadn't let them down yet.

Carter had worried he'd hardly see Kyle, that he would either stay at his mom and stepdad's or be out with his friends, but he'd found that his son would go from one home to the other happily. He was so glad he'd bought this house. It was close enough to Nora's that Kyle could walk over whenever he wanted.

"Don't worry. I'm not going to make you a granddad any time soon."

Carter shivered, suddenly realizing how his parents must have felt when he'd had to tell them Nora was pregnant.

"Good. I'm only just old enough to use dad jokes. I'm certainly not old enough to be a granddad. No following in our footsteps. Study, good grades, college, and university."

Kyle rolled his eyes. "You and Mom went to uni."

They had, but it had been difficult. They'd both planned to go away to university but changed plans when Nora realized she was pregnant. Instead, they'd gone to a local uni, worked, took care of Kyle, and didn't sleep for at least five years.

"We did, but we both want you to enjoy that time."

"I intend to. Partying, drinking cheap beer, and living in halls. All the good stuff you didn't get to do. You can live vicariously through me."

"Good, just don't have too much fun, yeah?" Aiden filled the kettle, and Kyle pulled himself up on top of the kitchen work surface like he used to do when he was a kid—though he didn't need a lift up anymore—and tapped his fingers on the counter. Carter glanced at him, a frown on his lips. Kyle only tapped when he was nervous.

"Everything okay?"

"Yes, I mean… it's just, Neil's family invited me to go on holiday with them during the summer holiday."

"That sounds fun. What's got you so worried?"

"They've got a villa in Spain, and they're going to be there for a whole month."

Carter nodded. A month without his son was a long time, but could he really complain when he was going to be busy?

"What does your mom say?"

Kyle shrugged sheepishly. "To ask you."

"I'm going to be working most of the holiday, so I don't mind, but what about your mom and Dennis? Your sister will only be five months old."

"I know that. I love her to pieces, and I'll miss her like crazy." Carter did know that Kyle was great with Bobby. "But it would be great to spend some time with Neil, go on holiday, get some sun."

Kyle deserved to do something he wanted to do. Everything had been about Bobby lately, so a trip away would probably do him a world of good. "I don't mind if your mom doesn't. You need to save your paper round money for spending, though, got it?"

Kyle nodded his head and grinned. His finger-tapping stopped, and he slid off the counter to give Carter a hug. "Thanks, Dad."

"No need to thank me. You deserve some fun. I'll speak to your mom later, and we'll figure it out with Neil's parents, okay?"

"Brilliant! I need to text Neil and let him know right away." Kyle already had his phone out as he headed back to the living room. "We're going to have so much fun."

CHAPTER ELEVEN

AIDEN

WYATT HAD BLANKED him. Nanny Biscuit was too old. Chrissy was too young. And no child had broken a leg, caught chicken pox, or dropped out of holiday club. Aiden was screwed, well and truly up shit creek without a paddle.

Now he understood what people meant when they said it took a village to raise a child. He had no village, no family to help out, and now he had agreed to go on a terrible trashy reality TV show so he'd have someone to watch his boys. How humiliating was that? Either way, he had to suck it up and take it.

"Am I going to be famous?" Ryan asked when he tried to explain it to them as they walked along the winding pathway that led through the woods at the bottom of the garden.

"I'm going to be famous," Luke said as he charged ahead. "Pine cones." He bent down and rooted through the cones on the ground, straightening in triumph, one clutched in each hand.

As he walked, Ryan picked up a stick and pretended he was an old man. "They're coming for the holidays? But I thought we was going to stay with Daddy Wyatt?"

Aiden stumbled over his own feet. Shit, they must have overhead him talking with Nio. He hadn't been as careful as he'd thought.

"Yes! Daddy Wyatt! I miss him. He didn't come to my birthday," Luke frowned.

"Or mine," Ryan added, making Aiden laugh.

"I know he didn't. He's just so busy lately. But you're going to have so much fun with the manny. He's going to take you to the park and play games. He's even going to be living with us, so you can show him all your toys."

Their little brows furrowed identically as Aiden tried his hardest to make it sound fun. They could probably sense his lie, but he couldn't tell them he was as wary as them. Not that he wanted them to go to Wyatt's, but he wasn't looking forward to being on TV. "Maybe he can help you fix the treehouse."

They'd reached the treehouse. It wasn't much, and it still wasn't safe enough for them to climb on, but Aiden had changed out the rope on the swing the last time they were there, and both boys raced towards it, clambering onto the tire, laughing as they spun.

"Swing us, Daddy!" Ryan shouted.

Aiden grinned at them and raced towards the swing, loving their shrieks of delight as he gripped the old tire and swung the boys around until he was dizzy from watching them. Perhaps with the manny there, he'd have enough time to come out here and fix the treehouse himself? All it needed was a few planks of wood and a ladder and it would be good to go.

CHAPTER TWELVE

CARTER

Interview with Carter from Manny SOS. Camera rolling. Day One.

Interviewer: How are you feeling going into a new family? Excited? Nervous?

Carter: I'm always excited to meet a new family, but the reel for this family has piqued my interest, so I'm doubly excited. I don't even know what they look like, so it's a complete surprise!

CARTER DROVE A Bedford camper van in the show. It was equipped with craft supplies, board games, toys, and so many more things that made his life as a manny easier as he went from one family to the next.

Each manny had their own camper, all rigged with childcare in mind. Carter's was a duck-egg blue, and each of the others had a different color to correlate to the rainbow. Not all the mannies drove their own motorhomes to the family they'd be staying with, but Carter loved to drive, and it reminded him of holiday trips with his family when he'd been small.

The house he pulled up to was a ramshackle farmhouse—only, without an actual farm—with a long gravel road up to the driveway and a fenced-in garden. With not much more information on the family than he'd started out with, Carter was as eager as the others to finally see the family Nio had talked about in the reel.

The crew consisted of a cameraman and Joe, the director, grips, and a sound guy; there was even a catering van set up outside. Thank God they'd only be there for the first day of shooting, and then the fly-on-the-wall cameras placed around the house would take over. There would be a cameraman who would go to different activities outside the home, but otherwise, it would be him, the kids, and the dad—when he wasn't at work. Occasionally the director would be back for an update interview with the family, but that would be their only involvement.

Carter jumped out of the van and stretched his arms over his head, working out the kinks in his shoulders.

"Carter, good, good. You're here," Joe said as he jogged over to him. "All set for the big reveal?"

"I'm raring to go. Let's do this."

Joe nodded and moved everyone into position. Carter enjoyed the hustle and bustle of the small TV crew. He'd been doing this long enough that he'd lost any awkwardness that came with having a camera follow him, and now he could almost forget it was there. Of course, there were always a few staged moments—like the parents opening the door and pretending to be surprised. But none of the children's actions were scripted, and Carter did look after them.

Carter could put up with a few staged moments because the interaction with the families was real. He rapped loudly on the front door with a flourish and a dazzling smile.

When it opened, his stomach dropped as if he was on a roller coaster, the wind roaring in his ears. He blinked, but the familiar eyes, the familiar lips, and that familiar face were still there.

Cinders.

How could he not know the father he would be helping was the man he'd picked up at Sparkle—or was it Thrust?

He cursed not having a full file—with photos and a reel of

the actual family—but this must be fate, because there was no way a meeting as crazy as this could be anything else.

"This is a joke, right?" Cinders said, his eyes on Carter's face.

Carter considered asking if he wanted to try the abandoned condom to see if it fit, but he had a semblance of professionalism to maintain. He forced a smile onto his lips and hoped he didn't look constipated instead. All the while, an inner monologue shouted, 'What the Fuck! What the Fuck?' in his brain.

Joe was looking at them with a frown, and Carter wasn't sure they should admit to knowing each other. He just hoped Cinders would play along until they had a moment to chat.

"Hi, I'm Carter, your manny for the holidays."

Cinder's—*Aiden, finally a name*—looked at Carter's hand but didn't take it. The long pause became awkward, and the weight of everyone's gaze on them made the hair on the back of Carter's neck stand on end.

Shivers ran down Carter's spine, and his throat became dry when Aiden finally took his hand.

"What are you doing here? Better question, *how?*"

Aiden would confuse the crew and give them away if he didn't play along.

"Cut!" Joe shouted, then jogged over. "I understand this is a bit overwhelming, but just keep it simple. Give your name, say thanks for coming. You'll soon forget about the cameras." He patted Aiden on the shoulder and went back to the camera.

"I'm Aiden, pleased to meet you."

Carter could hear the insincerity in the tone of his words, but Joe was oblivious.

"What are—I mean, how?" Aiden whispered. They'd been clasping hands for much too long. Carter reluctantly pulled his hand away.

MANNY SOS

CHAPTER THIRTEEN

AIDEN

THE THEME TUNE to the *Twilight Zone* played on a loop through Aiden's mind as he allowed the crew of *Manny SOS* and the cutie who'd picked him up at the club into his home. How insane was this? Frustration, annoyance, impatience, they all coursed through his body. He wanted to tell the crew to take a hike, pull Cutie—Carter—aside, and ask exactly what he was playing at.

This had to be a joke.

Instead, he did none of those things. He let the crew boss him around, tried to concentrate on what they were saying, but he couldn't stop staring from the corner of his eye. It was like being in line at the bar all over again.

Carter the Cutie looked so different, yet there was no mistaking him for anyone else. He wore a pale blue shirt, skinny jeans with rainbow suspenders, and brand new Converse on his feet. He was the PG-rated version of the man from Sparkle. And he was just as gorgeous, dammit.

Aiden's tongue stuck to the roof of his mouth as he allowed himself to be swept along without saying a word. He was completely out of his depth, and he wanted answers. When he spoke to Nio, he was going to—

Fuck—that was it. Nio. He had to be behind this. He didn't know how, but his friend had freaky superhero abilities, and he wouldn't put it past him to orchestrate a meeting between him and a manny beforehand.

Ryan and Luke were sitting on the sofa clutching identical Thomas the Tank Engine toys Aiden had bought to bribe them into sitting still. It had worked. They were still where he'd put them, eyes wide as they watched the cameraman.

"Do you have a slapper board?" Luke asked, and they all burst out laughing.

"Do you mean clapper board?" Carter asked with a smile as he knelt next to them.

"Whatever. I watched a video on YouTube. You're supposed to have a sl-clapper board," Luke pouted, looking very disappointed.

"They do. Want to see?" The boys' eyes bugged out, and they nodded as someone handed Carter the clapper board. He showed them what was written on it and how to use it. "I'm Carter. I'm going to help your daddy look after you while he goes to work." The boys were more interested in the board, and Aiden went to step in and remind them of their manners, but Carter bent his head over theirs, pointed out something else, then seamlessly turned it into a question. "What's your name?" He looked towards Luke first.

"Ryan," Luke said.

"I'm Luke." Ryan sat up tall and pointed at his chest.

"That's Ryan, and that's Luke," Aiden interrupted. They looked up at him with identical mischievous grins.

"We was just acting, Daddy." Ryan blinked up at him, his face so innocent Aiden almost believed it.

"Ahh, the famous twin-swap. I like it. I'm going to have to get good at telling you apart, aren't I?" Carter said as he looked from one boy to the other. They sent each other sly looks and gave toothy grins.

"Only Daddy can tell us apart," Ryan said.

"I can do it. You're Ryan, and I can tell that because the

dimple in your cheek is a bit bigger than Luke's."

They scowled at him, their hands reaching for their cheeks. He'd never admit it out loud, but Aiden was impressed. No one had ever noticed the dimple before. Not that it would help when they were running about or if you could only see the back of their heads, but it was a start.

"Do you want to see your room?" Luke asked with a swift change of subject. Aiden's stomach dropped, and he fought off a shiver when he realized that Carter—his cutie—would not only be looking after the boys but also staying in their house, in the room next to his.

He started to hum the *Twilight Zone* theme under his breath, and Carter frowned at him. "Sorry," he muttered.

"Yes, come and see your room. We picked the duvet," Luke said, and both boys shot off the sofa and raced up the stairs.

The spare room was small, only big enough for a single bed, chest of drawers, and a wardrobe. Aiden hadn't thought much about it before, but now he panicked about the single bed and what Carter would think about the worn furniture.

"Batman!" Ryan shrieked as he pointed towards the new duvet set Aiden had let the boys pick out. Why hadn't he vetoed that and gone with the blue striped set he'd wanted to buy? Because the boys hadn't been happy about being looked after by anyone other than Daddy Wyatt, and he'd wanted them to get involved and be excited. That's why. It was backfiring now.

He forced himself to look at Carter and felt his cheeks flush, but Carter had a large smile on his face. He was looking at the duvet like it was the largest piece of chocolate cake he'd seen in his life.

"How did you guys know I love Batman? This is awesome!"

"And you can put your T-shirts in here. And your toys over there," Luke said as he opened every single empty drawer to show him.

"Did you bring toys?" Ryan asked, eyes so wide that it made

Carter smile.

"Of course I did. See that camper van out there?" They walked over to the window. "It's full of toys and games and loads of fun stuff to do together."

"A whole van of toys. Wow, you must be rich!" Ryan pressed his nose to the glass, taking up all the room so Luke couldn't see. Luke went to pull his hair to get him to move, but just as Aiden started to reach for him, Carter stepped back and let Luke move in front of him, so they both got a good look without any meltdowns.

"Not rich, but I save my pocket money."

"Daddy, you got to save your pocket money so we can buy more toys, okay?"

"I want a robot."

"I want a talking dog."

They talked back and forth about what they wanted, and Aiden and Carter looked at each other silently. Aiden knew he was screwed. Well and truly screwed.

CHAPTER FOURTEEN

CARTER

A FEW HOURS later, the crew were gone, and he was alone with Cinders and the kids for the first time. Or as alone as you could be in a house rigged with cameras. Carter disappeared to his room to put away his clothes and give himself a little space. He was still in shock and needed a minute or two to compose himself.

As he laid out an array of multicolored suspenders in the top drawer, a burst of laughter escaped his lips. It was all so surreal. And despite the shock and confusion that had played over Aiden's face, he couldn't contain the spark of excitement that stirred in his belly. He had until he finished packing to savor it, but then he had to go back to being a childcare professional who happened to work in TV. He couldn't have feelings for a client. Even if he did know how well that client kissed and the tiny sounds he made at the back of his throat when he was excited.

Carter closed his eyes and took a deep breath. He needed to stop thinking of Aiden as Cinders and remember where he was. Ryan and Luke were a hoot, and he needed to concentrate on them and not on the fact that he knew Aiden intimately.

His phone vibrated, and Carter pulled it out of his pocket, seeing a message on the group chat he shared with the other mannies.

Evry1 settled? Howz hot dad?

Russ. Carter rolled his eyes. Trust Russ to be prodding him for details straight away. He shoved the phone back into his pocket without answering and went back to sorting out his clothes.

There was a knock on his open door, and he jumped.

"Sorry. Didn't mean to scare you. We're going to order pizza or Chinese... the boys are having a debate over which one. Do you want to join us?"

"I'd like that. Thanks."

Aiden took a step back, then hesitated. "Did you know?"

Carter knew what he was talking about. "No."

He nodded, face still serious. "And you don't know Nio?"

Carter lifted his eyebrows in surprise. "Reel Nio? He's infamous, but I've never met him in person."

"All right. Well, when you're finished, come downstairs. By then, the boys might have decided what they want to eat."

Carter hung his shirts in the wardrobe and abandoned everything else. When he entered the living room, Luke was racing around the coffee table chanting, "Pizza, pizza, pizza," so Carter presumed he'd won the lengthy debate.

"What would you like on your pizza?" Aiden asked.

"Ham and pineapple."

Aiden's whole face scrunched up. "Hawaiian? That's not a pizza."

Carter laughed and sat on the chair next to the sofa. "Tell that to Domino's."

While Aiden ordered himself a meat lovers and a plain cheese for Luke and Ryan, he turned to the boys. "Don't you like any pizza toppings?"

Ryan shook his head. "I don't like bits."

"Yeah, they get tangled in the cheese and covered in the

sauce." They made gagging noises, and Carter bit back a laugh.

The boys chattered and watched TV while they waited for pizza, and Carter did his best to concentrate on them and not their father. Their light brown hair stuck out in identical cowlicks, and they both had their father's grey eyes. But it was their matching grins with the same cute gap between their two front teeth that told Carter he was going to be kept on his toes. They had mischief written all over them.

It was a relief when the pizza came. Aiden got them all plates, and the boys knelt in front of the coffee table so they could carry on watching TV.

"Can we stay up late tonight?" Ryan asked as he wrapped cheese around his finger.

"You can stay up for fifteen minutes longer, but you've had a busy day, and you'll be up early tomorrow."

"Only fifteen minutes? That's not very long. We're not babies anymore. We should be able to stay up as late as we want."

"Yeah, a whole twenty minutes. I want to stay up twenty minutes longer."

"All right, twenty minutes it is." There was laughter in Aiden's voice, and the boys high-fived each other like an extra five minutes made all the difference in the world. When you were six, it probably did.

"It sounds like you'll be staying up longer than me. I'm tired already." It wasn't even a lie. The surprise of the whole day had wiped Carter out.

"You must be *really* old," Ryan said.

"Older than Nanny Biscuit, because she stays up all night." Who was Nanny Biscuit? As far as Carter knew, the kids didn't have any grandparents.

"That's because she naps all day," Aiden said.

The boys pulled faces at each other. "We hate naps!" they screamed, and Carter winced, ears ringing. Then, as suddenly as the noise started, it disappeared as they went back to inhaling their pizza.

Carter couldn't help but grin around his own food as he watched Aiden and the boys. Aiden was laid-back, and the kids were hyper yet sweet. Despite not being able to talk with Aiden yet, he felt right at home sitting in front of the TV eating takeout with them.

CHAPTER FIFTEEN

AIDEN

AIDEN TIPTOED AROUND his bedroom as he got ready for bed. Carter was on the other side of the wall... and they were very thin walls. For some reason, it was vitally important that Carter couldn't hear him as he got changed.

After hours of back and forth—which meant he hadn't been able to talk with Carter—the boys were finally asleep. Not that he could have said much, anyway. Not with cameras in the kitchen, living room, and hallway listening in. Aiden hated knowing those cameras would pick up every little thing he said and did. What if he said something the show didn't like? What if they twisted his words and made him look like an idiot?

His phone flashed with a text: Nio wanting to know how the first day had gone. Aiden didn't bother to reply but rang him instead. He answered right away.

"Well? How is it? Which manny do you have? Details, I want details."

Aiden's fingers tightened on the phone. He sounded oblivious. Carter had said he'd never met Nio—maybe he was telling the truth. Or maybe he was a good liar. "Carter," he eventually replied in a whisper.

Nio shrieked down the phone, and Aiden winced and moved it away from his ear until his voice returned to normal.

"They gave you Carter? He's been in the show since the beginning."

"Have you ever met him before?" There was a noise from Carter's room, and Aiden's eyes shot towards their shared wall, wondering what he was doing. Was he getting undressed? Was it the clatter of suspenders pooling at his feet? He shook the thought away. He needed to focus.

"Carter? No, why would you ask that? I spoke to someone from submissions, but none of the mannies."

"No, I mean, do you know him outside of the show?"

"Of course not. Wouldn't I brag about that?" Yeah, he would.

"I've met him before," Aiden admitted.

Nio gasped. "When? Where? How? Why didn't you tell me before now?"

Aiden rolled his eyes. "Because I didn't know who he was. Remember the guy I met at the club when the boys locked you in the bathroom?"

"Yes..."

"It's him. The manny. Carter. He's the one I was with." Did he have to spell it out?

"No. Fucking. Way." There was too much delight in Nio's words.

"Yes, way. Are you sure you didn't set this up? Because it's... too much of a coincidence."

"Yes, Aiden—from my bathroom, I organized for one of the *Manny SOS* nannies to seduce you, then wrecked it by calling you to come save me. That's exactly what I did."

"Okay, okay, no need to be sarcastic. I was just asking."

"So, does this mean you and Carter are sleeping under the same roof? Are there still sparks flying between the two of you? Do you still think he's—"

Aiden ended the call mid-sentence and crawled into bed. Of

course there were no sparks between them. That would be insane. Carter was a manny for a TV show. Aiden was a nobody with two kids, and he hated the limelight. Sure, Carter was still gorgeous, but now things had changed. He was here to look after the boys while Aiden worked, and that was all.

He groaned and pulled a pillow over his face. He was counting the days until this nightmare ended. How was he supposed to cope with a 24-hour manny invasion? Especially when he remembered the weight of Carter's cock in his hand.

The soft knock on his door made Aiden jump. His first thought was the boys had woken up, but they would never knock on his door, just barrel straight through and jump. Which meant it could only be one person.

What was Carter knocking on his bedroom door for? Nerves, heat, electricity—something he didn't understand—ran through his body. When he opened the door, Carter stood on the other side wearing Teenage Mutant Ninja Turtle pajamas and matching slippers.

"Do you want to come and catch some frogs?"

Was that a new euphemism for having sex?

Aiden's brow furrowed as he replied, "What?"

"The boys put frogs in my suspender drawer, and now I have frogs hopping around my room."

Aiden looked towards the ceiling and groaned. That's what the bang was. How on earth had they managed that between all the cameras and the crew? Perhaps Nio was right. They were turning into evil masterminds. Or chaotic gremlins. He wasn't sure which. Maybe he was lucky, and he'd got one of each.

The box-sized spare room was much too small for two grown-ass men to fit in comfortably. A frog hopped between them, and they bent to try and catch it, foreheads bumping with a sharp clash.

Their collision left a small red mark on Carter's head that Aiden desperately wanted to brush away, but...

"Got one," Carter said, a large smile spreading over his face.

They both looked down as he opened his cupped hands to reveal the tiny frog. It was the wrong thing to do. The frog jumped high out of Carter's palm. He tried to catch it midair again, but it moved through his fingers and propelled itself further into the air. Aiden craned his neck, tried to help catch it, but only managed to let it bounce off a knuckle and right towards his face. It crashed into his closed mouth, and Aiden fell back with a splutter, frantically wiping wet frog off his lips.

"Well, damn," Carter said. "It didn't turn into a prince."

Aiden saw Carter bite at his lip as, without even a 'sorry for bothering you,' the frog hopped under the bed. Apparently, that was the last straw. Aiden felt some of the tension leave his body when Carter laughed and slid to the floor. Scooting one of the frogs out of the way, Aiden slid down beside him.

"Maybe I should have slipped him some tongue."

CHAPTER SIXTEEN

CARTER

CARTER HAD AIDEN and the boys' daily schedule, right down to when everyone used the only bathroom in the morning. He'd set his alarm early so he could be ready for the boys as soon as Aiden left, and he didn't get in his way as he readied himself for work.

He'd done this plenty of times before. He'd stayed at houses smaller than this with larger families, but the house felt tiny, and everywhere he looked there were things that reminded him of Aiden. From cologne in the bathroom—the same one he'd worn at the club—to his brand of toothpaste. Even frogs reminded him of Aiden, for God's sake.

Carter was in the kitchen looking at the boxes of cereal when the twins burst into the kitchen, with Aiden following at a slower pace. His hair still looked damp from the shower, and he was wearing worn jeans and a faded black T-shirt.

"Good morning," Carter said, his voice higher than usual.

"Morning," the boys chimed.

Carter waited. It didn't take long.

"Ribbit," Luke said with a mischievous grin as Ryan jumped around the kitchen. Carter and Aiden shared a smile.

"There are two frogs in the kitchen. I should probably take

them outside. I prepared their breakfast. Two big juicy flies."

"Ew! Frogs don't eat flies," Ryan said and rolled his eyes.

"Yep, there are two flies on the barbeque outside," Aiden played along. The boys squealed and stopped being frogs in favor of sitting at the table and eating cereal, sans bluebottles. "Also, frogs live outside in ponds. Houses and little children scare them, so you probably shouldn't try catching them again. They might think they're lost."

Ryan frowned at his dad. "They weren't lost. We told them where they were."

"And we made them a house with water and mud and leaves. Until we—" Luke slapped a hand to his mouth, eyes wide as he realized what he'd been about to reveal. "Nothing. We don't know how frogs got into Carter's room."

"Yeah, I'll believe that when I see it," Aiden said, giving them a hair ruffle. "Just make sure you leave the wildlife outside, got it?" The boys nodded, though they didn't admit to setting the frogs free.

It had taken Carter and Aiden an hour to find all the frogs and set them loose in the back garden. Carter hadn't minded, though; it had been quite fun. And seeing Aiden kiss a frog?

"I thought I'd make a start on breakfast, I know you all like cereal, but I wasn't sure which you'd like today."

"You don't need to do that," Aiden frowned and leaned around him to grab a box of Frosted Flakes.

"I don't mind." He grinned at the twins, who whispered back and forth to each other.

"Daddy has to make breakfast," Ryan said around a yawn.

"You'll do it wrong. You might put flies in it!"

Carter wasn't sure how cereal could be made wrong, but he played along. "I promise not to feed insects to little boys—only little frogs!"

Aiden poured cereal into two plastic bowls while he filled the kettle and waited for it to boil.

"Shall I make tea?" Carter pulled out two mugs from the

cupboard next to the cereal, wanting to be useful. He was there to work and look after the boys, and that's what he was going to do. "Boys, what do you want to drink?"

"Orange squash," Ryan answered for the both of them.

The kettle boiled, and he went to pick it up, but Aiden's hand came down over his. "I need the water for the cereal first." Carter blinked but pulled his hand away and watched Aiden pour a drop of boiling water into each bowl, then fill it up with milk.

"We want warm cereal," Luke said.

Carter could think of nothing worse, but he nodded. "I can see that." He poured their juice and then made tea. "Milk, sugar?"

"Milk and two sugars. Thanks," Aiden said. Carter slid the mug over to him, and he picked it up, held it in his hands, and leaned against the work surface as he watched both boys eat their soggy breakfast.

"I'm going to make myself some toast. Do you want any?" Carter asked.

Aiden shook his head. "I should head off soon." He took a sip of his tea. "Are you sure you're going to be okay?"

"Of course. We're going to have lots of fun. I'll text you with updates throughout the day, and we'll FaceTime as well."

"Okay."

"I thought we might go to the park this morning," he said, turning to the boys.

"It looks like it's going to rain," Aiden said, staring out the window.

"A little rain never hurt anyone!" Carter said with enthusiasm.

"Aren't we supposed to be staying with Daddy Wyatt?" Ryan asked out of the blue.

"I already explained that he's got to go to work, so we needed someone else to look after you. Which is why Carter is here." Aiden seemed worried, but he kissed each boy and ran a hand through their hair. "I'll speak to you later, boys." They didn't respond, so he sighed and looked at Carter. "Ring me if you need me. I don't work far away, so I can be back no problem. They just can't come to work as it's a health and safety risk, and I'm on a deadline."

"I'll FaceTime you around lunchtime so they can talk to you. Is there a time that works best for you?"

"About one?"

He finally left for work, and Carter washed the bowls while they went to put on socks. When he was done wiping down the surfaces, the boys still hadn't appeared, so he went to find them.

They were sitting on the floor in the middle of their bedroom, toes still bare, crashing toy cars between them.

"It's time to put some socks on," Carter told them. They looked up at him with identical expressions. Today, the only reason he knew which twin was which was because Ryan had on a blue T-shirt with a football on the front, and Luke had on a green T-shirt with a dinosaur on it.

"We don't have any socks here," Ryan said as he pulled back his car and let it shoot towards Luke.

"Where did your socks go?" Carter asked as he pretended to look around their bedroom, picking up toy cars, pillows, and teddy bears. "No, not here." He finally opened all the drawers and looked in their wardrobes—and there were no socks. He did find a large empty drawer he was positive had housed socks at one point.

"Our socks are at Daddy Wyatt's. You should take us there."

"He's supposed to be looking after us."

Carter's heart broke for them. It must be very confusing, and they'd got their hopes up. "I bet you have lots of great socks at Daddy Wyatt's, but Daddy Aiden said he's got to work."

"His name's not Daddy Aiden, silly," Ryan said. "He's just *Daddy*."

"Thank you for letting me know." He gave Ryan a serious nod and a warm smile.

"Can we just go and see him for a little while?" Luke

pleaded.

Carter knelt next to them. "He's not at home right now. He has to work, like Daddy does. That's why I'm looking after you."

"Don't you have a job?" Luke asked, his brow furrowing.

"My job is the TV show, remember? But it means I get to play all day with you two, and I'm so excited about that!" The frowns on the boys' faces weren't quite so pronounced, and Carter hoped he was winning them around. "Can you help me find your socks so we can go to the park? That's if the sock monster didn't take them all."

"There's no such thing as sock monsters."

Carter gasped and widened his eyes. "Then why do I always lose one sock at home?" He stood up and started to look around the room again while the boys just watched him. "The sock monster usually only takes one sock, and he usually only takes them out of the washing machine, but I wouldn't put it past him to take pairs of socks. You know, if they're *really* good socks."

Ryan cupped his hands around Luke's ears and whispered. Luke nodded in response. "Ryan says he don't want to talk to you right now."

"That's okay. We're going to the park anyway."

Ryan rolled his eyes and jabbed a finger at the window.

Luke said, "It's raining now, dummy. It's too wet to go to the park."

Carter looked out of the window, surprised when he saw the rain. He hadn't even noticed the downpour.

"It looks like your daddy was right. Don't tell me you boys are afraid of a bit of water? We can still go to the park."

"Ryan doesn't want to go to the park."

"Neither does Luke," Ryan burst out. His vow of silence hadn't lasted long.

"Well, if you don't want to play in the park, I just might play in the back garden." Carter ran downstairs, put on his jacket, pulled the hood up, and ran outside. It wasn't raining so hard now, but the drizzle soaked through his coat, dampening his shirt. He had a raincoat in the camper, but he didn't want to take the time to fetch it and risk breaking the moment.

The boys had followed him downstairs and were watching from the kitchen. When he knew he had their attention, Carter jumped into the first large puddle he found. Inwardly, he shivered as cold water seeped into his trainers and soaked through his socks to his feet. He'd probably had better ideas than this, but both boys had come down to watch him, so at least he'd got them moving.

"You're going to get into trouble!" Ryan shouted. Luke nodded along.

Carter grinned at them, rain dripping from his hood and down his chin. He lifted his arms into the air. "By who?" He jumped again, and his jeans got wet. He was going to need a long hot shower later.

"Mrs. Brownlow." A teacher, Carter presumed.

"And Miss Goodman. And Daddy says so too."

Carter stopped for a moment, his feet in the deepest part of the water. "Well, that's true if you're walking to school or if you're in the playground with your friends because you'd have to spend the whole day in your wet clothes. But once we're done jumping, we can put on dry, warm clothes. Come on, little tadpoles, don't you want to have some fun?" Carter teased.

They looked at each other and whispered something he wasn't privy to, but they eventually both turned to him and nodded.

"Fantastic!" Carter fist-bumped the air. "Do you have wellies?" They both nodded, their faces still so serious.

"Then let's go get your wellies and raincoats and we'll play." He jumped again for good measure. He was getting used to the cold now, and even the wet jeans weren't bothering him too much. Jumping in puddles was always fun. It was the only good thing Peppa Pig had taught him.

Carter wiped his feet on the mat and followed them back inside to get coats and wellies. He still couldn't find their socks—

where did two six-year-olds hide a drawer full of socks? The only room Carter didn't look in was Aiden's.

It felt wrong to invade his privacy, so he pulled out pairs of his own. One pair had puppies on them, and the others had birds. They were much too big, but Carter pulled them up over their knees. With their wellies on, it wouldn't matter anyway.

This time, when they went outside, Carter took the small spare camera that was no bigger than a teacup and placed it on the windowsill. There were no cameras in the garden, but the spare was there to capture moments like this.

The twins both stared at the largest puddle, and Carter knew he was about to get drenched. He pretended to run towards it but let the boys overtake him, and they slam-dunked into the water, sending it everywhere.

They squealed, and Carter shrieked as the cold water dripped down his face. "Water fight!" he shouted as he found another puddle to splash in.

The boys relaxed enough to forget they didn't like him and had a grand old time ganging up on him and making sure he looked like a drowned kitten.

"We are so wet!" Ryan said, shaking his head. Luckily it had stopped raining, and the sun had come back out. "We made a mess!"

"We're acting a mess for TV. That's what actors do, isn't it? Are you acting?" Luke asked, the words tumbling from his lips.

Carter laughed and ushered the boys inside. "I work for TV, but I'm not an actor. Come on, let's all get out of our wet clothes. Then who wants hot chocolate?"

Both hands shot up with a chorus of 'me, me, me.'

The heavens opened again as they drank, so Carter pulled out their toybox. It was filled to the brim with pieces of a wooden train set and Matchbox cars. The morning passed quickly, and soon it was time to call Aiden.

Carter settled them onto the sofa with the iPad between them, and he stood behind them, leaning down.

Aiden answered right away and seemed relieved when he saw the boys. He instantly spotted the change in all their clothes, and worry flashed over his face.

"We had a fun day splashing in puddles, didn't we, boys?"

They started to chatter over each other, and Aiden grinned, his shoulders visibly relaxing. "One at a time, one at a time. You jumped in puddles?"

"We soaked Carter the most. We was the best at jumping," Ryan said proudly.

"And splashing."

"I can see that." He glanced at Carter through the screen for a second before looking back at the boys.

"I'm not gonna tell the teachers when I go back to school. They'll be mad."

Aiden shook his head. "They'll only be mad if you splash at school. I'm glad you boys—all three of you—had fun," Aiden said, eyebrow-raising and slanting a glance his way again.

Carter's stomach tightened. Despite still feeling chilled from the puddles, he warmed up inside and pulled on the neck of his new T-shirt to circulate some air.

Carter let the boys do all the talking and took the opportunity to sneak a proper look at Aiden. The pristine yet worn T-shirt he'd worn that morning was covered in dirt and sweat marks. He was in a bare kitchen. The units were off the walls, there were tools on the work surface behind him, and he had dust on his cheek that Carter's fingers itched to wipe off. There was a radio playing faintly in the background—classic rock—and Carter wondered if he liked that style of music or if it was just what happened to be on.

"Did you wear your coats and wellies?"

Carter blinked, coming back to the conversation with a start. He shouldn't be daydreaming. The question was innocent enough, but Carter knew Aiden wasn't asking the boys. It was aimed at him, ensuring he was taking proper care of them. Carter didn't blame Aiden. All parents were nervous at first. Leaving your kids, let alone with what amounted to a stranger, wasn't easy. DBS checks and references aside, parents still needed to trust the person they left their child with. He just hoped Aiden would learn to trust him.

"Coats and wellies," Carter nodded. "We were going to go to the park, but it's started to rain pretty badly, so we're going to have fun at the house until you get back. I'm just making lunch, and they're watching *Cars*."

"I'm glad you're all having fun. Have fun with lunch. I should get back to work. I'll see you all later. Love you, guys."

Carter knew Aiden was talking to the boys, but his body still tingled at the words.

He was going to call Dennis's strait-laced brother. Straight or laced be damned. He could not fall for a whole family that wasn't his.

MANNY SOS

CHAPTER SEVENTEEN

AIDEN

Filming with Aiden. Camera Rolling. Day One.

Interviewer: Hi, Aiden. It's good to meet you. How did you feel when your best friend nominated you for the show?

Aiden: I'm not gonna lie, I was a little shocked, but it's not so bad. Carter has been a huge help.

AIDEN LET HIMSELF in, and the boys launched themselves at him, both talking over each other. The tension he hadn't realized he'd been holding left his body as he laughed and lifted them both into his arms. Carter had texted him throughout the day, and he'd spoken to them at lunchtime, but he hadn't been able to brush all the worry away until he'd seen the boys for himself.

"I'm so happy that you had fun with Carter." The name sounded odd on his tongue, and Aiden's glance strayed across at Carter. His skin was shiny and flushed from being outside, and his hair wasn't quite as perfect as it had been that morning.

Aiden liked this rumpled look. He wanted to see more of this side of him. As soon as the thought formed, he tried to shake it off. He shouldn't be thinking about the twins' manny like that.

They had to keep things professional, not only for the boys but for the TV show. Carter wasn't just that cute guy from the club anymore.

No, he was Manny Fucking Poppins. Aiden groaned. When Carter shot him a curious look, he tried to cover it with a cough.

The boys talked about the puddles, how Carter had jumped in first, and about watching *Cars*, as though they'd seen it for the first time and not the thousandth. Aiden nodded in all the right places as he carried them into the kitchen and dumped them on the kitchen table. "I'm glad you had a good time. I bet you're starving." Ryan nodded his head, and Luke patted his tummy.

"Can we get pizza again?"

"No, it's Chinese next. You promised."

"Nice try. There's no way you're having another takeaway this week. You've got to eat something green. Did you manage to get them to eat anything for lunch?" he asked Carter.

"They had ham sandwiches. Plain. No butter, no mayonnaise, nothing."

"Yuck. I hate slimy sandwiches," Luke said.

"Butter touches the ham and gets all over it." Ryan's face twisted in distaste as he thought about it. Aiden would laugh if it weren't so difficult to get them to eat healthily.

"It's okay. I've got some tricks up my sleeve for tomorrow." Carter stepped closer to him and whispered while the twins were distracted.

Aiden's body tensed, hyper-aware that Carter was standing close. He remembered their whispering at the club, and goosebumps covered his arms. This was completely different, but still, it was oddly intimate as they talked about the twins while standing in his kitchen.

"You'll have to teach me, because I can't get them to eat a darn thing."

"My number one trick. Make it look cute. What are they having for dinner? I can help."

"I don't know…" Aiden opened the fridge, then the freezer,

and stared at the food there. "Fish sticks, fries, and... whatever veg is in this bag?" He needed to get a bit more adventurous with food and making things from scratch, but his mind went blank when he tried to plan, and who had the time after work to create all that?

"That's great. You start to grill the fish sticks, and I'll cut the fries. Where are the potatoes?" Aiden pointed to a cupboard under the work surface. He shoved the fish fingers under the grill and watched Carter as he thinly sliced the potatoes and cut each slice into a basic fish shape.

"You're not going to peel them?"

Carter wrinkled his nose. "It's good roughage, plus it makes it less time-consuming, especially when we're taking more time making it look cute." He placed potatoes in a bowl, drizzled them with oil, then hunted through Aiden's cupboards for a baking tray and lay them all flat.

"Why are you making fishes?" Ryan asked.

"Because it'll make dinner fun!" They didn't look convinced, and neither was Aiden, but if Carter wanted to give something a try—and if it got the kids to eat—he'd give it a go.

When the food was cooked, Carter placed the fish sticks at the bottom of the plate, then put the fish-shaped fries above, and gave each fish some peas to nibble on. Aiden could see a basic seascape, but the boys were mesmerized as their plates were placed in front of them.

They touched and played, moving the fish around as if they were eating everything on the plate. "Don't forget you need to eat as well," Aiden reminded them.

"Don't worry about them playing too much. It helps desensitize them if they're picky with textures."

"I bit its tail off," Ryan said as he crunched down on one of his fries.

"And I'm eating sand." Luke shoved half a fish stick in his mouth. It wasn't pretty, and they ate more of the fries than the veg and fish sticks, but he'd seen small pieces of carrot and peas pass their lips, so Aiden counted that as a win.

His own stomach started to rumble, and Aiden realized neither he nor Carter had eaten. Carter was helping the boys scrape their leftovers into the bin and place their plates in the sink, and something tightened around his heart. It was so domestic. How he'd pictured evenings with Wyatt when they were waiting for the twins to be born.

"I'm going to make myself some jar-al-a-pasta if you'd like to join me?"

Carter stared up at him, the smile he'd given the boys still on his face. "That sounds good, thank you. Tomorrow, I can cook for us."

Aiden nodded and turned to get the jar of pasta sauce. He had to remember that this was Carter's job. And they were going to be on TV very soon.

After the boys had eaten, they were raring to go again. Usually, Aiden would turn on Netflix—long enough for him to make himself dinner, at least—but Carter ushered the boys out of the kitchen with promises of a board game.

He hoped Carter knew what he was doing because board games and the boys never ended well. They'd not found a board game the twins couldn't cheat at, and neither of them liked to lose.

His ears strained for arguments or fights, but nothing came, and he went back to cooking—or his version of it. He should have said he'd make something better than pasta and jarred sauce, but in all his panic about having the TV show invade his house, mealtimes hadn't crossed his mind. Which was stupid; where else was Carter going to eat? And it would be rude to cook for himself and not offer to cook for Carter too.

Five minutes later, he was cooking ground beef to add to the jar of sauce. "Need any help?" Carter asked.

"No, it's all under control. The boys okay?"

"Yeah, I've got them making up stories using Story Cubes. Are you sure I can't help?"

The last thing he wanted was Carter standing too close to him. He was already having trouble thinking of him as the kids' manny. Cooking together would help. When they'd cooked for Ryan and Luke, the boys had been right there and a good distraction, but while they were in the living room, there was no buffer between them.

MANNY SOS

CHAPTER EIGHTEEN

CARTER

HE AND AIDEN ate dinner on their laps in the living room while watching the boys play with the Story Cubes. Each face of the die had a different picture, and they took turns shaking them and making up outlandish stories that mostly centered around Uncle Nio, slime, dragons who could drive cars, and snot. Carter had a feeling they were recreating the night they'd locked their uncle in the toilet.

"And then what did the dragon do?" Aiden asked.

"Sneezed all over Uncle Nio. Then he stole a car and raced a raccoon."

"Poor Nio."

While Aiden talked to the boys about their story, Carter took the empty plates into the kitchen and started on the washing up.

"I was going to do that when the boys were in bed," Aiden said.

Carter jumped and spun around, soapy suds spraying them both.

"Oh shit, sorry," he gasped, his heart jumping into his throat as the cooling water penetrated his clothes. Aiden got the worst of it, though. Suds were dripping down his face, and his T-shirt was almost see-through where the suds had soaked in.

"Don't worry about it." Aiden wiped the foam from his cheek and pulled at the hem of his T-shirt where it clung to his skin.

Carter told himself to stop staring. He dragged his gaze upward, looking at Aiden's face. There was still a trace of bubbles on his cheek, so that didn't help. "You missed a bit." He reached to wipe it away, his hand freezing when it touched Aiden's cheek, the slight scrape of stubble tickling his fingers, bringing back memories that made his whole body tight with want.

It was an automatic gesture, one he would do for any friend, but the moment his hand touched Aiden, he knew it was the wrong move. He still wanted him, though he'd tried not to. This man was essentially his boss. Carter was responsible for looking after his children. He needed to make sure Aiden didn't regret it. That he didn't think Carter was some slut who hit on any man he saw.

"Thanks," Aiden murmured. "I'll dry." Carter presumed he'd meant his T-shirt, but Aiden stepped in close and nudged him back towards the sink with his shoulder. He picked up a tea towel and started to dry the plates on the draining board.

Heart pounding, Carter plunged his hands back into the soapy water. He kept his gaze fixed firmly on the sink, washing and rinsing until there was nothing left to keep him occupied.

Thankfully, the boys racing into the room broke the tension. Carter took a deep breath and crouched down to check out their pajamas and fluffy dinosaur-claw slippers. "Look at you, both ready for bed."

"We're not going to bed right now, though. We want to watch *Paw Patrol*."

"An episode of *Paw Patrol* and then bed," Aiden said. The boys groaned but followed him to the living room and piled onto the sofa to snuggle.

"Are you going to watch with us?" Luke lifted his head off Aiden's shoulder. "It's my favorite show."

He looked at Aiden, who nodded a fraction, and Carter

smiled and sank into the chair he'd sat on earlier.

"No, don't sit there. I want you to sit with me," Luke said.

Carter froze, and his and Aiden's gaze locked onto each other.

"There's not enough room on the sofa. I'll sit here."

"No, no, no. We all need to sit together," Ryan said.

Luke scrambled off the sofa, almost kicking Aiden in the balls, and grabbed hold of Carter's hand. "Look, there's enough room."

There really wasn't. Not without being pressed against Aiden, anyhow. But that didn't matter to Luke.

"You can sit next to Daddy," he insisted. "And I'll sit next to you."

Carter couldn't find the words to say no without actually saying, 'Are you trying to kill me?' so he allowed himself to be pulled over to the sofa.

He tried his hardest to leave a gap between them, but by the time Luke climbed back on the sofa, snuggled into Carter's side, and braced his feet against the arm of the sofa, there wasn't much room left.

Luke fit perfectly against his side, and he smelled like soap and mint toothpaste. Carter gave him a tight squeeze and willed himself to relax.

"I've never seen this episode. I hope it's a good one," he said.

It was 8:45 p.m. before Aiden finally persuaded the boys they had to go to bed, and Carter's whole body ached from trying to stay as still as he could while they'd watched not one but two episodes of *Paw Patrol*.

It had been impossible to relax while he was so close to Aiden. He'd been so aware of the man sitting next to him that he could barely concentrate on the TV.

Now Aiden was putting the boys to bed, and Carter was contemplating running away because he needed space to get his emotions under control.

Would it be rude to shut himself in his room so early, though? If Aiden had a husband or partner, he might have done that to give them alone time, but if he did that now, it would look like he was avoiding him, and he wasn't. Though he wanted to.

Hiding out in his room might be rude, but moving off the sofa and to the armchair he'd claimed as his own just made plain sense. Not that they would be pushed together quite so close now the boys were in bed.

Carter would chat for a little while, pretend he was tired, then go to bed. That wouldn't be rude. He could do that. He was pretending to watch kids' TV when Aiden flopped down on the sofa and tipped his head back with a groan.

"Are they asleep?"

Aiden sat back up. "For the moment. You're not watching this, are you?" Aiden grabbed the remote but didn't change the channel until Carter shook his head.

"No, I didn't even realize what I was watching."

"Yeah, I've found myself aimlessly watching kids' shows when they're not even here."

They lapsed into an awkward silence, the air thick around them, and Aiden flicked channels until he landed on a weird science fiction film with bad special effects.

They both stared at the screen.

"This is weird," Aiden finally said, breaking the silence.

Carter had to agree. "For me too."

It looked like he was going to say something, but Luke padded into the living room, rubbing his eyes. "Daddy, I'm thirsty."

Aiden sighed. "You've already had a drink."

"I want cola."

He got up from the sofa and took Luke's hand. "You can have a glass of water and then back to bed."

Luke twisted around to give Carter a mischievous smile and a wave before they disappeared into the kitchen.

Aiden was back five minutes later and flopped down on the sofa. "He's back in bed now," he said, biting at his lip. "This isn't how I thought I'd... Shit, this is so hard to talk about with the cameras."

"I know. Maybe we can chat in the garden sometime?" And he would forget to take a camera out with him.

Carter noticed a movement from the corner of his eye and caught Ryan sneaking into the room on hands and knees. "Are you okay, buddy? It's late. You should be in bed."

From his crouching position, Ryan looked up at them. "The Loch Ness monster is under my bed. Can you check?"

"There's no such thing as Nessie," Aiden said, but Ryan gave him a wide-eyed look until Aiden sighed, sent Carter a shrug, and headed upstairs. Again.

MANNY SOS

CHAPTER NINETEEN

AIDEN

FOR ONCE, AIDEN didn't want to be at work, not when his house was turning into a home. He'd always thought he'd made a homely place for the boys to grow up in, something he'd never had, but he was now coming to realize that it had more to do with people than places.

Carter somehow warmed the place up—Aiden didn't know how he did it, but the way he was with the kids, how he cooked dinner for them and made them lunch, changed a ramshackle old farmhouse into something more.

The boys were feeling it too. They hadn't asked for Wyatt since the first day, and they were excited and happy to be with Carter. They were also eating much better, though their aversion to different foods touching was still there. He checked his phone and saw a photo of the boys on an adventure over the local nature reserve. He'd never taken them that far before—he'd meant to; he'd just never found the time.

They each had a pair of binoculars and were clutching bird-spotting guides. They were both beaming ear to ear, and Aiden had a weird feeling in his stomach that he couldn't describe.

'Looks like they're having fun.'

Fun. Without him.

Aiden caught himself frowning. Not because they were happy, but because he was missing out. He wished he could be more involved in the activities and adventures Carter was taking them on. He'd love to not go into work, but he had to earn a living, and if he played hooky, there would be no reason for him to need a manny.

He'd never have thought of taking the boys birdwatching or cutting sandwiches into stars.

"He's looking at his phone again," one of his two employees, John, said with a booming laugh as he carried the old kitchen sink out of the house and threw it into a skip in the garden.

"Have you got a secret boyfriend?" Daryl said, trying to peer over his shoulder at the message. "Is that who made you lunch? No way would you bring anything as fancy as that into work."

Aiden laughed and pushed him away. That's what you got when you hired friends. Nosy parkers who wouldn't leave you alone.

"No, actually, the childminder texted me a photo of the boys." He turned it around so they could see the twins. He hadn't told them about *Manny SOS*. All they needed to know was he had someone looking after the boys—they could find out about the show when it was on TV. Aiden hoped they'd never did.

"And your lunch?"

His cheeks flushed. Shit. "The m-nanny made lunch for me because he was making it for the boys."

They let out hoots and catcalls, and Daryl grabbed his shoulders into a hug. "It sounds very intimate if you ask me. Is he handsome?"

Aiden's ears burned. "He's all right. I've not noticed. He's there to look after the kids." He did not mention how he'd first met Carter. He'd never hear the end of it—and Nio was bad enough.

"Of course you haven't. Sure, sure. We can play it like that, though." Daryl gave him a wink. "We're going to get a bite to eat from that café down the road. I'm presuming you're not coming with us, considering you've got your fancy lunch?"

Aiden gave him a playful shove. "Get out of here. Don't be late back." They laughed as they left, and Aiden took his lunch and phone to sit in the garden.

The wind was a little chilly, but the sun was warm on his skin. He sat on a low brick wall and looked at his lunchbox. It was a narrow green box with two layers. Carter had brought it for him when he'd given the boys similar ones. It was a bento box, whatever the hell that was, but Ryan and Luke loved them. Carter made them lunch using them every day. He'd also made Aiden lunch this morning, which made him warm inside whenever he thought about it. No one had ever made him lunch before. Not when he'd been a kid and not when he'd been married. He and Wyatt used to sort their own lunches out.

Aiden had told Carter he didn't have to make anything for him, but Carter shot him a look that told him not to mention it again.

As if on cue, his phone vibrated, and the FaceTime alert came up. His heart skipped a beat as he opened it, and both of his boys' faces filled the screen, hands waving at him.

"We spotted lots of birds, Daddy."

"I saw a heroning."

"Heron," he heard Carter's voice correct him in the background.

"*Heron*. It was this big." He held out his arms, and Aiden laughed. The weird loneliness that had been churning in his stomach had disappeared.

"That's great. Are you having fun?"

They both nodded, and Ryan pushed Luke out of the picture so he could have more of the screen. "We're having a picnic."

Luke pushed back. "Will you have a picnic with us?"

"I wish I could, guys, but I have to work." They both groaned, and Carter said something he didn't catch; then the camera focused on his wind-swept face.

Aiden's throat went dry; his voice grew husky. "Hey."

"Hi. I know this is a bit out of the norm, but… are you going to eat lunch now?"

"I was just about to see what you'd packed me."

"Great. Do you want to stay on FaceTime? I'll put you on the picnic blanket opposite the tadpoles, and everyone can eat together?"

It made Aiden giddy to hear Carter's nickname for the boys. He couldn't have stopped the grin spreading across his face even if he wanted to.

"Please, Daddy!"

He laughed and set his phone down on the dusty unit. "If I can't be there with you, that sounds like the next best thing. Watch out for ants, though, okay?"

Carter set them all up, including the GoPro camera he'd taken with him to film their day out, and they chatted as they ate. Or rather, the boys chatted, and Aiden nodded as he chewed the chicken and salad Carter had put in his bento box. The boys had the same, though theirs had all the food separated to avoid anything touching, and they had cute little picks to eat with.

The smell of spices, onions, and garlic was mouthwatering. Aiden followed his nose to the kitchen, where Carter was standing at the stove, still wearing his skinny jeans and shirt, but the suspenders were loose around his waist, and his feet were covered in thick fleecy socks. He looked… at home.

Conflict warred inside him. He shouldn't be sappy just because some guy was cooking in his kitchen and was good with his kids. It was Carter's job to be good with them.

The boys were at the table, heads bent down. Luke's tongue stuck out in concentration as he slowly cut out a piece of paper. "You're being very quiet." Usually, when the kids were quiet, they were up to something, but he could see they were cutting, gluing, and coloring. And they weren't being horrible to each other or causing havoc.

"They're making dinosaur mosaics while I cook dinner."

"But we have to use these numbers and color cards to decide what color. See?" Ryan looked up with a card saying number two in one hand and another that was blue. "This means I need to stick two blue pompoms to my dinosaur. They're scales."

"Those look amazing, and I'm impressed with your counting," Aiden praised. He would never have thought of an activity like this to encourage them to learn their numbers and colors. He'd tried; it led to tears and shouting. Him as much as them.

"You didn't have to cook again. It was my turn," Aiden said as he turned to Carter.

"I don't mind. It gave me something to do while the boys play, and there'll be leftovers for tomorrow."

"Have the boys eaten already?"

Carter shook his head. "They're going to have chili with us. It's not too spicy, and I've done a separate pan without kidney beans and chunks of onion and tomato." Aiden barely ate the same thing as the boys because they were so fussy. It would be a nice change to all eat the same meal.

Carter glanced at the boys, but they were still busy making dinosaurs. "Don't worry, I blended loads of veg into the sauce, so they won't have a clue they're eating it." He winked, and Aiden's knees turned to jelly.

"I'm going to…" What? Kiss you? Make an idiot of myself? No. He needed to get out of the kitchen. Now. "… go take a shower before dinner. Be right back."

MANNY SOS

CHAPTER TWENTY

CARTER

UP EARLY ENOUGH that he'd been able to sneak out to the van to sort a selection of games and brew a pot of coffee—the instant stuff Aiden favored was killing him—Carter sat on the camper van steps, enjoying the chilly morning air against his skin and the silence of the countryside around him. He took in a lungful of air and slowly let it out. It was hard to relax around Aiden. Not because he was being rude, but because the air was thick with tension whenever they were in the same room.

He texted Kyle, who was having a grand time in Spain and was much too busy to speak to his old dad, and he looked at the dozens of photos Nora had sent him of Bobby. She was getting big. It hadn't been that long since he'd last seen her, but newborns grew so fast, so it seemed longer.

His first almost-decent coffee was halfway to his lips when the front door burst open and the twins erupted through it. They jumped and shrieked in delight as they zoomed across the gravel driveway, tagging each other back and forth.

"You're it!"

"No, you're it! Daddy's it!"

"Quick, run!"

Carter grinned, unable to work out which twin was saying

what because they were running so fast as they shouted back and forth. He was doing much better at telling them apart, even when they weren't laughing and he couldn't check their dimples. He loved their carefree laughter, but the way Aiden shouted after them made Carter jump. His hand tightened around his coffee cup, and his grin turned into a frown when Aiden shot out of the house wearing nothing but his boxer shorts.

"Ryan, Luke! Get back here!"

They cackled as they shot past Carter, craning back to look at Aiden and screaming in delight as he gained on them.

They ran towards the open gate at the bottom of the driveway and the long country lane beyond that.

Shit.

Carter's stomach somersaulted, and he dropped his coffee and sprinted after the boys.

"Don't go out of that gate!" Carter shouted. Too excited to listen to reason, they ignored him and carried on, giggling as they ran.

He just needed to stop them before they reached the road.

Carter had shoes on, and his legs were longer than the twins', so he quickly gained on them. When they still didn't stop, he grabbed the back of their T-shirts, pulling them to a stop and breaking their momentum. He slid to his knees, gravel spraying around them as he attempted to stop them without toppling the boys over.

Aiden got to them seconds later, skidding on the gravel next to him. His eyes were wild and his skin pale. "What were you thinking? Don't ever do that. We've talked about this before." Carter could hear the panic in his voice. The boys must have, too, because they froze, their laughter turning into wide-eyed confusion.

Aiden stood up, and only then did Carter realize his knees were red, raw, and bloody, dirt and gravel embedded into the skin. Carter winced; that had to hurt, he was glad his jeans made of tough denim. Aiden didn't even look down. His eyes were still wide as he stared at the boys.

"You're not going to run if I let you go, are you?" Carter asked. They shook their heads and looked down to the ground. Carter stood and walked over to the open gate and shut it.

"The postman must have left it open again," Aiden said through gritted teeth. "I always make sure it's shut."

"Why did you run off?" Carter asked.

Ryan looked at his feet and shrugged, while Luke crossed his arms. "We was just playing."

"Our legs wanted to run."

"You can't run out of the house, towards the road. It's not safe. There is a whole garden you can run in." Aiden raked his hand through his hair as he paced barefoot in front of them.

"It wasn't big enough," Ryan said

"The road is big. Like *Cars*." The twins nodded, as if the explanation should be good enough to stop the adults from fretting or being angry with them.

It didn't do anything for Aiden, Carter was sure. His agitated movements, the way he bit at his bottom lip, showed just how scared he'd been. "Back to the house. Now."

The twins slouched back at a much slower pace, bumping into each other's shoulders with little shoves. Aiden hobbled behind them, bare feet crunching over the gravel.

Carter placed a hand on Aiden's arm, and they both tensed at the shock of electricity that shot through them. "It's my fault. I opened the door to get games out of the camper. I didn't even notice the gate was open."

When Aiden's bicep tensed beneath his fingers, Carter pulled away and shoved his hand in his pocket.

"It's not your fault. How many times a day do they go out to play? They never run off then, but sometimes... They're so full of energy, like it's bursting out of them, and they don't think. They get silly, which means they get dangerous."

Carter nodded. "I'll still make sure the gate and door are locked in the morning. I'll do some activities about road safety with them too."

"Thanks." Aiden let out a slow breath as they followed the boys into the house. Carter locked the door behind him, then shook the handle for good measure before joining the twins and Aiden in the living room.

"What do you say, boys?" Aiden urged them on.

"Sorry," Ryan said with a pout.

"Sorry." Luke started to sniffle, and his chin trembled.

"Do you know why what you did was dangerous?" Carter asked. They both shrugged.

"We've talked about the main road before, haven't we?" Aiden said.

"We forgot," Ryan said. "It was a long time ago."

Aiden sighed and looked at Carter. "I thought they'd grown out of running off. They haven't done it in so long."

"Don't worry. I'll do some fun games about it and give you some tips for when I'm gone, okay?" Carter's heart clenched at the thought of not seeing them every day—which was ridiculous... wasn't it? Only minutes ago, he'd been outside to *get away* from Aiden.

"The road is dangerous. It could have real cars. Or strangers." Aiden became paler the more he talked about it. Carter itched to comfort him, but he didn't know what to do when it came to Aiden, so he concentrated on the boys.

"Come on. I'll cook you guys some cereal, just how you like it. Then you can do some coloring quietly while I get things ready for us to do later, okay?" They nodded their heads but didn't look at Carter or Aiden.

Aiden ran a hand through his hair and shifted from one bare foot to the other. "I need to go and put some actual clothes on," he said, and that was all it took for Carter to allow himself to look lower than his neck. "I don't want to give your viewers more of a show than I already have."

Carter had forgotten about the cameras.

He cleared his throat. "No. No, you don't." But it wasn't the viewers he should be worried about. His gaze lingered for too long as Aiden disappeared up the stairs.

Why were all these emotions warring inside of him? Mannies did not have feelings for the parents of the children they looked after. Only, he'd met Aiden before the TV show, and as much as he'd tried, it was impossible to be objective. He was screwed.

Luke slipped off the sofa and tugged on his hand. "Is Daddy mad at us?"

"No, he's worried. You could have been hurt. You mustn't run off. Your daddy would be very sad if either of you got hurt. You must ask if you want to go outside, and if you want to run, then ask, and we can figure out a fun game to play or go to the park."

"It's not fair. Cars get all the fun," Ryan said and shoved a pillow onto the floor.

Carter reached forward and messed up his hair, which made him smile briefly. "That's so true. They get to drive really fast and carry little boys and girls who like to eat and drink and leave sweet wrappers all over their floors. Come on, let's go get breakfast."

Carter gave the boys their cereal and juice, then set them up with coloring books and crayons in the living room, where it would be easier to keep an eye on them.

"You should color your daddy a really good picture to make him feel better, okay? I'm just going to check on him." He'd been a long time, and Carter was worried.

"Okay, Carter. Tell Daddy we're using the best pages for him," Ryan said.

"I will do."

The bathroom door was open, but no Aiden. His bedroom door was shut. Should he interrupt? It wasn't his place, but...

He just wanted to reassure himself that Aiden was okay.

Carter took a deep breath and knocked on the door. He didn't exhale until he heard the grumbled "Come in." Aiden was sitting on the edge of the bed, meticulously picking stones out of his bloody knees.

"Oh, I thought it would be the boys. Are they all right? Behaving?" He started to yank on some jeans, but he hadn't finished picking out gravel yet and gave a hiss.

"They're fine. Coloring you a picture. Shit, that has got to hurt. Don't do that. You've not got all the gravel out yet." Carter strode over and grabbed his wrist, yanking it to stop him from pulling the jeans any further up his thighs.

Aiden tensed beneath him, and Carter felt his cheeks burn when he looked down at his hand and realized what he was doing. He pulled away as if he'd been burned. "Don't be a baby about this. I've seen kids with much worse injuries, but you've got to get the grit out. Come on, let's go to the bathroom. I know where the first aid kid is." He chattered on as he pulled Aiden to his feet. Still gripping his wrist, and with Aiden holding his jeans together with his free hand, Carter slowly shuffled him towards the bathroom. "I'm not saying I needed to use it on the kids, but a game of thumb war did lead to teeth marks in said thumb."

Once Aiden was seated, Carter switched to his no-nonsense 'teacher' voice. "I'm going to clean the rest of the grit out. Now, let me see those knees."

Aiden didn't even blink; he just pushed the jeans down to his ankles and kicked them off. Which was… something to remember for the future.

Aiden's body was toned from manual labor. He didn't exactly have a six-pack, but he was solid in all the right places, with a spattering of hair that swirled around his belly button and disappeared into his boxer shorts.

Carter could feel his face burning—now was not the time to get turned on—so he rooted through the first aid kit until he could turn around without doing something stupid.

He filled a bowl with warm water, grabbed some cotton buds and a set of tweezers, then took a deep breath and lowered himself to the floor. The air around them felt thick as he nudged

Aiden's knees apart so he could sit close enough to inspect the damage.

"Are your feet okay?" Carter didn't understand why his voice shook.

"They were fine once I brushed the gravel off."

Carter nodded and placed a gentle hand on Aiden's outer thigh to steady him, dabbed at the scrapes, then used the tweezers to remove the tiny pieces of gravel embedded in Aiden's knee. He hissed, muscles tensing under Carter's palm, but didn't move away from his touch.

When Carter was sure he'd got it all, he moved Aiden's knee from side to side for one last inspection. The wound looked sore, it was still seeping a little blood, but he found no more gravel. He gave a small nod and twisted around to the other knee.

He rolled his eyes upwards before he began again. Aiden's jaw was clenched, and his eyes were hooded as they stared down at him. His nostrils flared as Carter shifted his position, his fingers grazing his inner thigh to steady the leg.

The silence between them was deafening. Carter concentrated on the dab of cotton balls and the gentle touch of his hand as he eased gravel out of the wounds, but it wasn't easy. He wanted to break the silence, to ease the tension between them, but words failed him. What would he do if he were tending a child's scrapes and bruises? He did his best to view Aiden as one of his charges, and he was sure it was working when his heartbeat returned to normal.

The water had shriveled his fingers by the time he was finished. He dabbed some antiseptic on each knee, and as he would for any child's scrape, he blew on them.

"There, all better," Carter said, voice shaky.

Aiden groaned.

Carter stood up with a wobble. His legs hadn't gone to sleep; why did they feel like jelly? Aiden spread his thighs wider and steadied him at the waist, which pulled him in closer. Aiden's hand was hot against his hip, and the skin under it tingled in the best possible way.

Face to face, chest to chest, with only a hair's breadth between them, Aiden's breath was soft and warm against his lips…

"Daddy? I need a wee," Luke said, legs crossed as he hopped back and forth in the hallway.

Carter flinched and jumped back while Aiden shuffled towards his son. He hadn't even heard Luke come up the stairs. Some manny he was supposed to be.

"Of course. Bathroom's free now."

They both stepped forward, shoulders colliding at the doorway.

"Sorry. You first."

"Sorry. I'll go check on Ryan." Carter's cheeks burned as he hurried towards the stairs.

"I need to put on some clothes," he heard Aiden mutter.

CHAPTER TWENTY-ONE

AIDEN

IT WAS DIFFICULT to concentrate on work. Whenever Aiden thought about the boys running through the gate, his hands shook, and if he wasn't picturing what could have happened if the boys had reached the road, he was thinking about Carter. About how Carter had caught them, about how he looked after them, and most of all, about how he trusted him. It had taken some time, but he did. Still, he didn't want the twins out of his sight right now. He wanted to be home. With them. All of them.

He was feeling so weak he finally texted Nio back after radio silence for the last three days—he'd ignored too many messages wanting more details than Aiden had been willing to give. That, and Nio wanted to meet his favorite *Manny SOS*.

So yeah. That was going to come back and bite him on the ass.

And to make a terrible day even worse, he'd forgotten his bento box. John and Daryl had persuaded him to go to their favorite café for lunch, but it wasn't until Carter FaceTimed him that the tension building behind his eyes lessened. The boys were clamoring to talk to him, and they'd taken the phone to talk about some elaborate thing they were making. It was so large they were painting outside and having "super fun."

He was glad they weren't still upset about that morning, though he wanted them to remember, if only so they wouldn't do it again.

He left work early, and when he got home, Carter and the boys were in the garden, still playing with the project they'd told him about at lunchtime.

"Daddy!" the boys shouted and ran towards the fence. "See, we stopped at the gate. We're good boys, aren't we?"

Ryan grinned at him. He had paint marks over his cheek, and his T-shirt was covered in grass stains and who knew what else. Aiden's heart swelled with love.

Luke came barreling over wearing a large cardboard box painted like a bus. "I'm a bus, see? And buses—and boys, stop at red lights."

Aiden laughed, all the tension suddenly fading. His eyes found Carter's, giving him a nod as he let himself through the locked gate. Somehow, the boys managed to hug him around cardboard boxes and an array of cut-out traffic signs.

"You've all been very busy." He scanned the chaos around him, the large paint sheet on the grass covered with pots of poster paint, coloring sheets, and another half-painted box-car.

"We've made cars *and* a racetrack. Come see." Luke tugged at his hand and pulled him over to the patio area, where a large track had been drawn in chalk. There was also a mini basketball hoop masquerading as a traffic signal with red, amber, and green lights.

There were different signs: 30 MPH. Stop. Beware of the deer. Signs they would have seen around town but probably never really understood.

"This means there are deer. See my coloring? I stayed in the lines."

Aiden crouched down so he could see all the signs. "I do. You've both done amazing. Did you make the cars too?"

"Yeah, Carter showed us what to do. And then we were driving on our racetrack. Wanna see?" Aiden nodded, and they raced off towards the chalk road where Carter stood beside the traffic lights. He showed the green light, and the boys zoomed off.

"What's this mean, boys? He showed them a 50 MPH sign, and they drove fast, then he waved the 30 MPH, and they slowed down. On their third turn around the track, Carter turned the lights to amber, and the boys slowed down and stopped when Carter switched the light to red.

"You have to stop in case other cars are coming or if people want to cross the road."

"Or deer."

"Yes, or deer. And monkeys, and rabbits, and hedgehogs and frogs."

Carter stood next to him. "Their toys have been taking turns crossing the road." Carter grinned as he watched the boys, and warmth spread out from Aiden's stomach. No one else had ever looked at them with such affection. Oh, their Uncle Nio loved them, but he was like another big kid when they were together.

"You did all this because of earlier?"

Carter shot him a sidelong look. "You're not my first rodeo. I had all the worksheets printed already. I collect cardboard boxes for craft emergencies, and I always have pavement chalk. I find this is a fun way to get them thinking about safety. That car there is for you. The boys couldn't wait to start painting it, but they're waiting for you to finish it."

A lump formed in Aiden's throat, and his eyes burned for some reason. He couldn't form words just then, so he nudged his shoulder against Carter's. They watched the boys, Carter's shoulder nestled familiarly against his, until the sound of a car pulling up outside the gate broke the comfortable silence. Both turned to see who it was.

Nio. Aiden couldn't stop the smile from spreading across his face. He'd missed his best friend. Still, trust him to break the mood.

"Uncle Nio!"

"Vroom, vroom, vroom!" the boys shouted as they raced along their side of the fence.

He was barely through the gate when the boys launched themselves at him, and he allowed them to plow him over.

"Oh no. I've been run over!"

"Don't be silly, Uncle Nio. It's just us. We'd never run you over."

"We'd stop at red lights and let you cross at the zebra crossing." They both chuckled.

"Well, I am glad to hear that." He tried to stand, but the boys wouldn't leave him alone.

"So, that's the infamous Reel Nio, huh?" Carter asked.

"Infamous is about right," Aiden said as Nio and the boys finally headed their way. "And brace yourself because he's a fan of yours."

Nio slapped Aiden on the back and then turned on the charm for Carter, kissing his cheeks and making the boys laugh. They'd abandoned their cars in favor of clambering all over their uncle.

"We want to show you our track."

"Carter, it is very good to meet you. I've watched all your episodes, and you're my favorite—don't tell the other mannies, though, okay?" He gave a wink and let himself get pulled away. "Oh, and Aiden, thanks for inviting me for dinner!"

"I didn't!" he shouted back, but Nio just laughed and let the boys drag him away to their track.

CHAPTER TWENTY-TWO

CARTER
Interview with Carter. Camera Rolling. Day Eight.
Interviewer: Have you met Nio yet?
Carter: [Laughs]

"WHAT ARE WE doing in the garden again?" Aiden asked, sounding puzzled. The patio light was dazzling in the darkness, and Carter had to squint to look at him.

"You don't have to do this. I just want to set it up for tomorrow so they don't see."

The boys had finally fallen asleep and hadn't been down for an hour. The books and bedtime routine Carter had helped Aiden with was finally working. They were going to bed at a reasonable hour and actually falling asleep—which was far better than when he'd first arrived.

"I don't mind doing it, but I'm still puzzled."

"When we made the salt dough earlier, I kept some aside and made dinosaur fossils."

"Huh, I thought we were burying cookies in the garden." Carter rolled his eyes and gave him a playful shove.

"Yes, I'm going to make sure your children hunt for their snacks tomorrow." Carter scoffed. "No, I rolled the dough out and cut it out like cookies, then pressed dinosaur shapes and footprints into it. Tomorrow we're going to hunt for them in the sand pit in that barren patch of dirt near the swing set."

Aiden looked mournfully towards the desolated flower bed and sighed. "Glad it's getting used for something, because plants do not thrive there."

"When they find the fossils, we're going to try and match them with the plastic dinosaurs we have and look through their dinosaur book to see if we can match their footprints."

"Did you do this because I'm taking them to the Natural History Museum at the weekend?"

Carter shrugged, hid another fossil, and then stood up. "Come on, you're supposed to be helping. They're numbered so I can make sure we've found them all. And they're so excited about having a day trip to the Natural History Museum. It's all they've talked about since you told them."

"And you just thought of this activity from the top of your head?"

"Of course not. I found something similar online a few years ago and stole the idea."

They hid the last fossils, and Aiden sat on the garden bench. Carter hesitated, but Aiden patted the space next to him. He sat down, nerves dancing deep in his stomach. The tension that had been blessedly absent a few moments ago as they laughed and hid things around the garden came crashing back

"Do you want a beer?" Aiden said eventually. Carter opened his mouth to decline, but Aiden interrupted. "Don't say you're working. You're technically off the clock as soon as I'm out of work. I'm in charge of the boys now, and I'm going to have one."

True. What harm could it do?

"Sure. Why not." Carter nodded, and Aiden headed into the kitchen but was soon back with two bottles of Coors Light. He handed one to Carter, sat down, and held out his bottle so they could clink.

"Cheers," Carter said and took a sip.

"Cheers," Aiden replied. Seconds later, so rushed that the words were almost strung together, he added, "I was thinking, why don't you come with us on Saturday?"

The question was so unexpected Carter almost spilled his beer. When he turned to look at Aiden, he was still staring up at the bedroom window.

"Come with us." He said it again; this time, his voice was steadier, more confident. "Not because I need help with the boys—though I probably will. Because they'd love it if you came."

"I don't want to intrude. It's family time." Aiden seemed to deflate, and Carter wanted to take back the words.

"I understand. You've been here every weekend. You probably want to go home and visit your family."

"No—I mean yes, I miss then, but that's not it. I have a son." Carter turned on the bench, tucking one knee under him so he could face Aiden. Now it was Aiden's turn to look surprised. Carter felt bad that he was only now mentioning Kyle, but he'd never broached the subject with previous families, and with Aiden… Well, everything had been so complicated right from the start.

"I… what? You do?" Aiden slouched, arm slung along the back of the wooden bench, and Carter was so tempted to skim his fingers over Aiden's arm that he clutched his beer bottle with two hands. "I guess I don't know anything about you."

"I didn't mean to keep him from you. It's just… I don't know how to bring him up. He's fifteen." Aiden's eyes widened, and Carter had to give a soft laugh. He got that reaction a lot.

"What were you, twelve when he was born?"

"Seventeen. His mom is my best friend. I was questioning my sexuality back then, and we agreed to have sex to see how I felt about it. I was hoping for a homo-cure, you know?" he said dryly with a self-deprecating roll of the eyes. "It didn't work, but it did leave us with one very large surprise."

"Jesus, Carter." Aiden's large hand moved from the bench

and landed on his bent knee. Carter stared at it, feeling the warmth spreading through the denim of his jeans.

"It all turned out good in the end. Kyle is a great kid, his mom and stepdad just had another baby, and he's gone on holiday to Spain with his friend, so he's not at home for me to visit." He shrugged, suddenly feeling lonely in a way he hadn't done since he was a teenager.

"I thought I had it tough with the twins when they were babies, but at least I was an adult. I don't know how you managed as a kid."

"We had our heads in the sand a lot of the time. We were just so determined to do it that we refused to give up. It was hard. My family wanted me to walk away. Her family wanted us to be in a relationship. But they all came around to our brand of parenting in the end."

"So you're just going to sit around all day on Saturday? Come with us. We're getting the train, we're going to eat McDonald's for lunch, and I'm hoping they'll be so tired when we get home that they'll sleep as soon as their heads hit the pillow."

As he spoke, Aiden's fingers were absently drawing small soothing circles on Carter's knee. Did he know he was doing it? Carter wasn't sure, but each circle was a brand so hot Carter had to hold back a shudder so Aiden wouldn't realize how much he was affecting him and pull away.

"Please," Aiden said.

"Okay. I'd really like that." He gave in quickly, resolve crumbling. Warmth settled in his stomach, and his heart did a little skip as Aiden grinned at him. He held his beer bottle out, and Carter clinked his against it.

"Cheers." Aiden tipped his head back and took a sip of his beer. Carter was definitely not watching how his throat moved as he drank. No, he was too distracted by the hand that now squeezed his knee.

CHAPTER TWENTY-THREE

AIDEN

THE TRAIN WAS packed with families who'd had the same idea as them. Fortunately they'd found a table, and each boy sat next to the window alternating between bouncing in their seats and looking at the passing scenery or sticking car stickers in a book that Carter had brought along.

It was working. They weren't racing up and down the aisle, and they weren't clambering over the table or pulling each other's hair. He wondered if Carter had ever written a book. If not, he should—because none of the child-rearing books he'd devoured gave the kind of practical advice Carter did.

They were both leaning on the table, ready to join in placing stickers in the twins' books if asked but allowing the boys to have fun while they chatted. Aiden's legs were long, and the table was narrow, so his knees nudged against Carter's whenever they went over a bumpy section of track.

This was what he'd imagined a family would be like when they went out on day trips. Like Hallmark, only better. Except Aiden needed to remember that Carter wasn't there for good.

A thought came to him, and he touched the back of Carter's hand. "Were we meant to let the producers know we're going out? Don't they usually organize a cameraman if you take the boys somewhere away from home?"

"Don't worry about that. It's Saturday, and I don't technically work weekends—what can they do? They wouldn't be following you if I wasn't with you, so there was no reason to ring them when you asked me along."

Aiden pressed his knee closer to Carter's. Good, he didn't want anyone following them about, pointing a camera at them, and having people gawk.

"We're almost there, boys. You must hold one of our hands while we're in the train station because it's so busy, and you mustn't hide or run off. At the museum, you're allowed to walk in front, but if you're too far ahead, one of us will shout 'stop,'" Carter said, reminding them what was expected. "You remember what to do from our day playing with the cars, don't you?"

They nodded. "Stop!"

"That's great, boys. Good listening and remembering." They glowed as he praised them, and Aiden made a mental note to do that more often. For so long, he'd felt like he was always telling them no and stopping them from doing something or moaning about something. He wanted to have fun with his kids. He didn't want to be telling them off constantly.

None of the books, TV shows, or the fossil game they'd played with Carter had prepared the boys for just how big dinosaurs were.

"We can't fit one of these bones in our bag, Luke," Ryan said as they craned their heads back to look at the T-Rex towering over them. They raced around looking at all the different displays, only running too far away a few times, and they stopped as soon as Aiden had shouted the magic word.

"Stand in front of the dinosaur, boys," Aiden said, wanting to take a photo of them with the skeleton towering behind them.

"You get in the photo too," Carter urged, giving him a shove towards the boys. He didn't have that many photos of him and the boys that weren't selfies or quick snaps taken by Nio or John, so he handed his phone over to Carter and went to stand between the boys, an arm slung over their shoulders.

Carter had only taken one photo when a lady interrupted him, said something, took the phone out of his hand, and pointed toward Aiden and the boys. Carter shook his head, and Aiden realized the stranger was offering to take a photo of all four of them. It hadn't occurred to him, but now... he wanted it. He wanted something other than the TV show so he and the boys could remember that it wasn't just about *Manny SOS*.

Carter's cheeks were flushed, and his hair was ruffled when he awkwardly came to stand with them, looking flustered and unsure where to place himself.

"Come here." Aiden reached out and tugged him to stand behind the boys. He placed an arm over Carter's shoulder and a hand on Luke's. Carter mirrored him with Ryan, but his free hand slid around Aiden's waist like it was made to be there.

"Sorry about this." Carter gave a nervous laugh.

"Don't be. This is perfect."

MANNY SOS

CHAPTER TWENTY-FOUR

CARTER

ON THE JOURNEY home, the boys' usual unending energy had flagged, and they were now sleeping, curled around each other like oversized puppies. Carter couldn't say he was any better. The steady movements of the train lulled him into a light doze.

He was pleasantly tired—the kind of tired you had after a good day. And it had been a good day. He was glad Aiden had asked him along. Seeing Aiden playful, carefree, and just enjoying the day with his sons was something he wouldn't forget.

They managed to rouse the boys long enough to get them off the train and to Aiden's car, which was parked across the road from the station.

Ryan clutched the T-Rex plush he'd picked out from the gift shop to his cheek as Aiden buckled him into his car seat, while Luke held a stegosaurus loosely under one arm. Carter helped him into his seat, buckled him up, and placed the dinosaur back in his arms without waking him.

He and Aiden shared a look through the car doors and over the boys' heads. Time stood still, and Carter's heart swelled. The emotions coursing through his body were heavy and thick like a warm blanket—he'd only ever experienced this with Kyle and Nora, but now Aiden and the boys felt like family too.

Carter knew it was too soon for that, but being in such close proximity had hurried along the feelings he already had for Aiden from the first encounter, and it was impossible not to love Ryan and Luke.

Even when they put frogs in his bed.

A car horn beeped in the background, and the moment drifted away as they climbed into the car for the short drive back home. Home, as in Aiden and the boys' home.

When Aiden turned off the engine, the silence was almost too loud. Carter was positive he could hear his own heart thudding against his chest. Could Aiden hear it too? He fumbled with his seatbelt, fingers not working.

Aiden's hand covered his, stilling his movements, and with a soft caress and a tangle of fingers that sent shivers down Carter's spine, he pressed the catch and released the seatbelt, then reached for his own.

Carter took in a deep, shaky breath. He had to get himself under control. This was a job, and there was no way his bosses would approve of—whatever this was. It wasn't as if they'd done anything, but looking after the kids, cooking dinner, and watching TV together was more intimate than anything else he could think of. Intimacy of the heart was a whole different ballgame to intimacy of the body, and he was realizing that at a rapid rate.

"I'll carry them in," Aiden whispered.

Carter wasn't sure if Aiden expected him to watch as he carried one boy in and then came back for the other, but that wasn't going to happen.

He walked around to the side of the car and unclipped Luke from his booster, carefully lifting him out. Carter gave a soothing "Shh" against his ear when his nose wrinkled and he let out a soft whine, but Luke still blinked his eyes open and grimaced.

"It's okay, little tadpole. Go to sleep."

"Not a tadpole. I'm a dinosaur," he said and promptly laid his head on Carter's shoulder and fell back to sleep.

Carter's heart stuttered at their small exchange. Luke smelled of sugar, fresh air, and sunshine and looked so content nestled in his arms. The boys were usually on the go 24/7. Carter hadn't seen them sleepy and heavy-limbed before. He could get used to it.

"They can sleep without brushing their teeth for one night," Aiden whispered as he pulled off Ryan's shoes. Carter did the same for Luke, and quietly, they got the boys into their pajamas and under the covers. They stood watching them for a few moments. When all stayed blessedly silent, they tiptoed out and back down the stairs to the kitchen

"Tea?" Aiden asked.

"God, yes." Now Aiden had said the word he was desperate for a cup of tea. He was achy, tired, and happy from their day exploring, and now all he wanted to do was curl up on the sofa with a hot drink and be quiet for a moment.

Aiden handed him his mug, and they walked into the living room. Carter hesitated when he saw the chair he usually sat on was full of clean washing waiting to be ironed and put away. It would be silly to move it when there was a perfectly good spot on the sofa.

He sat down, curling his feet into the middle cushion, and sighed. Aiden mirrored him at the opposite end of the sofa, both sharing the cushion in an oddly intimate way. They weren't touching, but the closeness was making Carter's body tingle.

"Thanks for inviting me today. I had a great time," Carter said softly, worried if he spoke any louder he might break the spell entangling them.

"I should be thanking you. The boys loved having you there."

They talked about the day—how good the boys had been; how much fun they'd had; how quickly they'd fallen asleep—sipped their drinks, and bickered about whether turning on the TV would be tempting fate. Within ten minutes of Aiden winning the goodnatured argument, Carter's eyes closed. The next thing he knew, Aiden was standing over him, shaking his shoulder.

With a gasp, Carter's eyes shot open. Somehow he'd slipped down the sofa and seemed to have taken up all the space. Aiden was hovering, hand still on his arm, giving him the cutest, widest grin while he floundered like a landed fish. Great. He'd probably snored too. Or worse.

"Did I kick you off?" Carter asked, running a hand over his face to surreptitiously check for drool.

"Nah, but I thought I was going to have to carry you to bed as well. Fireman's lift."

The words and Aiden's almost-cocky grin made Carter's body take notice. His skin suddenly felt too tight, and apparently, his cock really liked the idea of being carried upstairs. "I'm more partial to bridal style." He pulled himself up into a sitting position and winked. "It's more dignified." Though a fireman's lift did put him closer to certain… attributes he was fond of.

Aiden cackled at him and gave him a playful shove in the arm that made his insides flutter and turn to goo. "Don't you think I'll do it?" Aiden managed to lunge at him, and before Carter could stop him, he was lifted off the sofa and into the air, his belly swooping at the motion of their closeness.

"Aiden!" Carter's outraged yell was more of a breathless whisper so he wouldn't wake the boys, and despite struggling and poking Aiden in the chest, there was no real weight behind it. He was more than happy in Aiden's arms. "Put me down!" They both laughed, and Aiden only bumped into the handrail once as he made his way to the stairs, which tightened his arms around Carter. He couldn't say he was unhappy about that.

"Why?" Aiden's face was so close to his that Carter could see the flecks of hazel in his eyes. "I'm carrying you the way you wanted. *Bridal style.*"

God, he wanted to taste Aiden's laughter on his tongue. He shouldn't have mentioned bridal style. It was too intimate—it made him think of family and long term, yet they hadn't even had a chance to really talk. Still, he couldn't stop the shiver racing up his spine at the images it bought to mind.

Damned cameras. It wasn't fair.

Aiden stumbled up the stairs, and Carter bobbed in his arms, his forehead bashing against Aiden's cheek until they burst into giggles again.

"Shhh," Carter said, pressing a finger against Aiden's lips, which just made him snort and giggle even more.

This was ridiculous, for God's sake. They were two grown-ass men.

"Put me down, you crazy man." Carter flailed his arms, and Aiden slowly lowered him to the ground, bodies sliding against each other. Aiden didn't pull away.

Carter covered a moan with more laughter and hoped Aiden didn't notice exactly how he was affecting him. "If you have a bad back tomorrow, it's your own fault," he teased as he poked him in the ribs.

"Worth it," Aiden said.

"You're easily amused," Carter teased. Their smiles slowly faded, and the silence became heavy around them. Frustration clogged his throat. There was so much Carter wanted to say, so much he wanted to do, but *Manny SOS* cameras were literally everywhere except their bedrooms. He couldn't even sneak into Aiden's room without it being suspicious.

As it was, there was no way the cameras hadn't caught Aiden's crazy antics on film. Joe would already wonder what the hell they were doing, but Carter could play it off as having a bit of fun. If they did anything else, he'd not be able to explain it away. He'd never acted like this with parents before, and Joe knew that. Dammit.

Aiden's arm was still around his waist, and even knowing all the reasons why he should pull away, Carter couldn't make himself move.

The hallway was mostly in darkness, apart from the beam of light shining through from the bathroom, and Carter could see the sharp planes of Aiden's face, the way he clenched his jaw, and the reflection of light in his dark eyes. It seemed neither of them wanted to let the other go.

"Goodnight," Carter whispered.

"Night." Strong hands tightened around his waist as Aiden leaned forward. Carter's breath caught in his throat, and his eyes widened when Aiden pressed a fleeting kiss to his cheek and then let go, disappearing into his own room. He couldn't work out whether he was disappointed Aiden didn't kiss him on the lips or if he was relieved.

Carter braced a hand on the wall. His whole body burned, his cheek tingling where Aiden's lips had been. His legs were like jelly when he stumbled into his room and flopped onto the bed. How could a one-second kiss on the cheek be the best kind of foreplay he'd ever had?

He groaned and ran a hand over his face. Despite how tired he was, how he'd been falling asleep since their journey back home, he couldn't drift off. He checked his phone and scrolled some of the unread messages from the *Manny SOS* group chat he and the guys were in.

Many of them were asking how he was doing, but Carter knew they were trying to dig up dirt on Aiden and the twins. If only they knew the half of it. He'd been largely absent in their private chat since they'd started filming because he didn't know what to say about Aiden without giving himself away. How much was too much? Was he being too friendly? Talking about them too much? Being too nice? Would the other nannies notice?

Now he just needed someone to talk to who had an inkling of what he was going through.

Is anyone awake and free to chat? he typed after a moment's contemplation. One by they all read the message and replied. It was after ten p.m., and most of them were on their own time.

He tapped the back of his phone with a finger as he decided what to say.

Hypothetically speaking—if a manny fell for the single, hot dad he was working for—would it be wrong?

Two seconds after posting, one of the others invited him to video chat. He shook his head to himself. Nope, no way. He couldn't talk now. Aiden was on the other side of the wall. But they persisted, each of the nannies bombarding their chat until he hunted for his earbuds and accepted the invite. At least it would shut them up.

Each of his *Manny SOS* friends-in-arms appeared across the screen. "What the actual fuck?" Russ was the first to talk.

"Are you on drugs? This is the last thing I expected from the *king* of *Manny SOS*," Frey said with a grin and a wink.

Carter rolled his eyes and whispered, "That's *queen*, bitch, please."

It took a while— he was paranoid that Aiden would be able to hear him—but they eventually wormed the whole story out of him.

They were all conflicted. Half told him to go for it—Russ wanted every detail—the other half thought it was a bad idea. It wasn't professional; he knew that. His head knew that, but his heart didn't care. *Shit.*

He knew this shouldn't be happening, but he couldn't stop the fall, and the longer he was in Aiden's home, the more he didn't want to stop it.

"Did you know that our families only live a half hour away from each other?" Sebastian said. Carter shook his head; he hadn't known that. Usually they were scattered all over the country. "We should make a bit of *Manny SOS* history."

"What do you have in mind?"

"Let's get the kids together for a play date. I'll come over to yours."

"We'll have to tell the producers. They might veto that."

"Oh please, they'll love it. You know Ronnie will love it. We'll schedule a crew like we do when we have other activities. The kids can all play outside. While the cameras run after them, they'll be too busy to listen to us, and you can tell me all about it. What do you say? Shall we try and arrange it?"

"That is not fair. I want to come too." Russ pouted.

"You're in Scotland, sucks to be you," Isaac said and laughed when Russ gave him the finger.

"Talk in plain sight. That could work."

Sebastian's smile widened. "Exactly."

CHAPTER TWENTY-FIVE

AIDEN

Interview with Ryan and Luke. Camera Rolling. Day Twelve.
Interviewer: Hi, boys—
Luke: Did you know tadpoles turn into frogs?
Ryan: But frogs don't turn into princes.

IT WAS SUNDAY, the day of rest, but Ryan and Luke hadn't gotten the memo. They barged into his bedroom and launched themselves on the bed, knocking the wind out of him. Aiden groaned and grabbed the boys, tickling them until they giggled and he got his breath back.

"It's… five in the morning. It's too early to be up." Their early night had restored them to their usual high-energy, hyperactive selves.

"I'm not tired." Luke bounced on his belly.

"Why don't you watch TV for ten minutes while I wake up." He scrambled for the remote control and turned on the small TV hung on the wall opposite.

"Yesss!" Ryan said and snuggled down next to him. They always loved watching TV in his room, which was the perfect excuse to get a few more minutes of sleep.

The boys fought over the remote, but Aiden let it go over his head as he tried his hardest to wake himself up. It was futile. He didn't even get a full fifteen minutes before Luke was poking his cheek and Ryan was attempting to lift his eyelids, managing to prod him in the eye.

"I'm up. I'm up," he said and pushed prying hands away from his face with a laugh. He held his eyes wide with his fingers and stared at the boys. "See? Wide awake!"

"Goody! I want breakfast." Luke scrambled over him and ran to the bedroom door.

"I want bacon. I'm starved." Ryan patted his belly. "Let's wake Carter up."

Aiden managed to grab them both before they burst into Carter's room like a herd of hungry hippos. "Let him sleep. You can help me make breakfast, and I'm sure the smell of bacon will wake him up." Aiden wasn't about to get a lie-in, but that didn't mean Carter needed to be woken up on what was technically his day off.

"Do you want sausage and egg as well?"

"A fries up! Yeah, let's have a fries up. Can I get toast?"

"But with no butter."

"Yeah, you can have toast as well, and I remember you don't like butter on your toast." No, they liked it dry as a bone. He didn't know how they ate it, but they did, so he wasn't complaining.

On a go slow, he yawned his way through frying the sausages, gulping down coffee. How could the boys be in such high spirits today? He needed another day to get over their trip to the museum yesterday.

"I left my dinosaur upstairs," Ryan said.

Luke nodded a little too vigorously. Aiden might not know what they were planning, but he knew secret twin code when he saw it.

"Me too. I bet it's hungry too," Luke said.

"Mine wants bacon. Make extra, Daddy."

He gave an absent nod and poked the sausages. The boys ran

to get their dinosaurs, but what they brought downstairs was not small and extinct. It was adorable, though. Carter's bedhead rivaled one of their toy trolls, and his sleepy puppy pajamas made him look cuter than he'd ever seen him. And hot. Incredibly hot.

Don't go there.

His throat dried up, and he took a shaking sip of coffee. "Shi—I mean, sorry they woke you. I was trying to let you have a lie-in. Looks like the twins played me."

Carter snorted and wiped the sleep from his eyes. He'd never come downstairs in his pajamas before, and Aiden almost swallowed his tongue at the sight. Pajamas suited him, bedhead and all.

"It's okay, my nose followed the bacon." He was obviously trying not to grin, and Aiden lifted an eyebrow as Ryan held out the half-empty pack of bacon he must have swiped from the sideboard. "Apparently, the scent of bacon means I'll be joining you for breakfast—hope you don't mind."

"You devil, I told you not to wake him," Aiden scolded, but there was no heat behind the words.

"We was just making sure he could smell the bacon."

He rolled his eyes at them, and he and Carter shared a smile that warmed him from the inside out.

"Do you want any help?" Carter offered.

"Absolutely not. Sit, relax, and I'll feed you." Aiden added bacon to the pan, got the bread out, ready to toast, and listened as Carter and the boys played Eye Spy.

It was scary how seamlessly Carter fit in with… everything. Oh, Aiden knew he was a manny, that was what he was meant to do, but it felt like more. Since he'd arrived, there had been more structure and rules, but there'd also been more fun and warmth. It was starting to feel… complete, and that terrified Aiden. What would they do when Carter left?

He tried to shove that thought from his mind.

"It's going to be sunny today. What do you boys want to

do?" Aiden asked. "We could go to the nature reserve and paddle in the creek." Both boys cheered. They loved playing in the water and hunting for treasure.

"Is Carter coming?"

"If Carter wants to?" He turned to Carter, who cocked his head to the side and smiled, his blue eyes sparkling.

"Carter would love to join you tadpoles at the creek."

"Fantastic. Let's eat breakfast and then get ready to go."

Carter grabbed a bottle of orange squash from the cupboard and filled the boys' glasses. "Oh, before I forget, the producer might ring you at some point this week—nothing bad. It's just, one of the other nannies realized that we're only half an hour away from each other, and we thought it might be fun to get the kids together. Have a day in the garden or go out somewhere if you'd prefer us not to be here."

"Other kids to play with?" Ryan's eyes widened, and he practically vibrated in his chair.

"Can they come here? We've never had friends over before. Please, please, pretty please, with sugar on top?" Luke pleaded. Aiden felt guilty that he'd never let the boys have friends over, and he couldn't deny them some happiness when they were excited about it, even if it meant more cameras and more nannies invading his space.

"Sure. I don't see why not."

"Yes!" Luke and Ryan fist-bumped each other and grinned so wide their cheeks became red. "This is the best holiday ever."

Aiden had to agree with them.

CHAPTER TWENTY-SIX

CARTER

Interview with Carter. Camera rolling. Day Sixteen.

Interviewer: I hear it was your idea for a Manny SOS crossover special.

Carter: [Laughs] Sebastian and I kind of came up with it together.

THE SMALL GET-TOGETHER he and Sebastian planned had taken on a life of its own once the producers got hold of it. A bouncy castle was hired, the paddling pool was filled, and someone had bribed the sun gods to shine because the day was glorious.

The crew had arrived as Aiden left for work, and Sebastian and his charges not long after. Sebastian was wearing shorts and a red T-shirt, with a baseball cap covering his cropped blond hair, and he had a bag full of items for the kids slung over one shoulder. Spare sun hats, extra suntan lotion, a large plush teddy bear, and bright orange water pistols.

It hadn't taken the kids long to get over their initial shyness and race off together to play on the bouncy castle while he and Sebastian watched from deckchairs opposite.

Carter envied their ability to make friends so easily at that age. He and Sebastian watched for a while, ready just in case they were needed, but now they had other children to play with the adults were boring. Apart from the cameramen. They all adored showing off for the cameras.

It was fun to watch the boys interact with other children. Carter had only ever seen them play with each other, so it was nice to see how confident they.

Anna and Thomas were a little more reserved. The boys 'sharing' a face had confused Thomas for all of two seconds before the lure of bouncing became much more interesting. The cameramen moved around them like ghosts, peering over the top of the bouncy castle and following them to the paddling pool. They were even squirted with the water pistols Sebastian had thoughtfully brought with him.

Neither of them spoke about what was on Carter's mind until they were sure Joe and the cameramen's attention was focused on the kids and not on them. They sat on deckchairs on the patio, which gave them the perfect position to see the whole garden. The paddling pool was in front of them, and the bouncy castle to the right.

As they watched the kids running around the garden like maniacs, Sebastian prodded him on the arm. Carter glanced toward him, but Sebastian's perfect profile was already gazing into the distance. The cameras skimmed over them as they followed the children's antics.

"Tell me about you and hot dad," Sebastian hissed from the corner of his mouth.

Real subtle. Less James Bond, more secret squirrel. Carter rolled his eyes and turned to track the cameras. "Nothing's happened."

"But you want it to." Sebastian smirked, and Carter felt the urge to punch him because he was right, dammit.

"I am a shitty, shitty person."

"Why? What happens behind the scenes stays behind the scenes," Sebastian said. Carter raised an eyebrow.

"If only it was that simple."

"You're making it more complicated than it needs to be."

Was he? If he got this wrong it could mess with his career, disrupt Aiden's life, and potentially hurt the twins—which he didn't want to do. He watched them as they played, a smile forming on his lips.

"Carter! Come bounce with us!" Ryan screamed as he raced towards them, cutting off their conversation because—who could say no to bouncing?

They didn't have a minute to themselves until it was time to grab snacks. Carter pulled bowls of fruit he'd prepared in little star shapes out of the fridge while Sebastian grabbed sandwiches he'd cut into hearts.

Fuck.

Carter poked one of them disdainfully. "Subtle, Seb."

"I try. So why are you all cut up about this guy? It's not like you've been here long enough for anything deep and meaningful. Unless you're going to tell me it was love at first sight?"

Carter rolled his eyes and gave Sebastian's shoulder a shove. "Don't be stupid. Ass." He bit at his lip before carrying on. "After we wrapped up shooting B-roll for the Oxford job, I went to a club. Hooked up with a guy."

"And?"

"And? It was Aiden. I didn't have a clue until the door opened and the cameras were on us," he hissed. Sebastian burst out laughing, and Carter's gaze shot sideways to check the kids and cameramen weren't paying attention.

"Oh my God, that's hilarious. Talk about fate. You really had no clue it was the same man?"

"Of course not. Aiden's photo wasn't in the information, and the reel only had Nio on it. How was I supposed to know?" The world was throwing them together, teasing him because he couldn't make a move. It was unprofessional. Wasn't it?

It had taken Carter a while to put all the details of his first and second meetings with Aiden together, along with Nio's reel, but it was obvious once he had all the information.

"So, am I going to get to meet him?"

"He's coming home from work early, so yeah, you'll get to meet him."

Sebastian grinned. "For what it's worth, you're being too serious about this. Remember—whatever happens behind the scenes—"

"Stays behind the scenes," Carter repeated his own words back at him.

"I need to pee!" Anna screamed as she hopped towards them, crossing her legs and bouncing.

"Boys! Show your friend where the toilet is!" Carter shouted, and Luke and Ryan threw themselves off the bouncy castle and charged towards the house. Anna sent them a toothy grin and followed.

Carter had just put coals on the barbeque, and Sebastian was dousing the kids in sunscreen until they were slippery as fish when Aiden's truck pulled up. The twins shrieked when they heard his car, rushing to the fence and pulling themselves up to the top rail, where they whooped and waved at their dad.

Carter was glad they didn't attempt to open the gate or climb over the fence. "That's our dad," they said as Anna and Thomas wandered over to see what they were looking at. Carter had to swallow his own spit and stop himself from running to the fence just like the boys had.

Aiden looked good. A white T-shirt with dust marks strained over his chest, his worn jeans hugged his ass, and the smile he sent the boys made Carter's heart swell. He hugged them over the fence and looked up to search the garden, smile widening when his eyes found Carter's.

"Damn…" Sebastian muttered, leaning into Carter's ear. "He's eye-fucking you right now."

Carter jabbed his elbow into his ribs. "Don't be crude."

Aiden hopped over the fence and bent down to shake hands with

Anna and Thomas. He didn't see the small water pistol Thomas had hidden behind his back until he got a spray of cold water in the face instead of a handshake.

His look of surprise and shock had Carter bursting into laughter. Aiden glanced at him with a mock glare and wiped his face. "You could have warned me."

"Oh no, you're on your own here."

Aiden shook his head, and a few water droplets sprayed Thomas, who shrieked in delight and raced back to the paddling pool to fill up the gun.

"Water fight!" Ryan yelled and dragged Aiden with him.

"Come on, Seb, you can be on my team," Anna said. Sebastian shook his head with a laugh.

"I've only just dried off. I'm in charge of burning the burgers. Take Carter instead."

Anna grabbed hold of his hand, and he went willingly towards Aiden and the boys. "Traitor!" he called over his shoulder towards Sebastian, who just smirked and waved a pack of rolls at him.

By the time he got to the paddling pool Aiden was in it, clothes and all, while all three boys scooped out water and poured it over him. "Need some help there?" Carter asked with a laugh.

"Take pity on an old man?"

"It's your own fault. That's the oldest trick in the book," Carter snorted but reached out the hand Anna had abandoned in favor of helping the boys soak Aiden.

"You sure about that?" Aiden's wicked grin, the way the corners of his eyes creased, distracted him, and it was too late to save himself as Aiden grasped his hand and yanked him down. Carter landed on him with an 'oof' and a splash that had the kids squealing with glee.

It was much too small for two grown men, but that didn't stop Aiden from twisting and dunking him in the cold water. The kids giggled and shrieked, the twins jumped on top of them, and

Anna and Thomas picked up the water guns again.

"The war is on," Carter promised, reaching up towards Ryan and tickling him until he slid off and ran towards the bouncy castle to escape, with the others following. They lay pressed against each other for a moment, legs hanging over the edge, before Aiden pulled himself free and yanked Carter up with him. Still gripping his hand, Aiden dragged him to the bouncy castle.

It was slippery, and the kids flung themselves on the floor as Aiden bounced, screaming with delight as they were thrown into the air. Carter couldn't stop the grin spreading across his face or the joy that filled his heart when they glanced at each other.

CHAPTER TWENTY-SEVEN

AIDEN

THE KIDS HAD eventually let him go long enough to change into dry clothes. When he came back down, the burgers were grilled and all the kids were quiet, stuffing food into their faces. The cameramen were still there—which felt weirdly awkward—but they kept their distance, and it was easy to forget they were there. With no directors or producers telling him what to do, Aiden found himself relaxing.

Carter had changed as well and now wore shorts and a baggy T-shirt. His hair curled softly around his ears, still damp from their earlier dunking.

"I hope you're hungry. Sebastian cooked enough to feed a small army."

"I'm starving," he said, dragging his gaze away from Carter and smiling at the other manny. "Hi, I'm Aiden. Sorry I didn't introduce myself before." They shook hands, and then Sebastian shoved a burger into his hand.

"Sebastian, and that's okay. I feel like I should apologize for Thomas shooting you."

Aiden laughed and shook his head. "That's okay. I've had worse." He raised an eyebrow at Ryan and Luke. "Whoever invented slime should be thrown in prison."

Sebastian grinned and sent Carter a look that Aiden didn't quite understand. Carter's ears turned red, and he concentrated on his burger. "Ahh, slime, yes."

It took Aiden a second to realize, but then he groaned. "Don't tell me. You saw Nio's film?"

"Of course I did. We all did. I swear we almost had a duel when you agreed to the show, we were all so curious. But Carter here lucked out."

Aiden stared at Carter, and he shrugged. "Let's just say none of us had seen a reel like Nio's before."

While the children ate and wound down, tired from the day's activities, they sat and chatted. It was nice to sit with other adults and talk about nothing in particular while keeping half an eye on what the kids were doing.

Carter was good company, and his friend was fun. He'd not been sure what to expect when Carter had suggested the playdate, and he'd been worried that it would be awkward, that Sebastian would be one of the fake TV celebrities he thought Carter was before he got to know him.

Anna and Thomas raced up to Sebastian and begged him to come back to the bouncy castle. "I'm too old for this!" he told them, but they just dragged him even harder.

Ryan and Luke weren't far behind. "We want to push you and Carter on the swings," Ryan said.

"It's a race to see who can go higher."

"Daddy is stronger. He'll win."

"Hey! Are you saying I'm a weakling?" Carter asked in mock outrage as he bounced up from his chair and chased Luke over to the swing set. "I'll have you know, I'm an expert, and I'm totally going to win!"

Aiden shook his head. "Dream on."

Each boy gave them a shove to start them off, then ran around the front to cheer them on. Carter's swings were faster, but Aiden's were higher. He stretched out his legs and pointed his toes to gain an extra few inches.

Carter glared sideways at him and began to pump his legs faster. That would never do. With a sly smile, Aiden grabbed hold of Carter's swing, its metal links cool beneath his palm. Carter juddered sideways with a yelp, and their momentum swung them around in circles.

Carter's hand slapped sharply over the top of Aiden's as he grasped for purchase on the swing. Aiden's hand was probably just in the way, but he didn't adjust his grasp or try to pry Aiden's fingers away from the chain. He just gripped tighter, and that small touch made Aiden feel like they were flying.

"You're such a cheat!" Carter protested, making the boys laugh as they watched.

The swing shook a little more. Aiden didn't want Carter to move away; he wanted their connection to continue as long as possible. Only their hands were touching, but Aiden felt breathless, his whole body tingled, and the air between them crackled with awareness.

The boys whooped and cheered some more, and Aiden blinked and took a deep breath to calm himself.

"I won that one."

"You're delusional." Carter raised an eyebrow. His hand tightened around Aiden's, not moving, even when the swings slowed to a standstill.

Warmth spread through Aiden's hand, up his arm, and settled in his chest. "All's fair in love and war," he teased, even as the words sent shivers down his spine.

Sebastian left not long after they ate—Thomas was falling asleep, and Anna was fighting back yawns—and then the crew left, and people came to take away the bouncy castle. There were a few tears, but the boys were easily distracted with promises they would see Anna and Thomas again soon.

It had warmed something inside him to see his boys playing so well with other children. He hadn't been scared to death like he would have been just a few weeks ago. That might be because

Carter was there to step in if something happened, and all he had to do was have fun and not worry about parenting or looking after other people's kids. But it was a step in the right direction.

Maybe next year, he'd be able to invite them to Ryan and Luke's birthday. It didn't fill him with terror thinking about it.

The twins were adamant they weren't tired, even during their bath and putting on their pajamas, right until he and Carter put *Cars* on for them. Within minutes they were flat out, and without words, they carried the boys back upstairs and put them to bed.

When they got downstairs, Aiden went to collapse on the sofa, but Carter grabbed his arm and pulled him up again. He groaned. "Aren't you tired?"

Carter shook his head. "I'm not tired. I could stay awake all night!" he said, imitating the boys. "Come on. You can help me tidy up the mess outside so it's all fresh for tomorrow."

"Slave driver."

"You say that now, but you'll be happy when you get up tomorrow and it's all tidy out here." He knew Carter was right, but a part of him would still like to sit down and forget about the mess. That could be tomorrow's problem.

"Yes, sir." He gave a playful salute, feeling light and happy in a way he'd never felt before, even if he was being made to tidy up.

"Grab hold of the other side of the paddling pool." They carried it further onto the lawn, and Carter turned it over and dumped out the rest of the water on the parched grass.

The sun started to set, and Carter grabbed hold of the dirty plates while Aiden found all the water guns and threw them into a box. It didn't take that long, and something about doing it with Carter made it less like a chore and more intimate. These were the kind of moments he'd always pictured when he and Wyatt decided to have children. Family time, or finding quiet moments together between looking after the kids. It shouldn't be like that. Carter was a *manny*. He wasn't his boyfriend or the kids' other father… but sometimes it was hard to remember.

Carter picked up damp towels that the kids had used and scattered around the garden throughout the day, and they walked back towards the house. Aiden followed him and watched as Carter gave the garden one last look around before he nodded.

"That'll do."

"I'll shove those in the laundry basket." Aiden stepped towards him and went to take the wet towels, but they were wrapped around Carter's hands. He stumbled forwards, and Aiden reached out to steady him, hands wrapping around his warm, bare arms.

"Sorry," he whispered. He didn't know why he was whispering or why he couldn't move.

They were close enough that he heard Carter's intake of breath, felt his muscles contract under his palms, and warmth spread through Aiden's stomach. He didn't know who made the first move, but Carter's lips were under his, dry from the sun, tasting faintly of sunscreen. He'd never tasted anything sweeter.

It was more the press of lips and sharing of breath than a kiss, but it made Aiden's heart beat painfully against his ribs. He gasped into Carter's mouth and flicked his tongue out to tease the curve of his upper lip, sucking the point of that perfect cupid's bow until he could feel the vibrations of Carter's groan against his tongue.

The towels dropped between them and tangled in a heap at their feet. Aiden felt a soft touch graze his cheekbone, skim over his ear, and then fingers threaded through his hair. They kissed slowly, thoroughly, until they had to break apart to breathe.

Aiden's eyes blinked open. Carter's eyes were wide, pupils dilated, and his chest was rising rapidly. His hand slipped from Aiden's hair to the back of his neck, then down his arm until it rested in the crook of his elbow.

Carter licked his lips as if tasting Aiden on them, and Aiden's whole body tightened at the small movement. It was difficult not to lean forward again and capture that beautiful, perfect mouth with his own.

"I'm…" He was going to say sorry, but the words didn't want to leave his lips. "Not sorry. I've wanted to do that since I opened the door that first day and saw you standing there." It was true. Even through the shock, anger, and distrust, all he'd wanted to do was kiss him.

Carter gave a breathy laugh. "I'm glad."

Aiden wanted to say more, but he didn't have the words to describe his feelings. It was too early for love, wasn't it? They didn't know each other that well, but what he knew he liked.

A bang from inside made them both jump, then freeze. "One of the twins is up," Carter said.

Of course they were. His boys had the best timing ever. They pulled apart, and Aiden picked up the towels as Carter stepped into the kitchen.

"What do you want, buddy?" he heard Carter ask. Luke stood rubbing his eyes, hair on end, yawning loudly. "Do you want water? Or milk?" He shook his head and started to cry.

"What's wrong?" Aiden threw the towels in the basket and scooped Luke up and into his arms.

"I miss the bouncy castle, Daddy." Fat tears rolled down his cheeks, and Aiden had to bite his lip so he didn't laugh.

"I'm sorry, buddy. I know you had lots of fun." He rubbed Luke's back, and Luke lay his head on Aiden's shoulder. "But the bouncy castle has to sleep too, just like little boys need to sleep. Come on. I'll take you back to bed."

"Carter too." Luke reached a hand over Aiden's shoulder towards Carter. Aiden felt Carter take Luke's hand.

"Of course."

He was already asleep by the time Aiden put him back to bed.

CHAPTER TWENTY-EIGHT

Carter

IT WAS SLOW, sweet, glorious torture, Carter decided. He and Aiden were stuck pretending nothing had changed between them because they couldn't touch each other or speak freely. He'd never hated the cameras more than he did right then. Even outside the house, they had the kids with them, and those sweet, loveable little boys were more curious than any camera.

And having Aiden on the other side of the wall each night... he was going out of his mind. So close, yet so far away. He punched his pillow as he tossed and turned, unable to sleep. He was hard; his body felt like a tightly wound spring.

His phone buzzed, and he glared at it. Probably Sebastian or one of the other mannies.

Are you awake?

Aiden? Carter stared at it for a moment before answering.

Yes. Can't sleep.

Me either. I keep thinking of you. I want to kiss you again.

Carter looked at the wall and smiled. He imagined Aiden lying on the other side of it, looking toward him.

Me too. Once the cameras are gone.

The end of filming was an eternity and no time at all. On the one hand, he wanted to be free to pursue a relationship with

Aiden; on the other, he would miss being around them 24/7. Working with another family could take him across the country, not to mention he'd be busy with promotional work, but he'd gotten so used to being with the boys and Aiden every day. He'd never felt like this before.

Carter had worried about staying professional and kept his distance, but in the end, he couldn't regret that kiss in the garden. Chaste compared to the ones they'd shared at the club, it still made his heart flutter and had shown him what he felt for the other man was more than fleeting lust.

There's going to be an us once the cameras leave? Aiden replied.

This was such an awkward conversation to have via text, but he answered honestly.

I want there to be.

Good. I can be patient, then.

Carter grinned at his phone. Text message confessions was turning him into a giddy teenager texting his first crush. He gently tapped the wall between them. He wasn't sure it would be loud enough for Aiden to hear or if he'd understand, but when he heard a replying tap, he stopped trying to hide his smile. There was no one to see it, anyway. He could be as excited as he wanted without being embarrassed.

Can you sleep now? Aiden texted.

Maybe.

Carter settled back on his bed, less restless but mind still full of Aiden and what their confession meant. How was he supposed to act in the morning? That was a ridiculous thought—there was only one way he could act with spy cameras following their every move.

Sweet dreams, Aiden texted.

Carter was too lazy to reply with words, so he sent a sleep emoji along with a heart. He hoped that wasn't too forward.

He woke before Aiden and the boys the next morning.

Butterflies danced in his stomach as he remembered their kiss and the texts they'd shared the night before. There was no way he was getting back to sleep, so he pushed the duvet off and tiptoed down the stairs.

The scent of bacon was sure to wake the rest of them up. Warm cereal wasn't good enough that morning, and it wouldn't distract him enough to keep his mind occupied until everyone was awake.

Aiden came down just as Carter popped the sausages in the pan. He was freshly showered, hair slicked back, and wearing his work clothes. A faded T-shirt, ripped jeans, and work boots shouldn't look so sexy, but they were like designer labels on Aiden. Carter almost swallowed his tongue.

"What's the occasion?" Aiden leaned his hip against the worktop. He was close—probably too close for work colleagues—but frustratingly not close enough for Carter's liking. Now he'd had another taste of those lips, he was addicted and thirsty for more.

Damn cameras.

"I couldn't sleep, so I decided to cook breakfast instead. I hope you're hungry."

"*Starving.*" Carter glanced at him and saw the playful glint in his eye. He felt the tips of his ears start to burn, and he sent a glare back because he couldn't say anything, couldn't do anything.

What would it look like on the cameras if he gave Aiden a swift kick in the shins? Probably better than grabbing him and kissing the life out of him. He bit back a groan and turned back to the frying pan.

Aiden laughed, the bastard, then looked down at his phone, texting someone like he hadn't just made Carter think very lustful thoughts while he was at work.

The mobile in Carter's pocket vibrated, and he fished it out in time to see Aiden's name flash up.

This is me kissing you good morning.

Carter's whole face burned, but he couldn't stop smiling as Aiden opened the fridge, took out a carton of milk, and started to boil water for tea.

Sorry about my morning breath, he shot back, then looked up at Aiden and said, "I haven't brushed my teeth yet." Aiden checked his text, then back at him before he burst out laughing.

I <3 your morning breath, he texted before he shoved his mobile into his back pocket and poured water into two mugs. Carter put the bacon rashers into the pan, and not five minutes later he heard the thunder of footsteps running down the stairs as the boys ran into the kitchen.

"Bacon!" Luke said with enthusiasm.

"Hey, my little tadpoles, I hope you're hungry. We've got a busy day today, so you need a big breakfast."

"I could eat a horse," Ryan said with a serious nod.

Carter snorted. "Well, I don't have a horse. How about a pig?"

"That too." He shrugged and sat down at the table. "I could really eat some chocolate as well."

Carter pointed his spatula at him with a laugh. "Yeah, nice try. It's pig for breakfast, not chocolate."

Ryan sent Aiden a pleading look, but Aiden held up his hands in surrender. "The boss has spoken."

CHAPTER TWENTY-NINE

AIDEN
Interview with Aiden. Camera rolling. Day Fifteen.
Interviewer: What's the best part about having Manny SOS invade your home?
Aiden: Carter. I mean, the manny.
Interviewer: In what way?
Aiden: I'm a single dad; it's great to have another set of hands.

"YOU'RE IN A good mood," Daryl said as they ripped the old bathroom out in preparation for the new one that was going in that afternoon.

John was downstairs putting the finishing touches to the kitchen, singing off-key to the radio, so loud they could hear it upstairs. The renovation was going well. It helped that Aiden was relaxed. Since Carter's arrival, having someone he trusted looking after the boys, work seemed to flow much better.

Aiden's face ached from suppressing his smile, and he shrugged. "I don't know what you mean," he lied. He knew exactly what Daryl meant. He wasn't as tense, constantly waiting for a call from the school or childminder saying that one of the boys had gotten up to no good.

He didn't know what he was going to do when Carter left. It wasn't something he wanted to think about right then, they still had time together, and Carter had already promised the boys he'd visit once they were back at school.

"No frowning. I don't know what you're thinking about now, but stop it." Daryl jabbed a finger toward him.

"What? I'm not!"

"You are. I can tell you're overthinking. Stop it."

"Yes, boss." Aiden gave him a wink and got back to work. Still, it was difficult resisting the urge to check his phone. They'd gotten into the habit of texting each other the things they couldn't say out loud. When the kids were in bed and the weather was nice, they'd share a beer on the patio in the back garden, but they were still very much aware of the cameras in the house; neither of them felt truly comfortable talking out there. And there had been no other kisses, no matter how much they both wanted them.

Aiden enjoyed their evenings on the patio, their text messages, and the pseudo morse code they tapped out on the wall that separated them at night. He laughed and shook his head. He was being ridiculous, but he couldn't stop.

"What has you laughing now?" Daryl said.

He'd forgotten where he was for a second. "Oh, nothing. We're taking the twins over to Nio's tonight. I'm thinking about the trouble they're going to cause there."

For their trip to Nio's, Carter had put Aiden in charge of what he called 'damage control.' He'd been given a list of items to buy and was in the supermarket hoping to find everything he needed. If not, he'd have to improvise.

He found two backpacks, one blue, one green. Each had a football print on it. They were close enough that—hopefully—the boys wouldn't argue over who got what, but different enough that there wouldn't be any confusion.

Next on his list: fidget toys. What the hell were fidget toys?

He did a quick google search, then wandered up and down the toy aisle until he found fidgety things. Two spinners, mini pop-its that, in his opinion, still weren't half as good as bubble wrap, and neon wiggly worms that he knew would attract dirt. Then he picked up coloring books, mini packets of crayons, and a few sets of stickers each.

The boys already had loads of half-used coloring books, but Carter said they needed travel-sized ones, along with special yet inexpensive toys that would stay in their bags and only come out on special occasions, such as visiting friends or going out for dinner. Things that would distract them and keep them occupied. He was embarrassed that he hadn't already thought of it.

He quickly paid for his items and headed home. He hid the bags between the coats in the hallway and made his way into the living room to find Carter and the twins racing cars along the carpet on tracks made from books, cushions, and whatever else they'd found lying around the house. It was an impressive racetrack. There was a piece of thin card propped against the sofa that Ryan kept placing his cars on and then pushing them down until they crashed into the cushions at the bottom.

"You're having lots of fun." Three pairs of eyes looked up in surprise.

"Daddy, look how my cars crash," Luke said. He rolled another car down the cardboard hill.

"Is that the time?" Carter said, standing up. "I meant to have all this tidied up before you got home." The boys groaned when they heard that. "Don't be sad. We can play another day. Plus, we're going to Uncle Nio's tonight, do you remember?"

"Uncle Nio," Luke chanted and did a little dance.

"Come on, help me put all this into the box. Then none of us will fall over it, and it'll be easy to get it all out when you want to play with it again."

Aiden was surprised when the boys didn't do more than give a little whine before throwing their cars and toys into a box. It wasn't a perfect clean-up, but they put things in the box without tears or tantrums. That was impressive.

"Your dad got you boys a present," Carter said, kneeling once they'd finished. He looked up at Aiden with a grin and a nod. Aiden disappeared to retrieve the bags, then revealed them with a flourish.

"A present?" Luke's eyes widened.

"It's not our birthday." Ryan was more skeptical.

"We're going to Uncle Nio's today, and you boys need to behave yourselves."

The boys pouted, their excitement fading until Carter stepped in with a bit more explanation. "I know it can be really boring going to someone else's home, especially when there are no other kids or toys to play with. We thought you might enjoy these to play with while you're there."

They took the bags and yanked open the zips.

"Wow!" Ryan grabbed one of the straps and slid his arms into it. "There's stuff inside, Luke."

"Fidget toys! I always wanted one of these." Luke hugged the disgusting rubbery worm to his face.

"Coloring! And crayons. And stickers!" He pulled everything out to look at, as though he'd never seen or owned a coloring book before.

"This is a special bag for when we're visiting other people or going out to dinner so you don't get bored," Carter explained. "There's also enough space there, so if you want to take a few other quiet toys, you can. Why don't you go and pick something to play with at Uncle Nio's?"

When they both shot off to their room, talking over each other, Aiden let out the breath he'd been holding. "Why did I never do this before? And crayons instead of felt tips? Genius."

"Believe me, I learned that trick from experience, not a degree. Don't pack markers when you're visiting someone else, especially when they have fancy white tablecloths. Crayons are much easier to deal with."

There was a thundering sound as the boys raced back down

the stairs, their bags bursting to the seams. Carter laughed. "Well done, boys. You've done a great job, but you need to be able to close your bags, and I'm pretty sure Uncle Nio *doesn't* want to see your glitter collection. I bet he'd love to see your cars, though."

Carter helped each of them decide what toys to take—calm suggestions and praise so neither of them even realized he'd stopped them from taking their beloved slime, a bottle of hair conditioner, a water gun, and a toy keyboard that had sounded awful, even before the batteries started to go.

Aiden was almost certain Carter was a miracle worker. There was no other explanation.

MANNY SOS

CHAPTER THIRTY

CARTER

NIO OPENED THE door to his flat with a lavish bow. Both boys charged at him, and he allowed them to wrestle him to the ground with a loud laugh.

Aiden rolled his eyes and gave Carter a wink as they walked inside. It was only a few seconds before Nio called out, "Help, help!"

His hand reached towards Aiden through the boys, but Aiden ignored him.

"You've only got yourself to blame," he snorted, then turned to Carter. "Ever since they started walking, he's *always* let them do this. He can't expect help now they're getting bigger and he's too weak to take it."

Carter laughed but couldn't help feeling a little guilty for leaving Nio on the floor. "Don't be too rough, boys. Your uncle is getting old."

Nio spluttered and went to get up, but Luke jumped on his stomach, and he fell back down with an 'oomph.'

Leaving Nio to fend for himself, Carter headed into the apartment to join Aiden, who was in the kitchen filling the kettle.

"Will Nio mind where I put the camera?"

He'd brought one of the small spare cameras with him so

they could film the boys at Nio's apartment. Carter felt weird about doing it, but it was in their contract, and at least this way, they didn't have a cameraman tagging along.

"You should put it in there to show everyone how two six-year-olds got the upper hand of him—again."

"If I'd known that was going to happen, I'd have nipped ahead and set it up." Carter grinned, his shoulders relaxing. At least Aiden didn't seem too concerned.

He ended up placing the camera in the corner of the living room on a bookshelf that he was sure would get the whole view of the room. Nio was now sprawled on his stomach with the boys next to him as they pulled toys from their bags and showed him each one in excruciating detail.

"The bags are a hit. I should have got Nio one too," Aiden said before he pulled Carter back into the kitchen and shut the door on the three boys.

"What?" Carter went to say, eyes on the door, but Aiden swiveled him around, his fingers digging into the small of his back as he pulled Carter towards him and kissed him, hard and desperate, until Carter felt light-headed.

"Text kisses aren't enough," Aiden mumbled against his lips.

Carter couldn't agree more. He pressed his lips against Aiden's again, swallowing his words. Aiden's fingers spread out across his back, and Carter plunged his hands into Aiden's short, soft hair.

A bang from the other room made them both jump. Carter's breath hitched in his throat, and Aiden whined as he pulled away. "I suppose we should see what the kids are up to."

"Wait," Carter said, and he smoothed Aiden's hair back down.

A little old lady stood in the middle of the room. She leaned heavily on a walking stick, but her eyes were sharp as she looked at Carter.

"Nanny Biscuit," Aiden said as he slipped around Carter and

pressed a kiss to her cheek.

"Aiden dear. So good to see you."

"Why are you here, Nanny Biscuit?" Nio whined. She stood straight and lifted her walking stick, giving him a sharp, swift tap. "Ouch!"

"You said one of the mannies from my favorite TV show was coming around, so I thought I'd introduce myself." She turned to Carter and smiled.

"Hello, Mrs..."

"Just call me Nanny Biscuit. Everyone does. Have you eaten? I baked cookies." She shuffled towards him, obviously expecting him to kiss her cheek too, so he gave her what she wanted. She gave a little giggle, and her cheeks turned red.

"We want cookies, Nanny Biscuit." The boys crowded her, but they were gentle in a way Carter had never seen before—as if they knew they had to be extra careful so they didn't hurt her.

"And you shall have them." She pulled out a bag of cookies and handed them to the boys, who ran away excitedly, stuffing their mouths as they went. "So. Am I going to be on the telly? I dressed up for this." She pointed towards her lipstick and her perfectly curled hair.

Carter laughed. "You might be. We're filming this right now. Why don't you sit down? Nio was just about to make tea."

Nio crossed his arms and glared. "Was I? I thought Aiden was doing it."

"You're such a child," Aiden said but headed back to the kitchen anyway. Nio huffed, dragged himself up off the floor, and followed.

"Hey, boys, don't forget your bags," Carter said as he saw them start to eye the books on Nio's shelf. "Would you like to do some coloring?" He set them up on the floor, made sure Nanny Biscuit was comfortable, and went to see why it needed two fully grown men to make tea.

"Everything okay?" Carter asked. "I left Nanny Biscuit doing your crossword."

Nio cursed. "Honestly, that woman has no shame. I was saving that."

Aiden laughed. "Why are you being grumpy with Nanny Biscuit?"

"She thinks she's a bigger fan of *Manny SOS* than me. That's just not true. When we binge-watch it together, she always forgets your names. She calls you Carlson. Sorry, Carter."

"That's fine. I'm honored you're such a big fan. But what I can't understand is... How can a childless bachelor and an OAP watch *Manny SOS*, but a guy with kids didn't have a clue?" He gave Aiden a quick jab in the side with his elbow.

"Hey," Aiden said with a laugh. "Because the only things I've watched in the last six years are *Peppa Pig* and *Paw Patrol*,"

Carter went to say something else, but a shout from the other room stopped them all. Aiden was there before Carter could even give him a reassuring look. He followed behind, there for support if needed.

Nanny Biscuit still had her nose in the crossword, seemingly oblivious to the twins arguing at her feet.

"Oi, don't draw in my book!" Luke shouted.

"Sky should be blue, not brown." Ryan still had the blue crayon clutched in his hand, and there was a large, wiggly line of blue on Luke's picture.

Aiden took in a deep breath and looked at Carter.

"You've got this," Carter said. He hated how insecure Aiden could be at times. He was such a good dad; he just needed to believe in himself more.

Aiden knelt between them before the fight could escalate to more than just shouting. "Ryan, you shouldn't draw in Luke's book without his permission. It's not nice." His tone was calm and collected.

"But he did it wrong!" Ryan managed to glare around him at Luke.

"It's his book, and he can color it however he wants. Would you like it if he'd drawn in your book?"

Ryan pouted and shook his head.

"Exactly. Say sorry to your brother."

"Sorry." He still sounded put out, but an apology at all was something. Luke eventually nodded, and Carter saw Aiden actively relax.

"But I want a brown sky." Luke looked up at Aiden, his wide blue eyes swimming with unshed tears. Aiden brushed his fringe off his forehead and pressed a kiss to it. "You can still have a brown sky. It's darker than the blue, so I'm sure it'll go over it." Luke looked at his picture for a few moments before picking up the brown crayon and coloring over the blue scribble.

"We all deserve a drink after that," Nio said. "Tea. I wasn't sure how you take it, Carter. Milk and sugar?"

"Thanks. Just milk, please."

The boys were coloring quietly again, and the adults, not including Nanny Biscuit, gravitated towards the kitchen.

"That was pure magic," Nio said. "Are you some kind of magician, Carter? This would usually end in fisticuffs."

Carter shook his head. "It's mostly distraction, to be honest."

"I'm not sure if it's actually worked, or they're just biding their time." Aiden frowned as he looked back at the boys.

"They'll be okay for a few minutes. You need to give them a bit of freedom. Wait a few extra minutes, then go in, tell them how wonderful they're doing, and come away again. They'll soon forget about being annoyed at each other."

"I'm just waiting for them to break something or burn the flat down. We might need more than *Manny SOS* then."

"You're being overly dramatic," Carter said. Aiden grinned, but Carter could still see the worry in his eyes.

"I'm worried they'll break something else. It doesn't matter if they break things at home, but if they break something of Nio's, it matters more."

"That is why I moved my breakables and made this a slime-free zone," Nio said. He slapped Aiden on the back, and Carter saw the bond between the two friends. It was similar to his and

Nora's—lots of teasing and support. He was glad Aiden had that.

"That's why you go check on them every few minutes. If they're getting restless, get one of the other toys out, set them up, play for a few moments and come away. Rinse and repeat. Eventually, you can leave them for longer before checking on them."

"You make it sound so easy."

Carter shook his head. "Oh, it's not easy at all."

The boys started to talk rather loudly, and Aiden set his tea down. "I better start the rinse and repeat thing."

He brushed against Carter as he slipped through the open doorway back into the living room. He praised the boys as Carter watched, a smile playing over his face. He loved watching the three of them interacting.

When Nio cleared his throat, Carter tore his gaze away to find Nio looking at him thoughtfully. Smirking around his cup, he raised an eyebrow

"What?" Carter said.

"Aiden's a great guy, isn't he."

"Yes?" Carter didn't know where he was going with this.

"The boys are great too."

"I know."

"He's a bit clueless, but he'd make a good boyfriend."

Carter shifted awkwardly from one foot to the other. He wasn't sure he should be having this conversation with Aiden's best friend.

"Don't tell me you—" Thankfully, Aiden walked back into the kitchen, and Nio stopped mid-sentence.

"What did I miss?" Aiden frowned.

Nio grinned and sent Carter a wink. "Not much. I was just telling Carter that if the boys do burn down my flat, I'm moving in with you guys... and I want the biggest bedroom."

"In your dreams, Uncle Nio. In your dreams."

CHAPTER THIRTY-ONE

AIDEN

AIDEN HAD JUST finished a quick FaceTime with Carter and the boys. He was about to eat the lunch Carter had packed him when a car pulled up outside and a familiar figure got out and jogged up the front path.

Nio was Aiden's exact opposite, dressed in a suit, hair styled with wax. "What are you doing here?"

"We're going to lunch," Nio stated.

"I already have lunch." Aiden looked down at his bento box. He was looking forward to seeing what Carter had packed for him.

"Have that for seconds. We're going to a café down the road." Nio grabbed his arm, pulled him up, and then hustled him towards his car.

"What's this all about?" Aiden could have refused at any point, but if Nio wanted to buy lunch, then he wouldn't say no. He'd eat his lunch before he went home; he didn't want Carter to be upset if he left it.

"We can talk when we eat." He whistled along to the radio, and Aiden sighed, irritated.

The drive to the café only took a few minutes. They ordered and sat down with their drinks before Aiden raised an eyebrow at Nio. "Well?"

"I just realized we've not seen each other for ages."

"I saw you yesterday, or did you forget our visit? Obviously, the boys didn't do enough damage to your apartment this time."

Nio leaned forward and took a sip of his iced coffee. "That's not what I mean. We couldn't talk yesterday. The three Cs." Aiden gave him a lost look. "Camera, kids, Carter."

"That's not three Cs."

Nio shrugged his shoulders. "I know, but it sounds better than Camera, children, and Carter, doesn't it?"

Aiden rolled his eyes. Idiot. "What did you want to talk about?"

"You and Carter seem to be getting along well now."

Aiden concentrated on his drink. He wasn't ready to talk about his relationship with Carter when he couldn't even talk to the man himself properly. "We get along fine."

"Don't be coy. You two were close. Not manny and employer close, but intimate."

"Don't be stupid. Nothing we did at yours could be considered intimate." Nio hadn't seen the kiss, but that didn't stop the flush creeping over his face. Hopefully, Nio wouldn't notice. Or if he did… it was just because his drink was so hot.

"Oh, please. Intimacy is more than physical closeness. I could tell from the glances, the tiny touches, and how you both parented the boys."

"That's what he's there for."

"He's there to look after the boys, not to parent them. I'm not judging. It was sweet. I just want all the gossip because there's got to be a story there. And I'm your best friend and the one who brought you together."

Aiden snorted. "Please, you're the reason I had to run away from him at the club. Who lets a pair of six-year-olds lock them in the bathroom, anyway?"

"That was just lust. This is destiny. I'm Cupid. This way, you got to get to know him; he got to get to know you, Luke, and

Ryan. It's only right you tell me what's going on."

"At the moment, nothing." It was only a white lie. "There are cameras everywhere. What do you expect us to do?"

"But there are feelings, right? Mutual feelings? If you don't tell me, I'll tell Nanny Biscuit about my theory, and I'll give her your phone number."

"That's a low blow." Aiden winced.

"Don't think I won't." Their grilled cheese sandwiches arrived, and Nio was distracted for all of two bites. "Well?"

"Don't talk with your mouth full." Nio glared at him and opened his mouth wider.

"You really are such a child. We're... kind of in limbo until the show ends."

Nio swallowed. "That implies something has happened?"

"We've kissed. Once." Twice, if he included Nio's kitchen. "But it's impossible with all the cameras at home. We haven't had much of a chance to talk, but we're going to see where it goes once the show is over."

"See?" Nio grinned, picked up the other half of his sandwich, and waved it at Aiden. "Cupid, what did I tell you?"

MANNY SOS

CHAPTER THIRTY-TWO

CARTER

HAVE YOU DONE *anything for dinner yet?* Aiden texted Carter from work. He was at the park with the boys, watching them run off some excess energy while he got to sit down for a second.

Not yet. Do you have any preferences? he replied.

Let's go out to eat. The local pub serves great burgers.

Carter shouldn't be so happy that Aiden wanted them all to go out for dinner, but he was.

"Hey, boys. We're going to go out for dinner tonight," he said as they raced by.

Luke stopped running long enough to ask, "Pizza?"

Carter laughed and shook his head. "We're going to the pub in the village. I've never been. You'll have to tell me what's good to eat."

"You can have chicken nuggets," Ryan said.

Yeah, maybe not.

They played for a little while longer before heading home, where the boys entertained themselves alternating between playing with their Matchbox cars and building elaborate garages for them while Carter tidied the kitchen, putting away their breakfast bowls, wiping down surfaces, and making sure the place wasn't too much of a mess for when Aiden got home.

"Hey, boys. Do you want to take your bags to the pub with us? You can do some coloring or play with your fidget spinners."

They ran upstairs to find their bags, which Carter then double-checked in case they'd added anything they shouldn't have. Luckily there was no slime, shampoo, or anything liquid.

Nestled in the middle of the village, the pub was already bustling by the time they got there. They managed to find a table, and Carter helped the boys choose a toy to play with while they decided what to eat.

Aiden went up to order the food and get their drinks, and Carter had a glimpse into what it could be like in their future. A family. It was a weird but not unwelcome feeling. He could picture Kyle with them; he could even picture Nora, Dennis, the baby, and Nio there—a huge extended family.

Carter and Nora had never been in love or together as a couple, so even though they'd had family time with the three of them more times than he could count over the last fifteen years, it wasn't the same as being with someone who could—potentially—be your partner.

Goosebumps trailed up his arms, and it was hard to concentrate on anything else. Aiden's smile made his stomach jump as he sat back down. His foot pressed against Carter's under the table.

They chatted, but all Carter could concentrate on was how their legs nudged against each other. They each helped the boys color and attempted to do tricks using the fidget spinners, which failed when Aiden managed to shoot one across the table.

"Oops," he said sheepishly. "I should probably give that up in case it flies across the pub next."

The waitress brought their food, and Carter's eyes widened at the huge burger and chips he'd ordered. They ate in silence; even the boys were quiet as they munched their way through dinner. There was so much food that Carter couldn't finish his.

"No room for a dessert, then?" Aiden teased.

"Please, everyone knows there is a separate dessert stomach."

"Wow, is that true?" Ryan said, ketchup smeared across his face.

Aiden laughed and nudged Carter. "You can explain that to them, Mary Poppins." Well, that was a nickname Aiden hadn't used before. He was just about to try and explain the joke to the boys, but they'd already moved on.

"Why are you calling him Mary Poppins, Daddy?" Luke asked.

"I thought his name was Carter," Ryan said.

Aiden grinned, pulled a tissue from his pocket, and leaned over the table to wipe Ryan's tomatoey face. "His name is Carter, but he's a real-life Mary Poppins."

"I'm not quite sure about that. My outfit isn't half so good. And I don't fly."

The boys' eyes widened. "Who's Mary Poppins?" Ryan asked.

"Have we never watched *Mary Poppins*? We're going to watch it. You two will love it. It's about two children and their magical nanny."

"Are you magical, Carter?"

Carter shook his head. "Not magical, but I can sing pretty well." He started to hum and then sing softly.

The twins wrinkled their noses and shook their heads. "You can't sing."

Carter pouted, then opened his mouth in fake shock. "What do you mean? Tell them, Aiden—that was perfect."

Aiden was smiling and watching them all fondly. "The boys are right… you can't sing a note, *Manny Poppins*."

They laughed, ate chocolate fudge cake until Carter thought he was going to throw up, and had a great time—all without the cameras watching their every move. The only way the night could have been better was if Kyle had been with them too.

"Can we watch it tonight?"

"Please?"

"I don't see why not. I'm sure it's on one of the streaming channels. What do you say, Carter? Fancy watching another nanny on TV?"

"My idol, Mary Poppins? How can I resist?"

"We promise not to laugh if you sing." Ryan slipped his hand into Carter's as they walked towards the car. Carter's heart expanded as Ryan skipped next to him, warmth spreading throughout his body.

When they got home, the twins insisted they all pile onto the sofa together. The heat of Aiden's body pressed against his, and the boys practically sprawled out on top of them— an elbow jabbed Carter in the thigh, and at one-point little toes almost kicked him in the nose—it was the perfect end to a perfect night. He wouldn't change a thing.

"You're not singing, Carter," Luke said, and he realized he'd become sidetracked, so he started to sing, making sure his voice was a lot worse than it actually was, just to make the boys laugh.

All three of them.

The boys fell asleep before the end of the movie, and Carter helped Aiden carry them to bed. They'd probably demand to watch it over and over the next day, so there would be plenty of time for them to learn the songs and sing along. Carter was sure he'd get sick of it before they did.

"Want to watch a grown-up film for a change?" Aiden said softly as they padded back downstairs.

"Ahh, that sounds like music to my ears." Aiden laughed at his cheesy joke, and they settled down on the sofa—close, but not too close. Still, it was enough to drive Carter to the brink.

Would the producers notice if the cameras were accidentally turned off for an hour or two? He swallowed a groan and tried to concentrate on the movie.

CHAPTER THIRTY-THREE

AIDEN

IT WAS A Saturday. Carter was officially off duty, so they didn't have to feel guilty about going out without a camera. Aiden was relieved to have time with just the four of them.

The weather was warm enough for shorts and T-shirts. Aiden carried a rucksack with water and snacks as they followed a trail around one of the local lakes. The boys ran ahead, chattering away with each other in a world of their own as they looked at rocks, collected sticks, and made a game out of spotting birds. He and Carter followed, chatting and taking in the sun and scenery. They were so close that their hands brushed as they walked, and goosebumps ran up Aiden's arms.

It would be so easy to grab his hand and carry on walking. He wanted to desperately. Carter glanced at him, could probably see the want on his face, and he hooked his pinky around Aiden's just for a second. It made Aiden giddy.

"So, Kyle gets back from his holiday on Thursday," Carter said.

"That's great. I bet you've missed him."

"Yeah. It's the longest I've gone without seeing him. I wanted to ask you a question."

"Go ahead."

"Are you and the boys doing anything next weekend?"

Nothing came to mind. "I don't think so. Why?"

"I wondered if you wanted to come to mine for the weekend. You can meet Kyle. And Nora. Okay, you'll get bombarded by my family, but it'll be fun." Carter bit at his lip.

The thought of meeting Carter's son and his family filled Aiden with excitement and dread in equal measures. What if they didn't like him? What if Kyle hated him? But knowing that Carter wanted him to meet them made all his doubts worth it.

"I'd like that. What about the cameras?" Carter didn't work weekends, but the producers asked that they were given warning if they'd be doing anything that would be good for the TV show.

Carter shrugged, then gave a wicked grin. "We just won't tell them. I mean, if you're going away for the weekend, and I'm going home, that's none of their business, is it?"

Aiden was sure it wasn't that simple. A weekend at Carter's was more than a walk in the park, but he wasn't going to argue. He was happy for time away with Carter, even if he was scared about meeting his family.

"Great. I'll probably head home after dinner Friday, make sure the house is aired, and get everything ready. You can bring the boys Saturday morning?"

Aiden caught Carter's pinkie with his own. "Sounds like a plan."

CHAPTER THIRTY-FOUR

CARTER

BOBBY WAS SO much bigger than when Carter had seen her last, and though she still fit perfectly in his arms, she was currently draped over his shoulder, burping up a storm.

It was after eight on Friday night; he'd driven straight there from Aiden's to see Kyle, who was wearing an identical smirk to his mother as he lounged on the plush chair opposite him. Bobby wasn't the only one who was bigger. Kyle looked older than he had before his holiday. His hair had grown out, his skin was tanned, and Carter was sure he'd grown a couple of inches.

He looked so much like his mother when he smirked that it was uncanny, and he told him so, which just made Kyle laugh. Yeah, he got the crazy from her side of the family. Nora shuffled into the living room and put a cup of coffee on the table next to him.

"I can't believe that the guy you met at the—" Nora glanced at Kyle. "—*coffee shop* was the guy you ended up working with for the TV show."

Kyle rolled his eyes, obviously not believing them for a second.

"It's hilarious," Kyle said.

"You could at least not laugh," Carter said grumpily and pressed a kiss to the side of the baby's head. "Do you know how difficult it is to be around someone you like with cameras on you 24/7?"

Kyle nodded, and Carter raised his eyebrow. There was no way his fifteen-year-old son could possibly understand.

"What? I watch *Love Island*."

"This is *Manny SOS*, not *Love Island*." It was deja vu. His family was crazy, Carter decided. They were meant to be making him less nervous. He was meant to be telling Kyle he'd met someone he might—possibly—become serious with, but that didn't mean he loved him any less, but Kyle didn't seem at all worried. How the hell had he and Nora, two giant teenage fuck-ups, managed to raise a well-adjusted kid? He told Kyle so, and his son laughed even harder.

"This is going to be so much fun. We get to meet him tomorrow, and I'm going to tell him every single embarrassing story I know about you. I might even get some of the old photos out too. You know the ones. Me as a baby, and you with black hair and a straight fringe? Does he know about your emo phase?" Kyle teased. "Maybe he can explain what Myspace was."

"Maybe I need to duct tape your mouth shut before he gets here? I've got some cool colors at home. One even has penguins on it."

"Only you would have patterned duct tape, Dad. Only you."

"Let's not get sidetracked from what's important, boys," Nora said. "You've invited Aiden and his kids to yours for the weekend, right? We're all going to get to meet him, aren't we? You can't tell us everything and then keep him hidden away from us." Nora pouted and crossed her arms over her chest. "We are your family, after all."

"Please don't just descend on us. I don't want to scare him off. At least give him a little while to acclimatize. Perhaps you, Dennis, and the princess could come for breakfast on Sunday before they head home?" That should be enough time for Nora to meet Aiden but not enough for her to drive him away.

"Oh please, I won't be awake in the morning." Carter raised an eyebrow and nodded at the baby. "Being awake because of the baby doesn't count. It's the zombie hours. Surely you remember what that's like. Honestly, you don't know me at all. Come here for lunch tomorrow. You get to stay a few hours, then leave whenever you want. I get to check him out, and I'll leave you alone the rest of the weekend. Don't tell me that doesn't appeal."

It did appeal. He only hoped Aiden was ready for it. "Great. I'll bring them over for lunch." That seemed to mollify her, and they went back to asking him embarrassing and awkward questions.

"At least we know why he hasn't been commuting home despite only being a few hours away," Kyle said with a smirk. "I'm looking forward to meeting the man who kept my father away from me."

"Away from you? You weren't even here, you menace. I stayed away because I was heartbroken and pining because I missed my terrible son so much."

Kyle cackled with laughter. "I am the worst of sons. Did you find out about the drugs? Or did you spot me drinking alcohol at the bus stop with all the school dropouts?"

"Don't even joke about that," Nora said with a shudder. "I still see someone I went to school with drinking vodka at the bus stop down the road."

"See, Dad? I'm a good son," Kyle crowed and settled back into his chair with a big grin on his face.

"Okay, you're not so bad." Carter hadn't realized how much he'd missed this banter between the three of them.

"And now I get to vet the new boyfriend, make sure he's good enough for you."

Carter didn't know why his cheeks were burning, but the flush swept across his face. "Please don't give him a hard time… or run him off."

Kyle and Nora looked at each other. "Well, he didn't argue

about calling him a boyfriend, so that's got to mean something," Nora said.

CHAPTER THIRTY-FIVE

AIDEN

AIDEN TURNED INTO Carter's driveway just after ten a.m. It was a nice middle-class neighborhood with red-bricked houses and garages. It wasn't the gorgeous Victorian house he'd envisioned living in one day, but it had character despite being a relatively new build. The twins were so excited to be there that they were on their best behavior, and while they scrambled out of their booster seats, he picked up their bags from the trunk and sent a quick text to let Carter know they'd arrived.

The text had only just been marked 'delivered' when the front door flung open and Carter stepped out. The boys forgot about him and charged at Carter as if he hadn't helped put them to bed the night before.

Aiden wished he could get away with charging up the path and hugging him too. Aiden's mouth became dry as he watched Carter give them tight hugs before scooping them into his arms and twirling them around to an accompaniment of glee-filled squeals.

It was nothing Carter hadn't done before, but seeing him in his own home, wearing old clothes, hair fluffy from the shower and free of product, took Aiden's breath away. He'd always found Carter attractive—at the club, dressed in his signature suspenders for work, in his sweats, but this was on another level, and he couldn't get enough of it.

He was wearing low-slung jeans that hugged his hips but weren't tight enough to cut off the circulation, and a T-shirt with the rock band Pelamar across the front. Aiden knew of the band, but hadn't heard much of their music, unless he caught it on the radio at work. He hadn't expected Carter to be a rocker, and he tucked that nugget away for later. There were so many things he didn't know about him, and he couldn't wait to find them out.

It took all his willpower not to stride over there, pull Carter into a tight hug, and kiss him for everyone to see. For one, they had to be careful because of the TV show; secondly, the boys had no clue; and thirdly, he didn't want to give the neighbors a show. But as soon as he was within reach of them, he couldn't stop himself from enveloping him and the boys into a hug. The boys giggled and wriggled between them until they slithered out of their arms and into Carter's house. He worried about hurricane Ryan and Luke for a moment before Carter closed the space between them and wrapped his arms around his neck.

Hell, if Carter wasn't worried about what the twins would get up to, he wasn't going to worry either. Much.

His hands slipped easily underneath the back of Carter's worn T-shirt, and he splayed his fingers out, wanting to touch as much skin as he could, while he could.

The boys were too busy exploring Carter's living room to pay them much attention, so Aiden took advantage. He dipped his face into the crook of Carter's neck, the combination of his cologne and the spicy scent that was all him making Aiden heady.

"I want to kiss the hell out of you," he muttered into Carter's ear.

He felt Carter shudder. "I want to let you," he said as he stepped out of Aiden's arms and held out a hand. "Come inside before the boys decide to redecorate."

Luke sat in front of the fireplace ringing a brass bell while Ryan eyed a huge bookcase on the back wall. After deciding that Ryan could potentially do the most damage, Aiden lunged after him and grabbed his ankles before his little sticky fingers reached a book.

"What did I tell you before we got here? Luke, stop ringing that bell. You've got to ask and be gentle with Carter's things."

Ryan looked mournfully at the bookcase. "So many books."

"And this bell sounds so good." Luke rang the bell again but quickly stopped when Aiden went to take it off him.

"You've got your toy bags in the car. Let me go and grab them for you." He mouthed 'sorry' to Carter as he passed.

"It's not like I've never met them before." He winked. "Plus, I moved anything really breakable. I have a whole shelf full of picture books you can look at right here. *War and Peace* is a little too hard for you yet, Ryan," Carter said as he pulled out picture books. Both boys sat on the floor next to him as Aiden quickly grabbed the bags and brought them inside.

Carter, Ryan, and Luke were sitting cross-legged on the floor, with Carter reading from a picture book called *Oi Frog*. He was making up silly voices, and the boys were giggling. "What does a dog sit on?" Carter said, hiding the book against his chest so they couldn't see.

"I know! The bog!" The boys looked at each other and giggled. Trust his sons to turn to toilet humor.

"Clogs!"

Carter shook his head and opened the book back up so the boys could see. He didn't even say the last line out loud, just let the boys look at the picture of a large dog sitting on a small frog. The boys laughed and laughed until they cried.

"That sounds like a great book."

"It is, especially for little tadpoles," Carter said and ruffled their hair. "I kind of collect picture books. Kyle is too old for them now, but I still work with enough younger kids, and I love helping them realize just how fun reading is."

"It's a much better book than the Chip and Kipper books we have to read for school, Daddy," Luke said. And although he might have only heard the end of that story, Aiden had to agree. Getting the boys to read those godawful boring stories was like pulling teeth. He'd hated them when he'd had to read them at their age, and he still hated them now.

"I totally agree, buddy, but we still have to read those for school." They groaned, and he quickly changed the subject. "Is Kyle here?"

He saw evidence of a teenager everywhere: schoolbooks piled on a unit, thankfully out of the boys' reach; a skateboard in the corner he was surprised neither boy had spotted yet; a Nintendo underneath the TV, and many, many photos of Kyle and a woman Aiden presumed was Kyle's mom.

"He's at his mom and stepdad's. I hope you don't mind, but I kind of said we'd go there for lunch. She wants to meet you all, and if we don't go there, she will come here, and we'd never get her to leave. And I mean never."

Aiden laughed, despite feeling nervous at the thought of meeting Carter's family. It was nice that Carter had people who cared about him so much. "I don't mind. I'm just glad we get to spend time with you without Big Brother."

"Me too." Carter grinned up at him and hugged the boys to him.

"Me too," the boys parroted together.

"That's great, because they're all excited to meet you. But first, shall I show you where you're going to sleep?"

He stood and held out a hand for each boy. Then with one extra-large smile for him that made Aiden's heart want to burst with love, he took them upstairs for the tour.

The house was larger than theirs, but there was a homey vibe that was lacking in his. He worked every day renovating houses, but that wasn't the same as making a structurally sound building into a home. The only thing that made his house a home was the boys.

The room Carter took the boys to had a small double bed made up with navy blue sheets and a matching duvet. It was the spare room, but it had a huge bookshelf filled with even more books and shelves full of Funko Pops. Seeing how the boys' mouths dropped open as they gazed up at them, Aiden checked all the furniture to make sure they wouldn't be able to climb up to them.

"Kyle always gets me a Pop for my birthday or Christmas." There were some lower shelves with stuffed toys, a basket of old cars, and an assortment of action figures. "I put some of Kyle's old toys down for them to play with, nothing special, but everything is much more interesting if it belongs to someone else."

"We can play with them?" Ryan pointed at the lower shelves.

"Yes, anything there you can play with." They ran over to them and started to rummage. While they were busy, Carter turned to Aiden. "I thought the boys could share the bed. I have a blow-up mattress for you... if you want it."

Carter's words made Aiden's skin prickle with awareness. He'd not allowed himself to think about sleeping arrangements — he wasn't sure how the boys would sleep in a strange place. They'd only ever slept over at Nio's and their other father's, back when he took an interest in them, and that was years ago.

Aiden glanced at the boys, who were too busy discovering new old toys to pay them any attention. "I don't want it," he whispered. "But it depends how they settle."

Carter slipped an arm around his waist and hugged him. "Well, I'll blow up the bed for you, but I hope you won't need it. At least... not all night."

Aiden would much rather blow something else.

MANNY SOS

CHAPTER THIRTY-SIX

CARTER

THE BOYS DIDN'T run ahead as they had at his house; they'd turned shy and were stuck to Aiden's legs as they followed Carter into Nora's home. He'd let himself in—if she wasn't ready or half-dressed or had baby sick in her hair, it was her fault. Carter followed the sound of a wailing baby into the living room and took the baby from Nora with a kiss on the cheek. Bobby settled quickly in his arms, and he chuckled at the curse words Nora quickly stifled once she realized Aiden was there.

Her eyes widened, and the smile she gave was only half manic. "Aiden, isn't it? So good to meet you." She went straight in for a hug, and Carter hoped she didn't have sick down her front. Aiden awkwardly patted her on the back, and the boys looked up at her as if they'd never seen a woman before. He realized that they didn't seem to have any close women in their life, apart from teachers and Nanny Biscuit, so it was possible they weren't ready for Nora. Not many people were.

She quickly crouched down and shook each boy's hand. "You must be Ryan, and you must be Luke. Or is it Luke and Ryan?" She made a funny face that had them both smiling.

"I'm Luke, and he's Ryan," Luke said, and he wasn't even lying.

"I was right!" She clapped her hands and stood up. "Kyle, Kyle! Your dad and his guests are here." She yelled so loud, but Bobby didn't even flinch; she'd gone right back to sleep. Carter gently stroked her little fingers. Loud thuds were heard coming down the stairs, and Kyle walked into the living room. He grinned at Carter and walked straight over to Aiden. Carter held his breath, hoping this wouldn't go terribly wrong somehow.

"Hi, I'm Kyle. You must be Aiden, Ryan, and Luke." He shook hands with all of them, and Carter saw the boys fall in love with him like youngsters tended to do with older kids. Once they'd done introductions, he came over for a hug. Nora stole the baby back so she wouldn't get squished.

"Your coffee shop friend is hot… for an old guy," Kyle whispered.

Carter's mouth almost dropped open. Old? Aiden was hot, gorgeous, beautiful, and masculine, despite the slight grey in his hair, but he wasn't old.

"Mom decided we'd have a barbecue. Do you both want to play a bit of footie?"

Ryan and Luke nodded vigorously and ran into the garden after Kyle, all shyness completely gone.

"No mud pies until after lunch!" Nora called after them. Carter winced and dared to look at Aiden, whose bemused smile was much better than his terrified smile. Nora turned back to them and shooed them towards the kitchen.

"Coffee. You want coffee, don't you, Aiden? I'm making a pot. I hope you like it strong. Of course, I'm not drinking it because I'm still breastfeeding and trying to go without, but I love the smell of good coffee."

"I love coffee. Thanks for inviting us all." Aiden put on the charm. "Is this Bobby? Carter's told me all about her."

She nodded and thrust the sleeping baby into his arms. Carter tensed—Nora didn't exactly give him a choice, but it was like riding a bike. Aiden held the baby like a pro, and something tightened in Carter's chest.

Dennis got home just in time to oversee the grill, and they all ate themselves into a food stupor. Ryan and Luke followed Kyle around like he walked on the moon, and Kyle didn't get annoyed or bored with them. Watching the three of them, Carter could tell what a good big brother Kyle would be to Bobby once she got older. He couldn't stop imagining him with Ryan and Luke— playing with them, teaching them.

They made mud pies because… why not? Aiden had been sure it was just a joke, but Nora walked into the garden with a bucket full of water and poured it into a barren part of the flowerbeds, then started to give the twins instructions on making a perfect mud pie.

Once mud pies were over, and hands and clothes cleaned as best as they could, the living room turned into a shantytown. Dennis took it all in his stride as his wife and all three boys turned corners of the living room into forts using chairs and sheets. He even helped her turn the sofa over to create a crawl space from one to the other.

Carter just let her get on with it. Nora had missed out on lots of fun stuff when Kyle had been this age—so had he—so he wasn't going to stop her having fun.

"I thought jumping in puddles was way out there," Aiden said as Carter and Dennis sat under the table fort—Bobby luckily got to nap in her crib upstairs. Luke shrieked in happiness as he crawled under the upturned sofa, and Carter heard Nora make up a story about twin knights and dragons.

"She's got a list," Dennis said.

Carter and Aiden looked at him. Carter didn't know about any list.

"Fun stuff to do. Nora was always sad that you both felt like you had to be perfect because you had Kyle so young. And now she's older, she was worried she'd forget how to be fun." Carter snorted, and Dennis rolled his eyes. "I know. That woman will never forget how to have fun. But it's stuff like mud pies, forts, paper dolls, marbles, conkers… stuff she didn't get to do enough with Kyle."

Carter would hug Nora when he could catch her. He understood how she felt. They'd both tried so hard—almost too hard—and before they'd known it, Kyle was a teenager and only a few years younger than they were when they'd had him. They'd spent so many years trying to make up for what others considered a mistake.

"The twins are having a ball with her. I would never have thought to do this." Aiden looked around their fort and banged his head on the underneath of the table. Carter reached over and rubbed his head. Aiden leaned back into the caress, and he forgot how to breathe.

"That's my cue to move forts," Dennis groaned. He crawled from under the table, the sheet flapping back down behind him as he called out, "Luke, Ryan, can I come live with one of you?"

Carter's back ached from being stooped over, but he ignored it. He ignored everything except Aiden's breath hitching when he slid his hand down to cup the back of his neck and how Aiden leaned forward, sighing when their lips finally touched. His eyes fluttered closed, and he whimpered as Aiden's tongue pressed into his mouth. Carter held him in place, clutching the neck of his T-shirt, but Aiden wasn't going anywhere.

"You should probably both go for a *coffee*. Me and Den can look after the twins for a couple of hours."

Nora's gleeful cackle and manic grin as she poked her head between the sheets tore them apart so quickly that their heads bashed the table.

"What the hell, Nora?" Carter said.

She rolled her eyes and pushed her tongue in her cheek in a lewd gesture. "I mean, when else are you going to get the time alone to go for *coffee*? I can look after all the kids for a few hours, and if I need you, I know what coffee shop you go to."

Aiden frowned and looked at Carter. "I don't know… they might get a bit worried."

"Oh please. I'm so fun that they won't even know you're

gone. Ryan, Luke!" She yelled their names, and they scampered on their hands and knees, crawling under the sheets to join them.

"Are they the dragons, Nora?" Ryan asked.

Her eyes twinkled. "They are. And do you know what their punishment is for setting our mud pies on fire? They have to go to Carter's and put all your clothes away for the night. Boring, right?" They wrinkled their noses and nodded. "So while they do that, you don't mind staying here to help me defend the castle, do you?"

"We can also take turns playing Super Mario." By now, Kyle had crawled under the table too.

"It's getting very crowded under here."

"Well, go and get some *coffee*, then." Kyle used air quotes. Carter was never going to be able to have sex again.

"You boys sure you'll be okay?" Aiden asked. They nodded and chimed in with all the reasons why they should be allowed to stay and not made to go back to Carter's and do boring stuff.

"Oh well." Aiden put a hand on Carter's knee. "I guess it's just us, then."

That's when Carter decided that perhaps his previous thought had been a bit presumptuous.

MANNY SOS

CHAPTER THIRTY-SEVEN

AIDEN

ON THE WAY back to Carter's, Aiden pictured what would happen. They'd take it slow; he'd be romantic, sensual… But all those thoughts flew out of his mind as soon as Carter shut the front door behind them.

Being unable to touch him had been torture—knowing how he tasted but not being able to act on it. Aiden shoved him against the wall and pressed into him, so close Carter's erection hardened against his thigh. He thrust his own cock against him, needing the friction, and Carter flung his arms around his neck, nails scraping the tiny hairs on the back of his neck before spreading out in his hair and angling his head so they could kiss deeply.

His tongue lapped into Aiden's mouth and teased at his tongue. He took control of their kiss, stealing the air from his lungs until he was dizzy and the only thing holding them both up was the wall at Carter's back.

Carter ripped his mouth from Aiden's and breathed out something that might have been 'bed,' but he couldn't be sure because all he heard was the beating of his heart as it thudded against his chest. Carter pulled at his hand, and Aiden followed him upstairs into the bedroom. They kissed again, taking shuffling movements towards the bed until Aiden felt the frame at the back of his knees. He let himself fall backward and took Carter with him; the other man's weight on top of him sent shivers throughout his whole body.

"Off," he said as he yanked at Carter's T-shirt. It would have been much easier to undress before getting on the bed, but Carter wriggling on top of him as they both tried to pull his mud-stained T-shirt off over his head was much more fun.

From that night at the club, he'd known that being with Carter would be mind-blowing, but that was the kind of good sex strangers or acquaintances would have. This was so much more. He knew Carter now—the nuance of his laugh; how good he was with Ryan and Luke; how much he loved family; and how fun he was. It made each touch, each breath, and kiss electrifying. Every little touch meant something.

He finally got Carter out of his T-shirt and rolled them over so Carter was underneath. His chest was lean but well-muscled, mostly smooth with just a splattering of hair between his pecs and a light swirl below his belly button disappearing into his jeans. He sat back on Carter's thighs, rubbing his ass against his groin until Carter whimpered underneath him.

He leaned forward, and Carter tried to meet him for a kiss, but Aiden smirked and bypassed his mouth to nip kisses down his jaw to his collarbone, then lower. He sucked on each nipple, taking turns until they were tight little buds. Carter gasped, his hands rubbing against Aiden's thighs. His pupils were blown and his lips swollen. His hair was messed up, and Aiden couldn't stop himself from reaching out. It was so soft, especially when it was free from product. He'd wanted to touch for so long.

Carter's eyes fluttered shut, and he sighed, thrusting upwards. Aiden tightened his thighs around Carter's hips, and his stomach muscles clenched. He leaned down again and, this time, gave Carter what he wanted, kissing him. Carter's hands fisted his T-shirt, pulling it up under his arms. He scraped his nails down Aiden's spine, and he shuddered, his cock twitching at such a slight touch.

Aiden pulled away long enough to rid himself of his T-shirt, and Carter's eyes widened.

"I've dreamed of this chest ever since you ran half-naked down the driveway." He grinned and ran his hand up Aiden's abs, flicking at his nipples.

Aiden pressed Carter's hands to his chest and closed his eyes, willing his body to calm down. One touch from Carter and he was ready to shoot.

"I knew you were checking me out." He winked, then brought one of Carter's hands up to his lips and pressed a kiss to each fingertip.

"I mourned that you didn't sleep naked. I wanted to see more." With his free hand, Carter dipped into the waistband of Aiden's jeans, awkwardly pulling the zip down and attempting to free the button. Aiden laughed and took pity, opening his jeans for him. Carter lifted out Aiden's erection, and he shuddered. His touch was light, and Aiden's thighs began to tremble.

"Off," Carter bit out as he abandoned Aiden's cock in favor of trying to push his jeans over his hips.

Aiden gave a breathless laugh and crawled off Carter long enough for them both to remove their jeans, shoes, and socks. Carter settled back on the bed, and Aiden forgot how to move. He was beautiful. Carter blinked up at him and reached for his erection. He jacked himself so slowly that Aiden was hypnotized, and it was only Carter's small whimpers that got him moving. He pulled Carter's hand away and knelt between his legs. His mouth watered as he watched Carter's cock bob before him. The head glistened with pre-come, and Aiden swiped his work-roughed thumb over the top.

"Jesus." Carter arched off the bed, one hand grasping Aiden's arm, nails digging into his skin hard enough to leave marks. Or at least Aiden hoped so.

MANNY SOS

CHAPTER THIRTY-EIGHT

CARTER

HANDS FISTED IN the sheets at his side, Carter's whole body tensed in the hope it would stop his orgasm—he didn't want it to be over before it had even started. Aiden looked him in the eye and smirked as if he knew just how much he was affecting him, and then he swirled his thumb over the tip of his dick, the roughened pad scraping deliciously against his sensitive skin.

"Don't come yet," Aiden said, as if he had some choice in the matter.

Sadistic bastard.

Carter sucked in a lungful of air and held it in until his vision started to blur, and he let it out between his clenched teeth just in time to see Aiden shuffle further down the bed and dip his head over Carter's straining cock.

Aiden's breath was hot, but those delicious lips ignored his dick and licked the strip of soft skin between his groin and thigh. Carter lurched up at the unexpected touch, his cock bouncing against Aiden's cheek, scraping against his stubble. His eyes rolled back into his head, and he fell back onto the cushions and nudged Aiden with the heel of his foot against his lower back.

"Don't tease."

"I'm not teasing," he said, teasing. "It's called foreplay." He nipped at the skin on Carter's inner thigh, but they were both ready for it that time.

Carter lifted his head and glared at him. "All we've done since we've met has been foreplay."

Aiden only had to breathe in his vicinity and it was goddamn foreplay.

Aiden laughed, and the air blew across Carter's dick, making it twitch, and then without another word, he lowered his head until Carter felt the warm cavern of his mouth suck him in. His hips thrust unconsciously, and Aiden gripped his hip with one hand to control his movement, making it slow and tortuously sweet. His other hand massaged his balls, one finger sneaking into his crease.

Fireworks gathered behind Carter's eyes. With each movement of Aiden's tongue, each massage of his hand, another went off.

And another.

And another.

He wasn't going to last—but he wanted to—he didn't want to come without Aiden inside him. Aiden's eyes were dark and glassy, his mouth red and slick as it moved over his dick. Carter had to close his eyes again because that vision of him was too much. The warmth became chilled air as Aiden pulled off and crawled up his body, smashing their lips together.

He tasted salty and faintly of coffee. Carter groaned, threaded his hands in Aiden's hair, and locked his legs around his hips, thrusting upwards until their cocks slid against each other in a mixture of their pre-come. Aiden hooked one of Carter's legs over his shoulder, and his cock slid slickly underneath his balls and into his crease.

Carter's heart hammered in his chest, white noise roared in his ears, and he needed Aiden right that second. His arms felt heavy, and his fingertips tingled as he threw one arm outward, searching the nightstand. He grabbed the box of condoms, but the lube slid across the top and rolled under the bed.

"Shit. Fuck. Shit," he cursed against Aiden's lips. Aiden pulled away long enough to laugh at him; then when Carter glared again, he held his hands up in truce and twisted sideways, head and body disappearing over the side of the bed so he could find the elusive bottle.

It wasn't such a disaster once Aiden did that. Carter's gaze roamed over his firm ass and muscled thighs. He bit one ass cheek while one hand smoothed over the other, and Aiden almost fell off the bed. He used both hands to stop his fall, and eventually, he was back, the bottle in hand.

"You play dirty." He pointed the bottle at him.

Carter smiled, warmth spreading throughout his body. He spread his legs further apart, and Aiden settled on his knees between them. He placed the bottle securely next to his leg and grabbed a condom, ripping the corner of the foil with his teeth. Carter couldn't stop watching his hands; his pulse raced, and his ass clenched at the thought of Aiden's fingers and then his large cock inside him. He tipped his hips up and held his erection against his belly, giving Aiden a show.

Aiden growled and cursed something unintelligible that made Carter breathless. His eyes closed as Aiden pulled the condom free of its wrapper. He felt him reach for the bottle of lube, heard the click of the lid, and finally, his fingers pressed against him. He gasped, and his eyes shot open as he felt Aiden roll the condom down *his* erection. Carter's heart hammered so hard in his chest that he thought it would burst right out.

He grabbed Aiden's wrist, not to stop him—fuck no—but to make sure… he wasn't sure what, but to make sure. He hadn't expected this.

"This okay?" Aiden asked, voice low and rough.

How could he think anything else? Just because he'd expected it to be the other way around didn't mean he didn't want to feel Aiden's sweet, tight heat around his cock.

"More than."

Carter was lust drunk, and his words were slurred, but the

relief on Aiden's face was easy to see. He gave a wide grin and reached for the lube. Carter held his hand out, but Aiden grinned wider and shook his head. He squirted the liquid into his hand and reached behind himself. His eyes fluttered closed, dark lashes caressing his face. His breath stuttered, and his cock twitched with each movement.

Carter grabbed hold of his thighs, feeling each of Aiden's movements through the palms of his hands. He refused to breathe for fear of not being able to hear every grunt, sigh, and groan Aiden made as he opened himself out. Eventually, Aiden opened his eyes, and his pupils were blown. He used what was left of the lube to coat Carter's covered cock, and then he maneuvered himself over him.

Carter remembered to hold his dick still, and Aiden teased him for a few seconds before sinking down onto him.

"Jesus fucking Christ."

Carter thrust his hips upwards, but it was still Aiden who was in control as he sank down until there was nowhere else to go and his inner muscles clamped down tight around him. He leaned forward, and their lips met in a messy kiss, and then Aiden lifted up and slammed his hips back down.

He set a fast pace that drove Carter to distraction. They set a desperate rhythm, mouths sliding together as hands touched whatever bare skin they could find, and just as Aiden started to jerk, Carter rolled him over until he was underneath. Smaller he may be, but he was still strong, and he was going to rock Aiden's world. He hooked one of Aiden's legs over his arm and thrust into him.

There would be time for slow and tender later, but for right now, he'd wanted this man for so long, and he couldn't wait any longer. He wanted him more than he'd wanted anyone before. Carter sucked air into his lungs and bit down on Aiden's shoulder. He let out a strangled scream, and his hips stuttered. Carter felt warmth between them and realized he hadn't even touched Aiden's cock yet, something he vowed to make up for later, but now, in this moment, he was losing all rational thought, and all that was left was the warmth sucking him in and the glorious slide as their slick skin slipped together.

When the orgasm came, it was a surprise, ripping through him and making his toes curl. His body twitched in aftershocks. One minute he was sliding into Aiden's body, and the next, he was falling over the brink into a place that was nothing but one sensation after another. This was what falling in love was, he realized with the clarity that came with post-coital haze. He fell on top of Aiden and slid sideways. He held onto the condom and pulled it off, then threw it onto the pile of clothes on the floor beside the bed.

"Damn," he slurred when Aiden chuckled, pulling him closer.

If he'd been standing, he would be weak-kneed. He slid an arm over Aiden's chest and threw a leg over his, and all was right in the world.

"That was worth the wait," Carter teased, rubbing his lips against Aiden's five o'clock shadow.

MANNY SOS

CHAPTER THIRTY-NINE

AIDEN

THEY ALL STAYED at Carter's until early Monday morning when they couldn't put it off any longer. Aiden had to work, and it would look very odd on the camera feeds if none of them were there at the beginning of the work week.

He'd enjoyed meeting Carter's family and learning more about him, and it had been amazing not having to worry about what they said to each other or how they touched just in case the cameras picked it up. He wasn't sure how he was going to keep his hands off Carter now he'd had a taste.

As much as he was dreading the holidays coming to an end because it meant Carter wouldn't be with them 24/7, he was also looking forward to it because it meant they'd have more freedom.

The boys had pleaded to drive in the camper with Carter, so Aiden had a relatively stress-free ride back home. When he pulled up, the bright blue Bedford camper van was already parked on the driveway.

The camper's back door was open, and the boys were inside, rifling through the games and craft supplies Carter kept in there. Aiden grinned. The three of them were going to have more fun once he left for work.

He looked at his watch. He had enough time to get changed

and have a cup of tea, but then he'd have to be off. It didn't matter if he was the boss or not, he had work to do. That thought didn't make him move any faster once he caught up with Carter.

"What are you guys up to today?"

Carter grinned at him. "I'm not sure. But it's going to involve glitter. Lots of glitter."

"Hmm, maybe I'm not disappointed about going to work now," Aiden teased.

"Just you wait. If we're creating glitter masterpieces, who will have to treasure them forever? Possibly even put them on the fridge?" He raised his eyebrow.

"You're a sadist."

The eyebrow raise turned into a wiggle, and Aiden had to bite back a groan. "Don't you know it. Come on, I'll make coffee while you get changed." He then called out to the boys. "Have you finished choosing yet? Let's go get a drink!" They shot out the back of the camper, clutching boxes of glitter, glue, and other craft supplies that were enough to give Aiden nightmares. Shoving that thought out of his head, he raced indoors, taking the stairs two at a time. Changing quickly—he wanted as much time with Carter and the boys as possible before he had to leave—he headed down to the kitchen.

Carter pushed the mug of coffee into his hands, and their fingers touched. At first, he thought it was an accident, but the glint in Carter's eyes told him something different. Aiden looked down at his drink; saw it was tea. He took a sip anyway.

Carter blew on his own mug and took a sip. "Oh, oops. I must have given you the wrong cup. Here, this is yours." He swapped their mugs, and Aiden watched as he took a sip out of the one Aiden had just drunk from, his mouth in the same place. Could an indirect kiss take his breath away? Aiden decided yes, yes, it could, and knew that the groan he bit back wasn't fooling Carter in the slightest.

Two could play at this game. He twisted his… Carter's… mug around until he found the telltale mark where Carter's lips had been, and he brought it to his own, licking the trace of coffee away before sealing his mouth around the rim.

His whole body tingled with awareness—as if they were touching for real and not through crazy mugs that the kids had bought him for birthdays over the years. Carter's breath hitched in his throat, and Aiden knew he was just as affected.

"Cheeky." Aiden looked at him over the edge of the mug and watched in delight as the tips of Carter's ears turned red. He'd won that one.

Carter shrugged with a smile, then started to type something on his mobile. Excitement bubbled in Aiden's stomach. He knew what Carter was doing, and when he felt the tell-tale vibration in his pocket, he had to stop himself from checking it straight away.

He went to sit with the boys at the table, asked them a few questions about what they were planning to do, nodded in the right places, and once enough time had passed—a minute at least—he casually got out his phone and checked his message.

I've been demoted from sadist to cheeky. I'll have to rectify that soon.

Aiden gave his phone a hot glare, then replied. *Promises, promises. I can't wait to kiss you properly.*

"I have to head off to work. You be good for Carter, boys." He licked the coffee cup again and laughed through the hugs as the boys clambered over him, and Carter pulled the half-full coffee out of his hand before he spilled it.

MANNY SOS

CHAPTER FORTY

CARTER

THE BOYS MADE masterpieces until it was time to clean up for lunch. They'd be finding glitter in the kitchen for weeks, but it had been worth it. There was a pile of artwork on the side waiting for Aiden to gush over when he got home.

They FaceTimed with Aiden after lunch and then had a lazy afternoon watching movies while Carter sorted out all their dirty washing from the weekend. It was a boring chore, but Carter enjoyed the monotony, and it gave him a chance to daydream until Aiden came home.

The weekend had been perfect. Aiden and Kyle got along like a house on fire, the twins had followed Kyle around like little puppies, and Nora—well, she was a god for having the boys so they could finally spend some time alone.

Goosebumps raced up his arms, and he had to concentrate on the washing, folding, and putting away—anything but Aiden—so cartoon hearts didn't shoot out of his eyes. He was a sap, but he didn't care.

A knock at the door made him drop a pile of laundry. "Shit."

He scooped it off the floor, placed it on top of the washer, and then went to see who it was. The boys were already in the hallway but couldn't unlock the door, so they bounced impatiently on their tiptoes while they waited.

"We looked through the window. It's the cameramen," Luke said, excited. "Did they bring more sl-clapper boards? Are they here to see us?"

"Hurry up and unlock it. We want to show them our pictures." Ryan rattled the handle impatiently, and Carter tickled his ribs until he shrieked and moved away so he could unlock the door.

He didn't know why anyone from the show would show up at the house today; they had nothing booked and seldom arrived unannounced. Trying to ignore his clammy palms and the nerves bouncing around in his stomach, Carter took a deep breath and forced himself to smile as he opened the door.

"Hi, this is a surprise," Carter said with a feigned cheeriness that actually made his face hurt. Luckily the boys took over and grabbed Joe and Ronnie by the hands. The look of confusion on their faces was almost enough to chase away his nerves. Almost.

"Come look at our pictures. We used so much glitter. I drew Carter catching frogs," Ryan chattered happily, blissfully unaware of the tension.

"Well, I painted a picture of me, Ryan, and Kyle playing football," Luke said, trying to get one over his brother, but he only managed to incriminate Carter.

Crap.

Joe and Ronnie gave him identical looks over the boys' heads as they pretended to look at the pictures, while Carter busied himself filling the kettle, pulling out mugs, and making tea none of them wanted.

"Look at this one. It's baby Bobby crying really loudly. That's why I put glitter all around her. And this one is of all the dragons we saw on the weekend."

The boys were just digging his hole deeper and deeper.

"These are wonderful pictures. Who are Kyle and Bobby?" Joe asked the twins, though he knew full well who they were.

"Kyle is Carter's s—"

"Who wants to play Just Dance?" Carter interrupted in a desperate attempt to stop the boys from giving even more away. Their eyes widened, and their hands shot into the air.

"I do, I do!" they both chanted.

"Let's go set it up, then. You can… drink tea," Carter said to Ronnie and Joe as he followed the boys into the living room and set up the game Kyle had loaned them. Worry made his stomach cramp, but he smiled for the boys, set them up, and when he couldn't put it off any longer, he went back into the kitchen.

"We've probably got about ten minutes before they're back in here."

"So… you took them to visit your family?" Joe's gaze burned into him, and Carter wasn't sure how to answer for the best.

"You know you're meant to organize cameras and crew if you go on excursions. That includes taking your charges to meet your family." Joe sipped his tea. He had glitter on his face. Carter decided not to tell him about it.

"It was a weekend. I don't work on the weekend. Technically, we can do what we want. We didn't go together. I went home for a visit, and Aiden and the boys decided to join us." Carter knew he sounded defensive, but he couldn't stop it. So what if it wasn't exactly the truth? It was close. They'd taken separate cars.

"Not if you're doing it together. It's in the contract," Joe shot back. "This is a job, after all. And we need good content to make sure the ratings go up."

Carter ground his teeth until his jaw ached. He'd never hung out socially with any of the other families he'd mannied for; this was completely new territory. Plus, they'd needed time to be themselves. "The ratings will be fine. They got a *Manny SOS* Manny crossover."

"Yes. The crossover. Funny you should bring that up," Joe said.

Carter was rapidly wishing he hadn't now.

"Are you hooking up with Aiden?" Ronnie interrupted. His face wasn't as angry as Joe's, but the question was still a shock.

Carter glanced at the door, making sure the boys weren't in earshot. "How did you jump to that conclusion? Aiden and I are friends." His heart was thumping so loudly he was shocked no one else could hear it. He desperately thought back to their conversations and how they'd acted in front of the cameras. Nothing incriminating came to mind. What was he missing? He hated saying that he and Aiden were just friends, but he knew Aiden would hate anyone finding out about them in this way. He was wary enough about the show and cameras as it was.

"Are you really?" Joe placed his cup down and grabbed the iPad hooked underneath Ronnie's arm. He flipped open the cover and tapped the screen a few times before turning it around for Carter to see.

"What's this?" It was a video clip from the garden. The day Sebastian had visited. It showed Ryan and Luke pulling Aiden and Carter towards the swing set. Aiden cheating at their game, his hand grabbing the chain links on Carter's swing and staying there. A few moments later, Carter's hand moved down the chain links and covered Aiden's fingers as they swung in sync. Neither moved away for a long time. Was that all they had? A burst of relieved laughter fell from his lips, and he rolled his eyes. They hadn't even been together then.

"So what? This is nothing."

Joe raised his eyebrow but didn't say anything. He tapped the screen again, and the video clip changed. It was a wide shot, like the ones used with the small cameras set around the house.

Carter's stomach lurched as he watched himself and Aiden tidy up the garden. He knew how the night ended. But it couldn't be on camera. Technically this shouldn't be on camera either.

Carter watched as he and Aiden emptied the paddling pool; he picked up towels, and Aiden tried to take them. He didn't need to see this—he knew what happened—but he couldn't look away. How had their first kiss since the club been captured on film? Had the crew suspected before then? Had the camera been left there on purpose?

"What camera is this?" he demanded. "This was after the crew left."

Surely they deserved some privacy? It seemed Joe and Ronnie didn't think so.

"I'm presuming it's the spare you usually take into the garden when you're with the kids," Joe drawled and picked up his tea again.

Dread flowed down Carter's body like someone had thrown iced water over him. "No, I always…" He looked desperately towards the kitchen window where he usually kept the spare, but it wasn't there. It was on the other side of the glass, barely visible between the ivy. No, no, no. It couldn't be. There was no way he'd leave a camera out there.

Only… his mind had been full of other things, and nothing about this job was like the others. He'd let his professionalism slip and started to treat it more like home—as if Aiden and the boys were his family, not a family he worked for. He really wasn't firing on all cylinders.

Carter strode outside to the windowsill, as if staring at the camera from that side would change the outcome. The wind was chilly against his skin, and he shivered. He couldn't breathe. The neck of his T-shirt was too tight, and he pulled at it in an attempt to make it easier to suck in air. It didn't help. He closed his eyes and leaned into the wind, letting it wash over him. How could he have been so stupid?

"We didn't put it there," Ronnie said. Carter jumped; he hadn't heard them follow him.

"I forgot about it." He frowned, heart hammering in his chest. How was he going to explain this to Aiden?

"Tell me the truth," Joe said, choosing his words carefully. "Are you seeing Aiden?" At least he hadn't said hooking up. They were long past that.

"Are you going to fire me? Am I in trouble?" Answering a

question with a question, very mature of him.

"You're not fired. But what if I say you are in trouble? You crossed a line."

"What line? There's nothing in my contract. My private life is just that. Private." His words were clipped and angry. At himself as much as them.

"Until it affects the show, and this will have an impact. We just want to make sure it works in our favor. Both of ours."

"This is ridiculous. If I hadn't accidentally left the camera out here, you'd have no clue about our relationship. We were going to keep everything on the down-low until after our episodes aired. Nothing would disrupt *Manny SOS*."

Ronnie tipped his head back and laughed. "Aww, still so innocent. You don't think that people are going to be interested in one of our mannies falling for one of the parents on the show? You might not be Jason Momoa level of celebrity, but it'll be news."

"How you come out, even if you don't give a statement, will reflect on the show," Joe said. "Now, this is a presumption, but you introduced Aiden and his kids to your kid and Nora, so I believe it's more than a hook-up, more than close proximity, and you're both in it for the duration?"

Carter gave a small nod. At least they could tell that.

"This is our first *Manny SOS* romance, you know," Ronnie said, grinning. Carter wasn't sure why he was so happy all of a sudden. That smile made him uncomfortable, and he shifted on his feet, shoving his hands in his pockets. "We've got the perfect solution to any possible fallout or unwanted attention."

"We add your romance to the show." Joe was excited now, gesturing as he spoke. "Fans will be invested. We can control interviews, make sure the narrative goes our way. We show the kiss, some of the more intimate—yet innocent—moments captured on camera already, then film a few more. Who doesn't love a good montage? As Ronnie said, it'll be the first relationship, and you'll be our star couple."

Carter could practically see the horror in Aiden's eyes at the very idea of being *Manny SOS*'s 'it' couple. "Absolutely not."

"This isn't a choice, Carter. You're a brand, *Manny SOS* comes first and—"

"You want to capitalize on our relationship for extra views." He wasn't dumb; he knew what they were doing.

"You'll both get paid handsomely. Once your relationship is revealed as the show airs, we'll get you to do photoshoots together—go on TV for interviews, magazines. It'll be great publicity… for us and for you."

Carter heard someone clear their throat behind him. He flinched as he swirled around and saw Aiden's cold stare boring into him.

No, no, no. How much had he heard?

"Aiden…"

MANNY SOS

CHAPTER FORTY-ONE

AIDEN

RATINGS, PHOTOSHOOTS, INTERVIEWS, money all swirled around in Aiden's mind, disconnected words that held no meaning. It didn't take long for their weight to settle like stone in his heart.

It shouldn't hurt so much. In comparison to all the shitty things that had happened in his life, having a new boyfriend screw him over because of a TV show was small. His parents had cared more about their next fix than looking after him; he'd hopped from one shitty foster home to the next. He'd found what he thought was love, had kids, and then his husband had left not only him but the children they'd decided to have too. See? What was going on was nothing.

Then why did his heart ache? Why was his throat clogged with the tears he refused to shed? He must have made some noise because Carter spun around, eyes widening at the sight of him.

Caught red-handed, huh? Aiden didn't say a word. He didn't need to. His face said it all.

"Aiden. It's not what you think..." Carter stepped towards him, but Aiden stepped back. He couldn't let Carter touch him because he'd crumble, and he needed to be strong. He couldn't let them see how much it hurt.

"I don't know how much you heard, but I didn't agree to it," Carter tried again, but Aiden hadn't heard him disagree with Joe.

"Is that all we are? Ratings?" He could be hurt for himself, but the anger set in when he thought of what this would do to the boys. No one used or hurt his kids.

"You know that's not true." Carter reached for him again, but he shrugged him off.

Joe stepped between them, and all Aiden wanted to do was punch him. This wasn't even about him anymore. He wanted to hear what Carter had to say.

"You signed up for the show. You can't be surprised we want to use all the footage. It is, after all, a TV show," Joe said, and Aiden had to cross his arms so he didn't give in to temptation.

"Is that so?"

How could his life change in a matter of moments? He'd been so excited to get home that he'd left work early. When he'd heard voices in the garden and thought Carter and the boys were out there playing, this wasn't what he'd expected to hear after their weekend away. Had it all been a lie? Was Carter that good?

"What do you even have on camera?" Aiden looked at Carter, thinking back to their conversations in the garden, to the kiss they'd shared. Had he been secretly filming?

"They only have that one kiss. I forgot to move the camera, but it was an accident, I swear." Stepping towards him again, Carter reached for his hand. But Aiden shrugged him off.

"Show whatever you want." He glared at Joe. "It'll be the show that suffers when viewers realize we're not together after it airs, and you're just spouting a load of bullshit."

"Please don't do this, Aiden. You know my feelings have nothing to do with the show. You *know*." He grabbed Aiden's wrist, tried to uncurl his fingers, but Aiden couldn't let him, couldn't let him get close. This was all too much. Grim reality shitting on his life again. His skin crawled at the thought of cameras all over his house, cameras he didn't even know were there.

He had to get out. Instead of retreating, he pushed forward. Shoving past Carter and glaring at Joe, he walked into the house and heard the overly joyful music that made him wince.

As he stepped into the living room, he took a deep breath and pasted on a smile.

"What are you up to?" His voice sounded forced as he watched the boys dance to the movements on the TV, but Ryan and Luke were too distracted to notice anything wrong.

Only Luke spared him a glance. "Dancing, silly, can't you tell?" He turned back to the TV and wiggled his arms.

"You're right. Silly me. You're dancing so well, but I was wondering if you wanted to go to the cinema tonight." He had to get out of the house and away from Carter. Right that second. The boys abandoned their game with shouts of excitement. He hoped there'd be something suitable showing.

"Is Carter coming?" Luke asked. Aiden looked behind him and realized Carter had followed him out of the kitchen, worry and concern written over his face.

"No, it's a daddy and sons' night." Carter flinched at his words, and guilt made Aiden's stomach tie in knots. He pushed his warring feelings aside and ushered the kids out of the house as fast as he could. They could film an empty house for all he cared.

"Aiden..." he heard Carter say as they walked up the pathway to his car. He didn't turn around.

MANNY SOS

CHAPTER FORTY-TWO

CARTER

CARTER HAD NEVER been alone in Aiden's home before and hated it. He paced the carpet, wishing Aiden hadn't overheard their conversation. Not because he wanted to keep what had happened from him, but because he wanted to break it to him gently.

Did Aiden believe he was on board with Joe's plan for their relationship and the show? Carter wasn't sure exactly how much he'd overheard, and Aiden hadn't stuck around long enough for him to find out.

Aiden hadn't texted him, though Carter kept checking his phone just in case. It was stupid. They were in the middle of watching a movie. He wasn't going to be looking at his phone.

How could such a perfect day turn into such a disaster? He needed to explain everything. He opened his messages and hesitated. Should he text him? What would he say? Where would he start? He looked at his recent contacts, hesitating before finally pressing Sebastian's name.

He answered after a few rings. It sounded loud wherever he was. "Can you talk?"

"Sure, I'm in the garden watching the kids cheat at hopscotch."

"How do you cheat at hopscotch?"

"Beats me. The more obvious question would be—how do you even play it?" Carter gave a little laugh that then turned into a groan. "Now I know you didn't ring to give me pointers. What's wrong?"

"I fucked up big time."

Carter spilled everything, from their perfect weekend to the forgotten camera and the conversation Aiden walked in on.

"He's probably scared and a bit shocked. Give him time."

"He took the boys out to get away from me." Carter massaged his temples and leaned his head back. "You should have seen the look in his eyes…"

"Well, it's his house, he's got to come back, and you can clear up any misunderstanding. Look on the bright side. At least Joe didn't disapprove of your relationship."

"Oh, he disapproved, but he also sees potential for views to go up. I told him absolutely not, but Aiden didn't hear that." Carter bit at his dry lips. "I'm worried he thinks I did this on purpose."

"You can explain when he gets home."

Carter chewed his bottom lip even harder. "What if he doesn't think all this mess is worth it?"

Sebastian snorted. "Come on, we're not A-list celebrities. We still lead relatively normal lives. I rarely get accosted when I go out."

Carter tried his best to laugh. He appreciated Sebastian's effort to stop him from freaking out, even if it wasn't working. "Speak for yourself." Sebastian was half right. When Carter was dressed in his ordinary clothing, he barely got recognized in public, but being the face of the show had its drawbacks. He did a lot of interviews, TV appearances, and magazine photoshoots. Even if Aiden didn't appear in any of those, there would be people who would pry into his life; reporters would ask him probing questions, trying to find out as much as they could about him.

"I wish I could give you better advice, but all I can say is speak to him. Grovel about the camera, and don't let the producers bully you into something you don't want to do."

"Yeah. I guess. I just wish he'd get home already."

They should have talked about the reality of being with someone like Carter before their weekend away, before Carter had become addicted to him. Now he knew how the other man felt under his fingertips, tasted on his tongue, and had been inside him. It would be harder to walk away from him now. He prayed that wasn't what Aiden wanted.

"Just talk to him. He's a good guy. I'm sure it'll be fine."

"Yeah. I'll talk to him tonight. If he comes home."

"He will. It's his house." Sebastian sounded more confident than Carter felt.

Carter was giddy with relief when Aiden finally walked through the door with the boys. His gaze stayed fixed on Aiden's face, even as the boys talked over each other to tell him about the movie. He smiled and nodded in the right places, but he couldn't move his eyes away.

There were bruises under Aiden's eyes, and his mouth was on a downwards slant—not frowning exactly—but it was enough to make Carter's heart jump into his throat.

"Everything okay?" It was a stupid question, it was obvious that it wasn't, but Carter didn't know how to begin.

"We can talk when the boys go to bed." There was no emotion in his voice, but Carter didn't have a chance to dwell before Aiden turned away from him and ushered the boys upstairs into the bathroom to wipe sticky popcorn from their faces.

He didn't ask Carter to help him put the boys to bed, didn't ask him to read to them or brush their hair—none of the hundreds of things they'd done together until tonight. For the first time since he'd knocked on the front door, Carter felt like an unwelcome guest.

Aiden eventually came back downstairs. It was awkward, Carter couldn't read him, but he had a bad feeling churning in the pit of his stomach.

"I'm sorry you had to walk in on Joe talking like that."

Aiden didn't reply immediately; the quieter he was, the more nervous Carter became.

"You just happened to leave the camera there? Right where we kissed? Gave them prime footage."

Carter winced. "I forgot about the camera. I had no idea we'd even kiss. I've barely thought about the show, let alone ratings, since I arrived at your doorstep." It was true, Carter had crossed many lines he wouldn't usually cross, but pretending to like Aiden for the sake of the show wasn't one of them.

"Why didn't you just tell Joe no?"

Frustration built up inside him as the words burst out of his mouth. "I did. I did, Aiden. I had no clue Joe was going to turn up or that he knew about us, or that he'd want to air it on TV. I was in shock. You've got to believe I wouldn't do something as underhand as messing you, Luke, and Ryan about just for ratings? That I'd take you to meet my family if it was all a lie?"

"I heard the last series didn't do so well. Good people can do shady things if they're worried."

"How can you even say that?" His fingers bit into Aiden's arms and shook him, as if that would knock some sense into him.

"What am I supposed to think after what I heard?" Aiden shrugged free. "I've spent enough time with someone who lied and cheated, who messed my kids around. I can't do that again. I won't take the chance that they could be hurt."

Carter froze to the spot as Aiden walked away from him. His mouth was dry, the words disappeared from his mind, and his chest ached. This couldn't be happening. Just that morning, he'd been on top of the world, picturing their life together: family get-togethers, lazy Sunday mornings, and chaotic holidays with Nora, Dennis, and all the kids.

"Aiden…" Carter managed to croak out.

He stilled on the stairs but didn't turn around to look at him. "We should go back to being father and manny. I'm not going to risk the boys."

MANNY SOS

CHAPTER FORTY-THREE

AIDEN

HE SHOULDN'T HAVE blurred the lines. It was his own damned fault. He'd managed to avoid talking to Carter the next morning—he'd left early for work, and the boys had made a good buffer. They hadn't noticed the tension between them yet. Aiden was dreading their reaction when Carter left for good, but he knew it would be better than being part of some fake TV family. That would just hurt them more in the long run.

His phone buzzed, and Aiden clenched his jaw and ignored it as he worked out his frustration by demolishing the old fireplace. He'd thought the monotonous physical work would help stop him from thinking about the show, the lies, and Carter's part in it.

It didn't work. He couldn't stop thinking about Carter—how they'd met, the shock of their second meeting on his doorstep, and every interaction since. Were they all just for the show? Surely Carter must have liked him a little? Otherwise, he'd never have pursued him at the club.

Was Carter the kind of person to fake a relationship to gain higher ratings? He'd only watched a few episodes of *Manny SOS*, but they hadn't seemed fake. Not like other reality TV shows he'd watched. But what did he know? He was a builder; he fixed houses for a living. He wasn't privy to the glitzy world of TV.

Whatever was true or not, he couldn't risk it. The boys had had enough upheaval, and Aiden just wanted a nice boring life for the three of them. Their other father was a flake, he hadn't called once all holiday, and he'd disappointed enough times the boys had reached the point where they expected it. He didn't want another person in their life who would let them down. Especially on TV for millions of people to watch. He shuddered and tried to concentrate on hitting the bricks with a mallet.

He was nervous when he arrived home. He didn't want to see Carter, but he didn't have a choice. There was no avoiding him. Perhaps he'd take the boys out for dinner. Get them—and him—out of the house.

That idea was nixed when he opened the door to the scent of lasagna wafting through the house. Despite everything, his mouth watered and his stomach grumbled, so when the boys charged at him, he let them lead him into the kitchen.

Carter was fetching plates and filling glasses of orange juice for the boys. It was a scene Aiden had walked in on before, only this time there was tension to the set of Carter's shoulders, and he didn't text him his hello kiss or look at him with a sweet smile.

Shit. Was all that a lie? Aiden shook his head. He wasn't a good judge of character. He couldn't trust himself. Whatever it was, lie or real, he missed it. And he hated himself for missing it. He'd get over it; Carter wouldn't be there forever. Soon enough, he'd move on to the next family and find someone else to have an onscreen relationship with.

He scowled when he thought about that, not liking it one bit.

"Are you grumpy, Daddy?" Luke asked. He jumped, not realizing he'd drifted off. He forced a smile.

"Of course not. I'm just tired." He felt Carter's eyes burn into him from over Luke's head, but he didn't say anything.

"You looked mad."

"Not mad. Tired." He faked a yawn. "See?"

Despite the delicious food, Aiden couldn't eat a thing. He

pushed it around his plate and stole glances at Carter, who was doing the same thing. It was only when he finally forced himself to take a bite that he realized Carter would only be here for one more week. The boys would then be back at school, and he'd have no excuse to see him anymore.

A wave of nausea washed over him, and he pushed his plate away.

"Are you okay?" Carter's voice was quiet, tentative. Aiden frowned at his concern, anger churning in his stomach.

"Sure, I had a big lunch." He'd gone to the local café because he'd purposely forgotten the bento box Carter had left on the side for him.

"Aiden—"

"Boys, how about we go for a walk in the woods?" he interrupted Carter. He knew they wouldn't say no, and at least this way, he wouldn't have to be in the same room as Carter.

They ran to get their shoes while Aiden shoved his feet back into his boots. This time, Carter didn't come out into the hall with them, diving into the pile of crap that lived under the coat rack, digging around for an odd sock or a missing shoe. He stayed seated, and Aiden cursed himself for feeling bad for leaving him out.

"Isn't Carter coming?" Ryan asked.

Aiden looked at him, almost changed his mind, and said, "Yes. Of course, he's coming," but Carter shook his head and shot the boys a smile that didn't reach his eyes.

"Not today. I need to… do the washing up." It was a lame excuse, but the boys bought it, even though they weren't happy.

MANNY SOS

CHAPTER FORTY-FOUR

CARTER

CARTER WAS GOING out of his ever-loving mind. Aiden had been polite, cordial, and hadn't spoken about anything important since their big falling-out four days before, and Joe wanted to know what they were doing about the show.

Who cared about the show? He had to bite back the words so as not to say anything that would damage his career, but in no uncertain terms, he told Joe that they wouldn't play out their relationship for views. Why would Aiden even think he'd agree to that?

How was it even possible to avoid someone living in the same house? Aiden left for work early, and after two days of not taking his bento box, Carter was ready to cry. It was only a fancy lunchbox. It shouldn't hurt so much.

Though they still ate together, their conversation was stilted, and Aiden often whisked the boys away to do something, just the three of them. Carter hated it. Hated not being part of their family. He missed talking to Aiden; he missed their texts. And yes, he missed their kisses, brief though they were.

He'd managed to avoid telling Kyle and Nora that he and Aiden had split up because he hoped they could work it out. But there was no way they could work anything out if Aiden wouldn't talk to him.

The front door burst open, and Carter jumped up when he heard one of the boys crying. He hesitated for a moment, unsure if he should go and see what was wrong. It wasn't his place. Not now. But he couldn't stop where he was when those cries turned into loud sobs. He tentatively poked his head into the hallway and saw Ryan in Aiden's arms with Luke clinging to his side.

"Is everything okay?" Aiden's face was blank, but Ryan twisted around to look at him, fat tears rolling down his cheeks.

"I fell over," he wailed, struggling in Aiden's arms until he put him down. Ryan pointed to his skinned knees, and Carter winced as he knelt and pulled him into a gentle hug.

"It's okay. Daddy will clean them up and put a plaster on them." Ryan cried even harder and clutched Carter's neck.

"He doesn't want me to do it. He only wants you," Aiden said. He didn't seem very happy, but this wasn't the time or place to dig deeper into their problems.

Carter stood up awkwardly with Ryan in his arms. Aiden frowned but said nothing, just rubbed Ryan's back and gave Carter a nod. It was such a small thing and probably didn't mean anything, but Carter could feel the warmth spreading through his body.

"It's all right, tadpole. I'll sort it out for you." He carried Ryan upstairs. Aiden and Luke followed.

"Can I get a plaster too?" Luke asked when Ryan's cries turned to sniffles.

Carter cleaned Ryan's knees and blew on them, just like he'd done to Aiden's weeks before. He looked up at him and wondered if he was thinking about that too, but his face was closed off, and he couldn't read him at all.

He gave plasters to both boys, and Aiden didn't object when they asked Carter to read them a story before bed. Would it be wrong to pick the longest picture book they had, just so he could spend more time with the three of them?

He'd missed their bedtime routine more than he'd realized

and didn't want to leave the room when the boys finally fell asleep, but maybe now they could finally talk. Surely Aiden could tell how much he loved the boys—there was no faking that for TV.

But Aiden disappeared for a shower before he could corner him. Since the alternative was acting like a weird stalker waiting for him to come out, Carter headed into his own room and pretended he wasn't listening out for Aiden on the other side of the wall.

MANNY SOS

CHAPTER FORTY-FIVE

AIDEN

AFTER CARTER PATCHED up Ryan's knees, the boys had begun demanding he read them a story before bed. Sometimes Aiden managed to distract them, but other times only Carter's soothing voice as he read *Hairy McClary* would do. He shouldn't give in—what were they going to do when Carter left for good? But it was hard to say no to them when they were so sad.

Carter had made himself scarce that evening, so the boys didn't have a choice. He'd cooked them dinner—Aiden still felt like a complete jerk about that—and then he'd mumbled something about meeting up with Sebastian and hurried out.

The house was empty without him. He was angry at himself for thinking that. Carter was there for a job. Everything would go back to normal once he left, and they could all forget about him.

The boys picked at their meals and fidgeted restlessly at the table—they could tell something was wrong, even if they weren't sure what it was. He hated that he'd done this to them, but better that they be a little unhappy now than further down the line when they'd become more attached.

They continued pushing food around their plates, and Aiden couldn't scold them because he was picking at his dinner too. It was delicious. Everything Carter cooked was, but each mouthful was a lead weight in his stomach.

"Are you looking forward to going back to school next week?" he asked with fake enthusiasm, desperate for something to talk about and take their minds off Carter. The boys scowled at him as if he'd gone mad. Weren't kids meant to enjoy school at this age? Surely that look wasn't meant to be aimed his way until they were teenagers?

"We hate school. It's boring. I don't like wearing a tie, and Mrs. Gorman smells." Ryan banged his fork on the table to emphasize his words.

"But you get to see your friends." They blinked at him as if it was a confusing concept to understand. They had friends at school. At least he thought they did. They'd never had friends come back to the house, and they'd never gone anywhere else on a playdate, but that didn't mean they didn't have friends. He vaguely remembered hanging around with kids when he was at school, but then he'd be moved to a different foster family, have to change schools…

"Will Carter pick us up at the school gates?" Luke ignored his question about friends, and Aiden filed it away for a later date. They all had Carter on their minds.

Aiden shook his head. "No, you'll go to after-school club, and then I'll pick you up."

"But Carter will be here when we get home, won't he?" Luke gave up even pretending to eat.

Aiden had thought he'd made it clear that Carter was only with them for the school holidays, but maybe they'd gotten the wrong idea with how close they'd become, plus the trip to meet Carter's family. He'd blurred the lines, and now he'd hurt his kids. *Great job, Aiden.*

"You know we're going to be on TV?" He took his time trying to find the right words that wouldn't confuse or upset them. The boys nodded, though they weren't as enthusiastic as they used to be. "Well, that's Carter's job, so he'll go and help another family. What a great job is that? We can watch him on TV."

He hoped the boys had forgotten him by then. The last thing he wanted to do was watch Carter play happy families on TV.

Ryan and Luke's faces twisted, and he thought they might cry. He was doing a poor job of making it seem like no big deal.

"But he's going to visit?" Ryan said.

"He lives here. His bed is here." Luke sat back on his chair, bottom lip poking out, and folded his arms in front of his chest.

Aiden's heart broke. They'd become so attached and would miss him once he left, and so would he. But it was better this way. He didn't want the boys to grow up in the spotlight, always second-guessing Carter's real reason for being with them.

"He has his own house, remember?"

"Will we visit him, then?"

Aiden shook his head. "Probably not. He's very busy, and we're busy too. You with school and me with work. We'll be much too busy to miss him."

Perhaps if he said it enough, it would become true. It was his own fault the kids were hurting. He shouldn't have acted on his feelings; he should have left his crush buried deep down inside.

He wasn't cut out for the life Carter led, and there was no way he wanted what they'd shared aired on TV.

"Can we text him?"

Why wouldn't they shut up about it? Aiden's eyes burned, and he shoved a spoonful of food into his mouth just to give himself something to do.

"Can we?"

"You're going to be too busy having fun." Or Carter would be too busy with the new family he worked with, too busy promoting the show and charming the viewers. He shouldn't think about it anymore. He and Carter were over—if what they had was even real in the first place. He wasn't making the same mistake again. He'd trusted Wyatt, thought he would spend the rest of his life with him and the family they'd created. He hadn't even lasted eighteen months once the twins were born.

"It's not fair," the boys said in tandem.

Aiden agreed wholeheartedly.

CHAPTER FORTY-SIX

CARTER

CARTER HAD LIED about going to see Sebastian. Instead, he'd called a meeting with Joe, Ronnie, and his manager; this time, he was much more prepared.

His manager had been furious that they'd bombarded him with the change in direction to the show, and she was only mildly annoyed that Carter had kept it from her. Truth be told, he hadn't even thought of telling her. Most of the time, he forgot he even had a manager. He was just a live-in babysitter who happened to be on TV; what did he need a manager for? But Carter had to admit, she was a godsend at times like this.

They met in a private boardroom at a hotel not far from Aiden's house, which gave them the privacy they needed for this conversation and was on neutral ground.

By the end of the meeting, Lissa had given his producers an earful, told them in no uncertain terms that his personal relationships weren't up for air, even if he had started said relationship while working on the show. She had given them holy hell, and it had been glorious to see.

Carter headed back to Aiden's a little lighter, though still unsure how he was going to fix things with him, terrified he wouldn't be able to.

The house was quiet. He checked his watch. He'd lost track of time; the boys would already be in bed. It was too early for Aiden to have gone up, though.

Nerves clenched in his stomach as he walked through the darkened hallway to the living room. The lights were out, but the TV flickering in the corner cast broken shadows over Aiden sprawled out in the chair, head tipped back, mouth open, a leg hooked over the arm.

He'd be in pain for days if he slept all night there. Carter hesitated at first, then told himself off and strode across the room to shake his shoulder. Aiden whined, his brows furrowed in sleep, but he didn't wake up.

"Aiden," Carter whispered, which was stupid because he was trying to wake him up. "You shouldn't sleep like that."

Aiden's eyes shot open, and his body tensed. Carter tensed, too, quickly removing his hand and stepping back to put some distance between them. "You'll get a crick in your neck."

"What?" Aiden blinked up at him and slowly untangled himself from the chair.

"You shouldn't sleep like that." Carter bit at his lip. "Can we talk?" It was now or never.

"We haven't got anything to say to each other."

"Perhaps you don't have anything to say to me, but I've got something to say to you. I talked to my manager, and we've talked to the producers and said in no uncertain terms that our private lives are not entertainment and won't be on the show."

Aiden didn't say anything, and Carter ran a frustrated hand through his hair. He'd hoped Aiden would be relieved, that they'd make up and all would be well.

"I know you thought you walked in on the three of us plotting and scheming. What you heard was them railroading me and me objecting. There's no way I'd do that to you. I might be in the public eye, but I didn't sign up for the start of our relationship to be on TV."

"Sure." Carter hated that cold, passive tone in his voice.

"You don't sound like you believe me." If Aiden thought he was telling the truth, he'd be happy. He'd tell him he was sorry for the misunderstanding and pull him into a comforting hug. They'd be fine.

But he didn't move from his seat.

"Say I do believe you. All this is still your life. The cameras, the TV, the backstabbing, people recognizing you—you even have a manager. I signed the kids up for a month of the spotlight because I was in a bind—I didn't sign them up for life."

Anger stirred in Carter's stomach. How could Aiden be so blind? Carter was popular with a small demographic, but not so popular that he was hounded by paparazzi Hollywood-style. He was a small fish in a big pond.

Kyle led a normal life. Carter's job allowed Kyle to live in comfort. He wasn't spoiled, but he and Nora didn't have to struggle to provide for him the way they'd had to when they were younger. His job had done only good things for Kyle, and Carter wasn't going to allow Aiden to suggest it was bad. He loved his job, he enjoyed working with kids, and he even enjoyed most of the media aspects of it. He wasn't going to apologize for it.

"I have a son who grew up in this so-called spotlight. Perhaps you could talk to him and see how he feels about it? I wasn't planning on parading the three of you around like a trophy family."

"People are going to be interested in the kids featured on *Manny SOS* once they find out their father and the manny are together. It's not the same."

"It'll be a bit of gossip. It'll die down. I don't want to lose you. Or the boys. You're overthinking this." Why wasn't Aiden listening? Why didn't he understand?

"I'm sorry. I can't. Maybe we rushed into a relationship. I just want a quiet boring life. You can't give us that."

"So you're just going to throw what we have away so you

can stay tucked up in the country all alone?" Aiden didn't reply. "I never thought you were a coward." Carter's eyes burned, and there was an ache in his chest right above his heart.

"To someone who didn't have stability as a kid, to someone whose ex ran off and barely sees the kids—that sounds like heaven."

Carter gave a little cry of frustration. How could Aiden be so blind? "I'm not saying it isn't. But wouldn't it be better to share it with someone?"

Aiden lowered his head, his eyes trained on the floor, without saying anything.

That was it, then? Aiden wasn't even going to try. Carter wasn't important enough to give them a chance. He swallowed the lump in his throat and nodded. What more was there to say? He wasn't going to win this argument.

CHAPTER FORTY-SEVEN

AIDEN

WHAT THE HELL is going on with you? Daryl and John said you're being a bastard to work with, and you've not answered any of my calls or texts..." Nio eyed the store-bought sandwich Aiden was picking at. "And where's your swanky bento box?"

He hadn't taken one of Carter's homemade lunches with him since they'd argued, even though Carter had made him one every day without fail. The guilt got stuck in Aiden's throat, and his chicken mayo tasted like sawdust.

"I'm working. Why are you here? Don't you have to work?" He didn't want to talk about this, especially not with his best friend, who apparently was *still* Carter's biggest fan.

"It's lunchtime, and you're moping in the garden on your own. I thought I'd eat with you before meeting my next client." Nio was entirely too proud of himself, and Aiden was too tired to deal with his crap.

"Tell me what the hell is going on." His voice gentled.

"Nothing. Nothing is going on."

He raised an eyebrow, obviously not fooled by Aiden's denial. "Look, the boys FaceTimed me and told me all about your visit to Carter's house and how you met his family. You don't have to tell me any details because I can read between the lines.

You and Carter are together, aren't you? No need to be shy."

He should take away the boys' tablet or at least block it so they couldn't WhatsApp with Nio. He didn't want to talk about this. He already felt sick to the stomach. He didn't know if he was doing the right thing, but the thought of him and the boys living in Carter's celebrity world was terrifying. The look of greed in Ronnie's eyes had been nauseating.

The sandwich got stuck in his throat, and Aiden coughed. He took a sip of water before pushing the sandwich away from him.

Nio's gaze bore into him, smile shifting to concern. "What's wrong? I thought perhaps you were sad because Carter's leaving soon, pining because you won't get to see his pretty face every day. But that's not it, is it?"

"We're not together." Nio nodded, urging him to explain. "Not anymore. The show found out about us." Aiden could still hear their words as they talked about his and Carter's relationship like it was a commodity to be used.

Nio gasped and reached across the table to grab Aiden's arm. "What? Did they tell you that you can't be together? Can they do that?"

"No. *Worse.* They wanted to add our relationship to the show. We accidentally kissed in front of a camera, and they found out."

Nio became all misty-eyed as he finished off his salad and reached for Aiden's half-eaten sandwich. "That would be so sweet, wouldn't it? Watching your love play out in the show. Who wouldn't want to watch that?"

"Me, that's who. I'm already dreading being on TV. I don't want even more of my life on there. I walked in on Carter and the producers talking about how it would drive up the ratings."

"It would." Why wasn't Nio as outraged as he was?

Aiden glared at him and resisted the urge to kick him under the table like the twins did when they were angry at each other.

"Didn't you hear what I just said? They want to use our private relationship to get more viewers. Carter says he's told them no. His manager told them no. Can you believe he has a manager? I had no clue he had a manager." Aiden's palms started to sweat, and he wiped them down his jeans. No, that wasn't for him. He was content to live a quiet life. It's what he wanted. He wanted the boys to have that idyllic childhood he never had. He didn't want them to look back and only remember cameras and interviews and no privacy.

"That makes sense because he's working in the entertainment industry. Of course he'd have a manager."

Aiden didn't know what to say to that. Was he just naive? Despite the show, Carter had never seemed like one of those typical TV entertainers.

"I don't want to live in the spotlight, Nio. I don't want the boys to either. I'm a simple creature. I spent my childhood getting bounced around from one foster home to another. Now I just want peace, quiet, and stability for me and the boys. Nothing about Carter's job can give us those."

"But what about Carter himself?"

He couldn't stop thinking about what Nio had said. Aiden's heart raced as he shifted restlessly, thumping the pillow before rolling over to stare at the wall. Carter was on the other side of it and would be for another week. Then he would be gone, and apart from a few interviews for the show, he'd never see him again.

His stomach dropped at the thought, and that just made him angry at himself. He'd made a decision, the best decision for him and his family, and he should be relieved, not dreading it.

Stupid brain and stupid heart. He was too old for this shit. He turned over and thumped his pillow again, trying to get comfortable. He closed his eyes tightly and eventually drifted into a fitful sleep.

Aiden woke with a start, hair slicked to his forehead with

sweat, T-shirt clinging uncomfortably to his chest, and blinked, trying to orientate himself in the dark room. How long had he slept for?

It was late, and his brain was slow to process, confused. He didn't know what had woken him up, but he was restless and unable to drop back off. He got out of bed and crept down the hallway, hesitating outside Carter's door, but didn't hear anything. He wanted to knock and see if he was awake, but he resisted the urge. That would only muddy everything between them even more.

He carried on to the boys' room and eased the door open so it didn't squeak and wake them up. The room was dim but not pitch black, thanks to the nightlight casting a gentle hue over the twin beds.

It still took him too long to realize neither Ryan nor Luke was in their bed. Toys were scattered around the floor, which wasn't unusual, and their chest of drawers was open as if they'd been rummaging through it.

Aiden frowned, and his heart rate increased. There was no need to panic; they'd probably snuck downstairs to watch TV. That must have been what woke him.

The relief lasted until he got to the living room. They weren't there. The TV was off; the lights were off. Where were they?

He strode into the kitchen, ready to catch them having a midnight snack—ready to scold them and secretly be relieved. They weren't there either.

His hand scrambled for the light switch, flinching when the fluorescent light flooded the kitchen.

"Ryan, Luke?" he called, willing his voice to stay calm, but then he noticed the back door was open a crack, and there was a chair pulled up close.

He yanked the door open fully and ran into the garden. He couldn't see them. "Luke, Ryan! Answer me right now!" he shouted into the darkness. They didn't answer.

A madman possessed, he raced around the garden. They

weren't there. His heart pounded inside his chest, his mind racing with images no parent wanted to see. He didn't know what to do. He ran back inside and checked every room in case they were hiding and he'd just missed them. He wouldn't put that past them.

Nothing. Terror burned through his veins, vomit scorched the back of his throat. His hands shook as he turned on every light in the house, hoping they were hiding in a shadowy corner, that he'd missed them in his panicked state.

They were nowhere to be found. He was going to be sick. Aiden's stomach cramped up, and he bent over and retched. This was not happening. It was some weird joke.

Where were they? Had they snuck out? Aiden straightened up and stumbled towards Carter's bedroom. The only room in the house he hadn't been in. He banged on the door and didn't wait for an answer before shoving it open and grappling for the light switch.

Carter shot up in bed, hand shielding his eyes. "Wha'?" he slurred.

"The boys are missing." Aiden's voice cracked as he spoke, and he had to lean against the wall when he felt himself sway.

All his sleepiness disappeared as Carter jumped out of bed. Aiden steadied him when he got his foot caught in the sheets. "What do you mean missing?"

"They're not in the house. A chair was pulled up to the back door, and it was open. They're not in the house or the garden." His voice shook. What if someone had taken them? What if they were lost or had wandered onto the main road?

"Come on, let's take another look." Carter grabbed his mobile, shoved his bare feet into his trainers, and steered Aiden out of the room while shouting for the boys. He was greeted with silence too.

They both searched, calling for the boys, Aiden getting increasingly hysterical with each yell of their names. How could Carter be so calm? He searched the house and the garden methodically, but he didn't find them either.

"I've already searched the house and garden," Aiden snapped. "We're wasting time." This wasn't getting them anywhere. Why wasn't Carter doing something?

Carter glanced at him but didn't say anything. His pacing the only thing showing he wasn't as calm as he appeared, Carter pressed something on his mobile and placed the phone to his ear.

"Are you calling the police?" Aiden asked. They should call the police. It had been too long since they'd gone missing. It could have been hours ago for all he knew. Some father he was. He hadn't even heard them sneak out of the house.

"Joe? I know it's late. No time to talk. Do you have access to the camera feeds? The boys have gone missing from the house. We need to see which direction they went." He put the phone down. "He's going to call us back in a few minutes."

"Oh God, where are they, Carter?" Had Wyatt taken them? Aiden threw that thought away as soon as it entered his mind. Wyatt didn't care enough about them to put in this much effort.

Carter grabbed hold of his arms, his fingers biting into his skin. "We'll find them. We know they managed to unlock the back door and get out. No one broke in and took them."

"They climbed on a stool."

"Exactly. They can't have gone far. Joe's sent something." Aiden and Carter huddled over Carter's phone and watched a video of the boys running into the kitchen around two hours ago. They tried opening the door, and when they couldn't unlock it, Luke pushed a chair over to the door and Ryan climbed on it, easily unlocking it.

"Shit," Aiden muttered, his heart still slamming against his chest as he watched them slip through the door. The camera caught them running past the window and off into the distance.

Aiden's stomach lurched, and he ran outside. He knew where they were heading. "The treehouse." That had to be it. He didn't know why, but he was sure that was where they were going.

Carter caught up with him and jogged a few steps behind, following his lead. "Are you sure?"

"They ran towards the woods. Remember they kept talking about it at the beginning of the holiday?" Aiden pumped his legs faster and cursed as his trainer caught on a tree root.

"Slow down, we can't see a thing. Here." Carter turned on the torch on his phone and flashed it ahead of them.

Aiden wanted to run, but he knew Carter was right. Even with the phone's light, it was still pitch black. What if they were lost or hurt? How could they see to get to the treehouse?

"Luke, Ryan!" Carter called out. Aiden jumped. He'd been so fixated on getting to the treehouse that he'd forgotten to call for them.

They might not have even made it that far. It was dark and cold, and the boys were so little…

"What if they're not there?"

"How long until we reach the treehouse?"

"A minute or two." Quicker if he lengthened his strides.

"If they're not there, then we call the police. Then we call our friends and neighbors and get everyone out here looking. But they're going to be there." Carter's voice brooked no argument. Aiden wished he was that confident.

"Ryan, Luke, are you there?" Aiden called out. He thought he heard something and stopped, peering around frantically. Nothing. Did he imagine it? Was he just hearing things he wanted to hear? "Luke, Ryan! Where are you?"

"*Daddy?*" There it was again; this time, Aiden knew it wasn't his imagination.

"Luke?" They both ran towards the small voice, Carter's phone flashlight bouncing in front of them until it found Luke's tear-stained face. He clutched a small plastic torch with a weak orange light that barely lit his face, let alone his surroundings.

Aiden dropped to the ground in front of him and pulled him into his arms. He clung to Aiden, shaking so hard he dropped the torch. The light went out. It didn't make much difference.

"Thank God. Are you okay? Where's Ryan?"

Luke leaned back in his arms and pointed towards the tree. Aiden swung around, and Carter pointed his phone upwards until Ryan's form appeared like a ghost.

Ryan's pale face stared out of the branches. He was clutching the tree with both arms, and Aiden's heart jumped into his mouth when he realized the rotten planks of wood had collapsed under his weight. He was only keeping himself upright by his arms and one foot wedged onto a small broken section of wood still attached to the trunk with rusty nails.

Ryan's eyes were wide, his teeth biting into his bottom lip as he tried his hardest to hold onto the branch above his head and keep his tiptoes rooted to the rotten piece of wood. "Don't move," Aiden told him and swung around to Carter.

Without speaking, they were in sync. Carter reached for Luke and handed Aiden his phone so he could light his way as he climbed.

"Be careful," Carter said.

Luke wrapped his arms around Carter's neck and clutched him tightly. "I'm sorry," he repeated. Carter rocked him and ran a soothing hand down his back as Aiden turned towards the tree.

Wedging his feet into grooves, Aiden pulled himself up on smaller branches, closing the distance between him and Ryan as quickly as he could. His palms were scraped, his nails broken, but soon he was close enough to touch Ryan's knees.

"I'm almost there, buddy," he panted. He tested one branch, and though it swayed under his weight, he hoped it wouldn't snap. He stretched as far out as he could and managed to wrap an arm around Ryan's waist.

Carter's phone slipped out of his other hand, and the light he had was lost. He blinked, trying to get his eyes accustomed to the darkness, but suddenly the light was back from below. He looked downwards and saw Carter pointing the phone upwards. Aiden sucked in a deep breath and tried to send Ryan a comforting smile.

"Daddy..." His voice was so small and scared that it broke Aiden's heart.

"Don't be scared. I've got you. When you're ready, let go, and I'll pull you towards me. Then you hang on to my neck, got it?"

"I'm scared."

So was he. Aiden watched the scrap of rotten wood that was the only thing keeping his son from falling. He didn't know how much longer it would last.

"I know you are, but you're brave." He hooked his fingers into the elastic of Ryan's pajamas. Why wasn't he wearing jeans? A belt loop would be much easier.

"Just let go and lean towards me." His arms were burning with the pressure of holding onto the tree and clutching his son.

"I can't." Ryan started to sob, huge silent shakes of his body that made one of his feet slip. Aiden hissed and tightened his grip, shoving Ryan into the tree trunk to try and stop him from falling. He managed to regain his footing but was still crying.

"I can't."

"You can," Aiden encouraged, though his heart beat wildly. "You're Superman." He remembered how Ryan had attempted to jump from the childminder's garage roof with a sheet as a cape, so sure he could fly. He needed that fearless boy back.

"On the count of three, Clark Kent. One...Two...Three."

Aiden held on with all his might, and Ryan let go. Arms flailing, he dropped further down in Aiden's grip, but Aiden tightened his fist in the elastic of his pajamas and, using the trunk to brace himself, he pulled Ryan into his side.

Ryan's arms grabbed at his neck, and Aiden climbed downwards, only sighing in relief when his feet hit the ground.

He staggered for a second, legs weightless and head spinning, but Carter was there to ground him, steadying him with one arm.

And then suddenly, all four of them were hugging—Ryan still in his arms, Luke in Carter's. Tears burned his eyes and slipped down his cheeks. Both boys were still sobbing and saying they were sorry, but Aiden couldn't be angry at them. He was too relieved to have them back, too scared about what could have happened.

CHAPTER FORTY-EIGHT

CARTER

AIDEN'S ARM WAS tight around Carter as he held Luke, and Carter wrapped his free arm around Ryan's back, his fingers stretched out to grab hold of Aiden's T-shirt as if that were the only thing grounding him.

The image of Ryan hanging precariously from the tree was etched into his mind, and he knew he needed to be strong for the three of them. Still, just for a moment, he allowed himself the comfort of Aiden holding them all, even though he should be the one comforting him.

'I'm sorry," Aiden said, his voice low, his body shuddering. Carter thought he was saying it to the boys, but how he dipped his head and hid his face against Carter's neck left him wondering something else.

"I don't want to run away anymore," Ryan wailed in the cocoon of their arms, and Luke shifted to hug him, his little arms comforting his brother.

"Me either. I don't want to live in a stinky treehouse," Luke sniffled. "There's no TV."

"That's good, because I don't want you to live in a stinky treehouse," Aiden said. "I don't want *any* of you to live anywhere else."

Did he emphasize 'any,' or was he hearing things he wanted to hear? Carter was too exhausted to process any of it, so he gave all three of them one last squeeze and shifted to face the direction of the house.

"Then let's get you boys home. Hot chocolate is in order."

The walk back was slower; neither one wanted to put the boys down, and with how Luke was clutching at his neck, Carter was sure he didn't want that either.

The woods were dark, and his phone's screen was cracked and almost out of juice, but they carefully made their way through the trees and shrubs without incident. They were quiet, apart from the odd sniffle, but Carter wasn't ready to break the silence surrounding them. His mind was noisy enough as it was.

When something touched his hand, he flinched, expecting a bug or a spider, but when callused fingers threaded through his, he realized it was Aiden, and he relaxed. Tears burned at the back of his eyes, filled with emotion, relief, and love.

Relief could make you reckless or crazy, but Carter was selfish, and he would take what he could get, savor the feel of their fingers threaded together, even if it was just for tonight — just for the length of time it would take them to get home.

Home. He wanted it to be.

The house came into view, and they walked through the open gate into the garden. The back door was still open. Neither of them had even thought to close it as they'd run in the direction the boys had gone.

His phone vibrated in his pocket, but he ignored it as they carried the boys inside, wrapped them in blankets like burritos, and sat them on the sofa. They needed to talk to them about the seriousness of running off, but right then, Carter was too relieved to be angry at them, and one look in Aiden's direction confirmed he felt the same.

His phone vibrated again, and he fished it out, double-checking it wasn't Kyle. It wasn't. It was a missed call from Joe and at least a dozen texts asking if they'd found the boys, with a

PS that said he was asking because he was genuinely worried, not because of the show.

"It's Joe. He's asking if we've found the boys. I'll just text him quickly so he doesn't worry and send in reinforcements."

Found them. All ok. Thanks for your help
"Tell him thank you from me," Aiden said.
Aiden says thanks too.

He had just enough battery to send it before his phone died. He should charge it in case Kyle needed to get hold of him, but the thought of finding a charger and plugging in his phone was too much to cope with. He placed it on the coffee table instead. He'd charge it in a moment.

He gave the boys a shaky smile when he realized they were all staring at him. Aiden was practically swaying on his feet, and Carter was afraid he was going to fall, so he steadied him, hands on his shoulders, and gently pushed downwards until he sat between Ryan and Luke on the sofa.

"Are any of you hurt?" Carter asked each of them, including Aiden. Ryan looked at his hands. There were a few scrapes, but otherwise, nothing to show he'd almost fallen out of a tree. Luke shook his head.

Aiden blinked at him but stayed silent. Carter raised an eyebrow, and Aiden finally gave him a hint of a smile. "Just a bit achy. I'm fine." His eyes were still wild and haunted, probably the shock taking over. A swift drink would probably help, but hot chocolate would have to do.

"All three of you stay there. I'll make hot chocolate."

Once he was out of their sight, Carter's knees buckled under him, and he grabbed hold of the table to stop himself from falling to the floor. He hadn't realized he was in just as bad a state as Aiden.

His head pounded, his heart hammered so hard in his chest he thought it would burst right through, and his vision started to swim. So many images crashed through his mind. Awful things that could have happened. Kidnappers, the boys getting lost, frostbite, broken bones, broken head—*dead*. Ryan could have died if he'd fallen from that tree. Suppose they'd gotten there later, or if Aiden hadn't managed to hold on to him tight enough.

Nausea churned in Carter's stomach, and his mouth tasted sour. He clenched his teeth and willed himself not to retch. He didn't want Aiden to hear and be worried.

Ryan and Luke were okay. No one had taken them; they weren't hurt, not even a splinter. They'd just run off and got into a little trouble, but they were fine. No need to feel like the ground had been ripped out from under him.

What was he doing? Hot chocolate, yes. He needed to concentrate on that. Something small, something he could control, something that would make them smile.

He filled the kettle, picked out the boys' favorite mugs, got the cocoa powder from the cupboard and the milk from the fridge, and let the easy task fill his brain until nothing else remained.

When he was composed and the hot chocolate was made, he carried four mugs into the living room. Each boy was still wrapped in their blanket, but now they were huddled tight into Aiden's sides as he talked softly to them.

Carter took a step towards them, his heart clenching at the sight of them all snuggled together. For just a moment, happiness filled him; then he remembered that they weren't his, and this was a moment for family—not for a manny or a TV personality or an ex, no matter how brief.

Aiden may have clutched his hand out in the woods, he'd maybe said sorry, but that didn't mean he'd changed his mind about them.

He placed the mugs on the coffee table, then picked up the one he'd made for himself. All three of them turned his way with identical eyes.

Carter forced out a smile. "I'll leave you to it."

He turned to go up to his room, but Aiden leaned forward

and grabbed his wrist. His thumb caressed the soft skin above his erratic pulse, and goosebumps ran up his arms. His hot chocolate sloshed over the side of the cup and landed on the back of his hand. It didn't hurt.

"Don't go." Aiden's voice cracked, and it made Carter want to cry. What did Aiden want? He wasn't a mind reader. Aiden had given so many mixed signals, and Carter wasn't firing on all cylinders right then. All three of them already meant more to him than any family he'd worked with ever had. He didn't know if he could draw the line... or keep to the line Aiden had set.

"I..." His throat closed up again.

"Please." Ryan's fragile voice was his undoing. How could he ignore him?

"Don't go," Luke added, as if Ryan's plea wasn't enough.

"I'm right here," Carter said and handed each boy their hot chocolate, then sat on the coffee table opposite them. Close, but not so near that he encroached on Aiden's space. He didn't know what any of this meant.

"We're sorry we ran away from home," Ryan said as he looked into his mug. His cheeks started to burn with embarrassment.

"Why did you run away?" Carter asked when Aiden didn't say anything.

"We was sad that you're leaving, so we decided we'd leave too," Luke said, bottom lip trembling.

"And live in the treehouse forever and ever."

"Or until Carter came back."

"But... why run away?" Aiden looked so confused, but Carter knew that kid logic was lost on adults, and he didn't attempt to dissect it. His headache would only get worse if he tried.

Luke's bottom lip trembled, and he scowled. "You said Carter was leaving and never coming back, but Kyle told us you was boyfriends. We know what boyfriends are. We thought we'd all be together, but... but you said Carter was going to live with another family." Luke's face turned red, and he started to cry.

"We like Carter. We like Kyle and Bobby and Nora and Dennis. We want to keep them."

Carter wanted to keep Ryan, Luke, and Aiden too. He had a hard time not voicing it and bit at his lips to stop the words from falling from his mouth. This wasn't something he could decide. It was up to Aiden.

Carter didn't want to look at Aiden, afraid of what he'd see in his eyes, but he couldn't move his gaze away. He was stuck to the spot.

"You're not scared?" Aiden looked away first as he spoke to the boys. Carter was confused about where the conversation was going, but he didn't interrupt. He was worried whatever he did or said would make it end badly for him.

"Of what? We're never scared," Luke said, puffing his chest out.

"Except for tonight. I was scared up in the tree. But only a little bit." Ryan grabbed hold of Aiden's arm and snuggled further into his side. "Daddy said I was Superman. But I wasn't."

"You were," Aiden said.

Ryan shook his head and poked Aiden in the arm. "*You* was Superman. You weren't scared."

"I was terrified. I was worried I'd drop you. I was worried that you were hurt. I get scared a lot, boys." Aiden glanced at him. "And not just tonight. I was scared Carter's job could hurt us."

The boys frowned. "How can a job hurt?" Luke asked.

"You're not scared that Carter's on TV and strangers will want to photograph us or be mean to you because he's famous?"

They scrunched their noses up. "Marian Miller's stepdad was on *Pointless*, and she was trying to sell his autograph on the playground, but no one wanted it. Can I sell your autograph?" Luke cocked his head at Carter.

"Yeah, we'd make much more money because *Manny SOS* is much more fun than *Pointless*," Ryan agreed.

"I don't even know what *Pointless* is." Luke's eyes got wide as he spoke. "I bet we could make at least two pounds!"

Carter couldn't help laughing. "I'm honored you think you could get so much from my autograph." How ironic that the fate of his heart came down to this conversation. Aiden smiled down at the boys, and then when he turned his attention back to Carter, he took a deep breath.

Carter found himself holding his breath too.

"I'm sorry. For blaming you for Joe's actions, for running scared because of your job, and for thinking all the things that could happen were more important than you. Than this— *us*."

Aiden detangled himself from Ryan and Luke, and then he was standing right in front of Carter. So close he wouldn't be surprised if Aiden couldn't hear the beat of his heart.

"Forgive me?"

Carter was still clutching his hot chocolate. He set the mug down, and Aiden whimpered and grabbed hold of his arm. "Hey, I'm just putting this down so I can do this…" He slipped his arms around Aiden's neck and pulled him in close.

"I'm still semi-famous. You might still get hounded because of me…" He had to make sure Aiden understood.

"I know. And I'll be awkward and grumpy and not know what to say, but I'll have you and the boys, and that will make up for it." Aiden closed his eyes and licked his lips. "There was a point today when I thought I might lose all of you, and I never want to feel like that again. That was the most terrified I've ever felt."

Carter trailed a finger down Aiden's nose, across his cheekbone, and then cupped his cheek until his eyes fluttered open. "You'll never be alone again," he promised.

They had more to talk about, but that could be addressed later. Right now, Aiden was offering up exactly what he wanted, and Carter wasn't going to say no.

They grinned at each other, and when Aiden's mouth touched his it was brief, sweet, and perfect.

"Gross. Kissing is disgusting." Carter wasn't sure who said that, but he laughed against Aiden's smiling lips.

"But we don't mind if it means Carter stays—and Kyle becomes our brother."

"And Bobby becomes our sister."

Aiden pecked his lips again and hugged him tightly. Carter liked the image the boys portrayed. It was exactly what he wanted too.

"Does that mean Nora will be our mommy?"

A snort burst through Carter's lips, and he cackled. He'd have to tell Nora about that... or maybe not. Perhaps he'd just let the twins call her Mom and watch her have a heart attack.

"Let's ease Nora into it before you scare her off, okay?" Aiden said.

Carter nudged him with his hips. "Spoilsport."

"Hey, I'm just trying to get on the good side of your family."

Aiden pressed their lips together again while the boys made gagging noises that had them laughing into the kiss before Aiden pulled away and turned to look at them.

"All right, you got what you wanted. Carter and I are officially boyfriends. That doesn't mean we're not going to talk about you sneaking out of the house and running into the deep, dark woods all alone."

CHAPTER FORTY-NINE

AIDEN

NONE OF THEM wanted to be alone that night. Aiden knew he had a lot to make up with Carter, a lot to explain to him, but it was after three a.m., and he didn't want to go to bed alone, and he definitely didn't want Ryan and Luke out of his sight.

They ended up in a den made of pillows and blankets on the living room floor with the TV playing cartoons quietly in the background, giving out just enough light that Aiden could see Carter's profile on the other side of the boys snoring softly between them.

The twins had fallen asleep as soon as their heads hit the pillows, and he and Carter had settled on either side of them.

They were quiet, Aiden just listening to their breathing, as if he didn't trust his eyes to show him they were right there and safe. He placed an arm over the boys' waists and felt the slight movements they made as they slept. Only then did he relax.

A part of him thought he was stuck in some perfect dream, and he was terrified none of it was real.

He jumped when Carter's fingers skimmed along his arm and threaded through his. Then Carter smiled, that small, intimate smile that was for Aiden and Aiden alone.

It was as if he knew what Aiden was thinking without him

saying a word. How could he have thought he'd be better off without this man?

As scary as it had been to realize the boys were missing, as terrified as he was when he saw Ryan balanced in that tree, it had made him realize just what he would be giving up.

"Go to sleep. We'll be here in the morning," Carter whispered.

He was so tired, the muscles in his arms and back were still tense from grabbing hold of Ryan, and his heartbeat still raced so fast it roared in his ears. But...

"I'm afraid to close my eyes," he admitted.

"You don't need to be strong right now."

Why did Carter say that? It was as if his words unlocked something inside him. The tears burning the back of his eyes swam in front of his vision, trickling down his cheek and into the corner of his mouth.

Carter leaned over the boys, neither of them so much as stirred, and wiped away his tears. More fell, as if he'd burst a dam. He'd never had this before. Never had someone care about the boys as much as he did; never had anyone care about him as well. Not Wyatt. Nio, to a certain extent, but Aiden never wanted to burden his best friend with his problems. He hadn't signed up for that.

Aiden fell asleep as Carter's fingertips wiped away his tears, the boys' quiet snores between them and Sponge Bob Square Pants playing quietly on TV.

The boys woke too early the next day, full of beans, happy to start the day. Carter made them breakfast while Aiden showered and tried to ease his aching muscles.

He was glad it was Saturday so he didn't have to go to work. Carter was just handing him some painkillers when Joe's face appeared in the kitchen window, making him choke on his water. Carter patted his back absently, then went to let Joe in.

Aiden wasn't sure why he was there, but he was too happy to care.

"Hi, hi. I thought I'd check in, see how you all are?" Joe's eyes scanned each of them before nodding, as if he'd assured himself they were no worse for wear.

"We're fine," Carter said and ruffled Luke's hair. He was the closest, and Ryan was too busy shoveling cereal in his mouth for hair ruffling. "Even the tadpoles."

"And just so you know, I'm not here as a producer. I'm here as your friend."

"Thank you. And thank you for getting the footage so quickly yesterday." Aiden shuddered. Five minutes later and he might have seen Ryan fall from the tree. For once, he was thankful they had cameras watching their every move.

The boys were suddenly very sheepish, looking down at their warm, soggy cornflakes, the tips of their ears pink.

"Do you have something to say to Joe, boys?" Aiden asked.

They rolled their eyes up to look at him, shifting in their chairs while shoving their spoons into their mouths. "Fank you," they said around their cornflakes.

Aiden rolled his eyes and grinned. Nothing was going to annoy him today, not even bad manners.

"Do you want some breakfast, Joe?" Carter asked.

Joe eyed the cereal dubiously. "No thanks."

"Don't worry, I'm making us all bacon sandwiches. They were just ravenous, and I wouldn't let them eat chocolate biscuits."

"Then, yes. I'd love to stay. As long as I'm not intruding?"

"No, not at all."

"I like bacon," Luke said as he slurped the milk in the bottom of his bowl.

"Me too," Joe said. "So… are you two…?" He looked between Aiden and Carter but didn't finish his sentence. He didn't have to.

Aiden smiled, which made Carter grin as he grilled the bacon. "Yeah, we're together."

"Don't worry, I remember our meeting. No relationship stuff will make it into the show."

Carter nodded, his shoulders relaxing. Aiden found he wasn't as worried about that as he'd been just a few days before. He hugged Carter from behind, then turned to stare at Joe. "Maybe in a few years, we can do a Where Are They Now episode..."

CHAPTER FIFTY

CARTER
Interview with Ryan & Luke. Camera rolling. Final Day of Filming
Interviewer: I heard you ran away?
Ryan: Only because daddy and Carter were fighting.
Luke: Now all they do is kiss.
Ryan: It's disgusting. It's like spitting in each other's mouths.
Luke: [Makes gagging sound]
Interviewer: ...We're going to have to cut that out.

THE BOYS WERE in bed, and Carter and Aiden were alone. Finally. They tiptoed out of Ryan and Luke's bedroom and stopped outside of Aiden's room. Butterflies fluttered in Carter's stomach, and his breathing caught in his throat as Aiden turned to face him.

Was it hot? He pulled on the neck of his T-shirt, and Aiden's hand found his and pulled it away from the material, placing it right above his heart. The thump-thump against his palm made something stir deep inside him, and he inched closer to Aiden, eyes zeroing in on his mouth.

Aiden leaned toward him, and Carter lost his ability to function. He froze; the only thing moving was his heart as it beat in sync with Aiden's.

When Aiden's kiss came, it was tentative and full of promise. He pecked Carter's bottom lip, then sucked it into his mouth until Carter groaned and swayed towards him. Aiden's hands cupped his shoulders, and as he deepened the kiss, they slid up his neck and cupped his cheeks, angling his head and sliding his tongue into Carter's mouth.

Carter sighed, and his eyes fluttered closed. The slow, torturous kiss sent a shiver down his spine. It was a simple kiss, but there was weight behind it, the promise of more, the assurance that this was more than one night. This kiss showed him that they were for real, that their relationship was strong despite their ups and downs, despite being so new.

It felt like Carter had known Aiden all his life. Maybe it came from living in his house and working so closely with him; maybe they just clicked and were meant to be. Whatever it was, it didn't matter.

Aiden fumbled behind him and placed a hand on the door handle, but he didn't open the door. He nipped at Carter's lips, then pressed tiny kisses to his nose, his chin, and each eyelid.

What a sap, Carter thought, unable to hide the grin forming around the kiss. *Who would have guessed he'd be so sweet?*

"Are you going to open the door before we give the editors a real show?" Carter asked against Aiden's mouth. He felt the other man smile, and then the door opened, and they stumbled through.

Aiden shut and locked the door, then turned on the bedside lamp. Any other day Carter would love to explore the room, but the only thing he wanted to explore right then was Aiden.

Lust had been bubbling away just under the surface all day. Now it was near boiling point, and Carter couldn't contain it anymore. He stepped out of his jeans, yanked his T-shirt over his head, and smirked at Aiden's appreciative stare.

He grabbed the front of Aiden's T-shirt and walked them back towards the bed until his legs hit the side; then he topped backward, making sure he brought Aiden with him.

The sheets at his back were wrinkled and cool, while Aiden's weight was hot and heavy as it pressed him into the mattress. They both hissed, and Aiden leaned on his forearms, their faces so close Carter could reach out and lick the seam of his lips if he wanted to. So he did.

Energy crackled around them and flowed throughout his body as Aiden shoved his thigh between Carter's legs, grinding his erection against him. Fireworks burst behind his eyes, and Carter became dizzy as the kiss carried on.

When Aiden pulled away and sat up, Carter whined and reached for him. It was Aiden's turn to smirk as he undressed, and then he was pressing Carter back into the bed, his hands roaming Carter's arms until he threaded their fingers and held them against the pillow.

He was at Aiden's mercy and was perfectly fine with that. The tender slide of flesh drove Carter so wild he was sure he could come like this; he just needed a little more...

A ragged cry fell from his lips as Aiden nibbled a pathway down his neck and then bit his shoulder. Carter's cock twitched between them, and blood soared through his veins. He wrapped his legs around Aiden's waist, holding him as tight as he could. It wasn't tight enough.

His stinging kisses made Carter writhe beneath him, and he grunted as Aiden made his way down his body, kissing his chest, his abs, laving at his belly button, then over his hard cock.

His legs rested on Aiden's shoulders, his heels tapping against his back. "Don't tease." He couldn't cope. He was going to come before Aiden even touched him. He was so worked up, and his body was so highly strung it was ready to break.

Aiden didn't reply, but he did suck Carter deep into his mouth. *Fuck!* He half sighed, half groaned as Aiden's tongue worshipped his cock, and his talented mouth sucked him so deep he saw stars.

His back arched, heels sliding off Aiden's shoulders and digging into the mattress. It was torture, but at least he was touching him. The slow slide of his tongue, the gentle suck that had him teetering on the edge, but never enough to send him soaring.

Bastard. Carter thrust his hips, slipping in deeper, and Aiden grabbed him in a bruising grip, controlling his movements.

"Come on," Carter hissed. Every nerve ending was on fire, and when Aiden pulled off him, he whined. He wanted more, not less.

Oh. His eyes widened as Aiden reached for a condom and lube, setting them on the bed beside them, and then he smiled down at Carter, that kind, sweet smile full of dirty promises that made Carter want to cry because it was aimed at him.

Carter lunged upwards, grabbing hold of Aiden's shoulders, and slotted their mouths together in a messy, breathless kiss that was all tongues and clashing teeth.

Aiden's hands were everywhere, and when they eventually came up for air, he rolled Carter onto his stomach and started the sweet torture all over again. His hands scraped along Carter's shoulder blades as his tongue licked strips up his spine before he lay his whole body on top of him.

Carter whimpered, Aiden's weight pressing him into the mattress turning his limbs to jelly, yet making his cock ten times harder.

The click of the lube bottle was music to Carter's ears, and he shivered when Aiden nipped at the back of his neck, his fingers teasing the crease of his ass before pressing into the ring of muscle and opening him up.

His heart thudded when Aiden curled his fingers upwards and found his sweet spot, electricity racing throughout his body before it coiled in the pit of his stomach. His cock leaked, and he moved restlessly against the mattress, groaning at the friction of the sheets and the way Aiden's fingers played him so well.

Aiden maneuvered him until his knees were under him, ass in the air. Carter couldn't even help. He had no control over his limbs. It was hard enough to suppress the ragged gasps, let alone anything else.

Carter heard the crinkle of the condom wrapper, the slick slide as Aiden rolled it on, and when Aiden put a hand on the base of his spine to steady himself, his skin tingled. He turned his head to the side and watched from the corner of his eye as Aiden sank into him.

They groaned. Carter's heart expanded in his chest, and the fire in the pit of his stomach raged to life as Aiden slid all the way into him, then pulled out, only to slam back inside.

The yell that fell from his lips was enough to make them both jump. They froze for a second, but when nothing happened, Aiden started his onslaught again. He set a brutal pace, and Carter gritted his teeth and let the sensations flow over his body.

MANNY SOS

CHAPTER FIFTY-ONE

AIDEN

THERE WAS NOTHING as beautiful as Carter spread out beneath him, trying his hardest to muffle his screams, the arch of his back glistening with a thin layer of sweat and Aiden's cock disappearing inside of him. He kept up the brutal pace, his heart racing, body desperate to find release, but his mind wanting to make it last, to make it good for Carter.

He leaned over Carter's back, his breath coming in heavy spurts as he pressed a kiss behind his ear. His hair was damp and stuck to his forehead, his mouth was swollen, and his eyes were blown. Aiden had never seen anyone as beautiful as Carter in that moment.

His lips were bruised where he bit them, and Aiden tasted the sweet tang of pennies before he took a deep breath. His orgasm was just under the skin. His spine tingled, his back arched, and his hips stuttered.

It wouldn't be long, and he wanted Carter to come with him. He leaned over his back, took a deep breath of his woodsy outdoor scent, and pushed a hand under Carter's hips, grasping his long hard cock in his palm and working it in time with each thrust.

Carter tightened around him, pushed backward, then thrust forward into his hand, and Aiden angled his hips until he hit that spot inside Carter with each movement. Aiden's heart galloped in his chest, and blood raced through his veins. Sweat dripped into his eyes, and he blinked it away, unable to move either hand to wipe his forehead because he didn't want to stop touching him.

He had no control as he came. One moment he was enjoying the pleasure-pain as he teetered on the edge of orgasm, and then he was soaring over it without any knowledge.

Carter came mere seconds after him, coating his hand and the bed beneath him. Aiden managed to roll them onto their sides before they collapsed in a tangle of limbs, and they lay there gasping, waiting for their breathing to return to normal.

They were messy and sticky, Carter's come smeared over them both, and he needed to dispose of the condom but was too lazy to move. He needed a moment. They were trashed, and Aiden had never been so happy.

He grinned, and Carter blinked lazily at him and pressed his face into Aiden's sweaty neck like it was the most natural thing in the world.

Soon they would have to shower, put on pajamas and unlock the door. But not just yet.

CHAPTER FIFTY-TWO

Epilogue
Carter
Three Years Later
Manny SOS. Where Are They Now? Special. Cameras Rolling

A LIFETIME CAN happen in three years, Carter thought as he stood in the kitchen doorway of their new family home, looking out into the garden.

Rainbow bunting lined the fence, a glittery Happy Anniversary sign made by the twins and Bobby hung above it, and there was a long table full of party food just waiting to be devoured.

It was a quiet morning for them, but it wouldn't stay that way for long. It was the calm before the storm, and Carter was going to enjoy every moment of it before the rabble descended.

Two cameramen moved silently around the perimeter of the garden, setting up. Joe, Ronnie, and Sebastian stood off to the side, talking quietly.

Some things didn't change, he thought as he looked at the familiar crew. This was the first time Aiden and the boys would be back in front of a *Manny SOS* camera, and a sense of nostalgia washed over Carter.

Sebastian was going to be the unofficial interviewer for Carter's segment of the episode 'Where Are They Now?' and he was taking his job seriously, scanning through the pre-approved questions he would spontaneously ask throughout the day. His hair had grown out over the last three years, and he absently ran a hand through it to stop his bangs from falling into his eyes as he read.

Hurricanes Ryan and Luke chose that moment to shoot out in front of him, kicking a football back and forth. They were practically vibrating with excitement as they waited for everyone to arrive and the filming to begin.

"Don't kick the ball near the food, guys!" The twins shot him identical mischievous grins as they aimed the ball in his direction instead.

He jumped off the back step and lunged for it, kicking it in the opposite direction of the table and hitting the back fence. The boys charged after it. "Goal!" Carter shouted, and fist bumped the air. The party food was safe for the moment.

The twins had grown a lot in the last three years. They were still daredevils, still kept him and Aiden on their toes, but they'd grown in confidence, were more content, and were as sweet as ever—when they weren't trying to be cool. Nine was a precarious age, and cuddles were few and far between. Carter was honored to call them his sons, and he was so glad he got to watch them flourish and grow.

Becoming a family hadn't been easy, but they'd persevered and made it work. He never thought life could be like this. Sometimes he needed to pinch himself to make sure he wasn't dreaming.

He'd managed to keep Aiden and the boys out of the spotlight after they'd gone public. The hype had died down quickly, and their family life soon became private again. There was the occasional photograph of them—Aiden came to a few TV award shows now and then—but they'd lived a quiet, chaotic life together.

It wasn't perfect by any means, but it was his and exactly what he wanted. A family, kids, even a lazy cat called Toad.

Aiden's arm slipped around his waist from behind, giving him a one-armed hug as he rested his chin on Carter's shoulder.

"Enjoying the silence?" Aiden asked.

The twins screamed, and Carter shook his head with a smile. "Call this silent?"

Aiden dug his chin into his shoulder a little harder. "It's silent for us." He wasn't wrong.

Something cold, wet, and sticky slapped the back of his neck, and he let out a very manly shriek as he swiveled and grinned at the baby held in Aiden's other arm.

"Are you trying to get my attention, little miss?" He kissed one of her drool-covered hands, then stole their daughter away from Aiden and danced down the garden with her, laughing as she shrieked in joy and curled her wet fingers into his T-shirt.

Life certainly didn't get better than this.

"I see how it is." Aiden had caught up with them. "I'm never going to get to hold her today, am I?" He slid his arm around Carter's waist as they walked towards the covered veranda in the back corner of the garden and their eldest daughter.

"Just wait until Nora gets here. We'll not be allowed near her." To say that everyone loved their baby daughter was an understatement.

She was adored. Even Ryan and Luke were putty in her hands. They were such good big brothers. Great little brothers too.

Janey had come to them from the hospital at a few months old, not long after he and Aiden became foster parents. She was alone, mother dead, father unknown, and they'd fallen in love with her immediately.

It was only when they were going through the process of adopting her that they realized she wasn't as alone as they'd believed. She had an older sister in the system called Star—a sister who had looked after her in the few months she'd been with her birth mum.

Then they'd wanted her too. Wanted to reunite the sisters and give them both a good home. It had taken a while to get there.

Star had been desperate to see the baby when they'd first started visiting, but she didn't want to show any weakness or give them any ammunition to hurt her. When she finally came to live with them, she'd been hopeful, suspicious, and afraid.

Carter couldn't blame her.

Star was thirteen years old, all gangly legs and arms, with an attitude and fighting temperament behind which she hid a broken, loving heart.

It had taken a lot of time, love, and therapy for her to realize that they didn't want her for the money they'd receive for being her foster parents or for free labor and babysitting.

It made Carter furious at her previous foster placements. Aiden wasn't surprised at how she'd been treated, but he was just as frustrated and sad that things hadn't changed that much since he'd been a child. There were still children falling through the cracks.

Star had finally figured out that they weren't going to send her back no matter how awful she thought she was, and she'd been officially their daughter for three months.

Carter's heart swelled with happiness when he looked at her as she concentrated on the book she was reading. Sometimes he couldn't believe she was his, that she wanted to be their daughter. That she'd been brave enough to go through with it even though she was scared it wasn't real.

Star looked up when she heard Janey babble and put the book down as Janey reached for her. Carter placed her on the floor just in front of Star so she could crawl into her big sister's lap.

Star gave a shy smile and kissed the top of her head. Carter plonked himself down next to her, spread his legs out in front of him, and leaned back on his elbows.

"Are you ready for the show?"

She shrugged and wiped away baby drool with the corner of her T-shirt. "Do I have to say anything?"

"Not if you don't want to. You don't have to be on camera at all if you don't want it."

"I'll see how I feel."

Aiden kicked the ball a few times with the twins, then dropped down on the other side of Star and picked up the copy of *Heartstopper Volume 2* she was reading.

"How far have you got? We need to talk about it when you're done."

"I can't believe you've finished it already," Star said. Carter knew what she meant was she couldn't believe he was reading it so they could talk about it together.

"I may have taken a longer lunch break to finish it," he admitted with a wink that made her laugh softly.

"Oh, here comes trouble," Carter said when he heard arguing coming from inside the house.

Nanny Biscuit carefully stepped into the garden, leaning heavily on her walking sticks. Her eyes were narrowed and her lips pursed. Nio walked sheepishly behind her, holding a gaudy pink handbag.

"Nanny B!" Luke shouted as the twins ran towards her, skidding to a stop so they didn't barrel into her and gently hugging her. She was the only one that got hugs on tap.

Her scowl turned into a bright, happy smile as she hugged the boys back.

"Look at you two. You've shot up!" They grinned at her like angels. She said that to them every time she saw them. "Nio, stop standing there. Take the biscuits out of my bag and put them on the table."

"I told you that you didn't need to bring anything. Look at all the food. There is no room for Custard Creams or Party Rings."

"There is if you don't want me to hit you with them," she said sweetly.

"I better go over there and stop World War Three," Carter said. "Quick, hand me the baby. She'll be a great distraction." Star lifted Janey, and Carter carried her over to Nanny Biscuit and Nio.

"My grandbaby," Nanny Biscuit said. "You, find me a chair so I can hold the baby." Nio didn't say a word as he went off to steal someone else's seat.

She quickly had Janey cuddled on her lap, and the argument between her and Nio was forgotten. Unfortunately, there was no time to relax as Nora, Dennis, Kyle, and Bobby burst into the back garden and the chaos began.

Both twins tackled Kyle to the ground, then dragged him off to play football. Nora and Dennis made a beeline for Nanny Biscuit, who would not release the baby no matter how hard Nora tried. Carter snorted in laughter and left them to it. He didn't know which one would win, but it would be fun to watch.

Joe's eyes were slightly crossed at the chaos of children running all over the place when he and Sebastian wound their way around to Carter. Sebastian didn't look out of place at all. Like Carter, he was used to lots of children running about. Not that Kyle was a child anymore. He was eighteen now. Carter didn't quite believe he had an eighteen-year-old son.

"This is a lot of people. And kids. How are you not exhausted all the time?"

Carter snorted. "Who says I'm not?"

"You must thrive on it, then. So, are you ready to do this? We'll just film the day and do a few interviews with you, Aiden, and whoever wants to do them. Sebastian knows what questions to ask." Sebastian gave him a thumbs-up.

"That sounds good to me."

"Poppy!" Bobby spotted him and shouted as she ran towards him. Carter leaned down to catch her, swinging her around into a big bear hug.

"She calls you Poppy too?" Sebastian asked, using one of the questions on his list.

Bobby stuck her tongue out at Joe and Sebastian, then hid her face in Carter's neck as if she was shy. Which was so far from the truth it was laughable.

Carter was just about to answer Sebastian when Ryan appeared next to him. "'Course she calls him Poppy. It's his name, and she's my sister. Can I eat yet? I'm starved." He rubbed his belly.

"I want biscuits too," Bobby added.

Carter put her down. "Yes, you can all eat. Make sure Bobby eats more than Party Rings, okay?" he said, but they were already racing towards the table.

"Why do they call you Poppy?" Sebastian's next question.

Carter grinned when he saw Aiden make a beeline in his direction, then sling an arm around his shoulders. "They call him Poppy because he's our very own Mary Poppins."

He pressed a kiss to the side of Carter's head, and Carter rolled his eyes. He'd turned into such a softie.

"Aiden used to call me Manny Poppins when we first met— it kind of stuck," Carter said. And it stops any confusion," Carter added. "He's Daddy, I'm Poppy."

When they'd moved in together, the boys hadn't wanted to carry on calling him Carter, but they didn't want to add to the confusion because they already had a daddy and a daddy Wyatt, though he'd been mostly absent since Carter came into the picture.

Carter loved the name the twins had come up with for him and couldn't imagine being called anything else by them. He'd actually teared up when Bobby started to call him that too. Even Kyle occasionally called him Pops.

"Poppy sometimes calls Daddy Cinders, but I don't understand why," Luke said, his face twisting into a frown.

With a cough, Aiden grabbed a Party Ring from the table and shoved it at Luke. "Here, have a biscuit."

Carter bit his lip, trying not to laugh as Aiden became flustered. It was true. Occasionally, he did still call Aiden Cinders because he knew it drove Aiden wild, and he loved to tease him with reminders of how they first met.

"Cinders, huh?" Sebastian teased. He knew full well where the name came from because Carter had confided in him at the time.

"Oh look, it's Nora. She wants to show you the family tree she made for Bobby to take to school," Aiden said loudly, not-so-subtly changing the subject. Carter laughed, shook his head, and pressed a kiss to his cheek.

"You're all one big family, then?" Sebastian asked. Carter and Aiden nodded. Warmth flooded through Carter's body.

Nora beamed at them as she bounced baby Jane on her hip, having wrestled her away from Nanny Biscuit, who was sending her death glares. She pulled out an A4 piece of paper from her back pocket. It was wrinkled, had a coffee stain in the corner, and there was a tree drawn in crayons on the front with all of their names branching off it. It looked complicated.

"So... Bobby is mine and my husband Dennis's daughter. Kyle is mine and Carter's son. We share custody... or did when he was a child. He's all grown up now, eighteen, can you believe it?" She hugged Kyle until he rolled his eyes.

"The twins are Aiden and Carter's, and so are baby Jane and Star." She beamed at Star, who gave a shy smile back and looked towards the floor. "They adopted her five months ago and Star three months ago. But all the kids think of each other as siblings. If you ask Bobby, she's got three brothers, a cool big sister, and a baby sister. Carter and Aiden are second parents to her. I tell you, it was a nightmare when she was making a Father's Day card at school."

"And Nora and Dennis are second parents to Ryan, Luke, Star, and Janey," Aiden added.

"Did that make sense? Oh, I forgot one. Nio. Well, we all share custody of him." Nora wrinkled her nose and looked back down at her paper. "Shit, I told you I'd need a bigger piece of paper."

"You forgot Nanny Biscuit," Ryan added. Aiden nodded. Somehow, they'd adopted a nanny, and she'd become a part of their lives and family celebrations. He didn't know how it happened, but Nanny Biscuit and Nio were kind of a package deal now. She came to all their family occasions and celebrated Christmas with them. She was as much a part of the family as anyone else in it.

Ronnie looked dizzy with all the information, but Sebastian nodded. He'd met a few of the family before and found it easier to get his head around all the different people.

"There is one other thing." Aiden looked toward Carter, who raised an eyebrow. He had no clue what Aiden was going to say. "Carter has been a dad to the twins practically since he first met them. He's loved them like a dad. He cares for them and treats them the same as Kyle and now the girls. We have a surprise for him."

He nodded at the twins, who jumped up and ran over to him. He pulled an envelope out of his back pocket. He handed it to the boys, and they took it to Carter, each holding a corner.

Butterflies fluttered in his belly. He didn't know what was happening, but he knew it was going to be momentous.

"What's this?" He was too nervous to open it, conscious of all eyes on him and how quiet it was. Nanny Biscuit had even given up trying to regain custody of Janey so she could watch what was happening.

Janey sat happily in Nio's arms playing with his shirt collar as all eyes were on him. Carter's cheeks started to burn, and his hands shook as he opened the envelope. The words swam in front of his eyes, and he couldn't take in what they said.

"What is this?" His voice shook. It couldn't be what he thought it was. No way. His eyes looked for Aiden, who stepped forward, face determined. He grabbed hold of Carter's hand, holding it tightly.

"You're their father as much as I am. We wanted to make it official. More official than when we got married. Then we will all have the same name."

"We want you to 'fficially be our Poppy," Ryan said, and Luke nodded. Carter bent down and swooped them up into a tight hug. Not wanting to be left out, Bobby ran over and joined in. This day couldn't get any more perfect.

"And Wyatt agreed to this?"

"Yes." There was probably more to it, but not anything they wanted to say on camera or in front of the twins.

"I love you both more than Mary Poppins loves medicine," Carter said as he stood up, Bobby still in his arms. He pulled Aiden in for a tight hug, never wanting to let him go.

Nora pulled the paper from Carter's fingers while they hugged, and Kyle grinned knowingly. "Holy shit, these are adoption papers!" There were a few shrieks, more hugs, and lots of brilliant footage for Ronnie to dig his teeth into.

"I don't know how you kept all this a secret," Carter said, leaning his head on Aiden's shoulder during a rare quiet moment. Aiden pulled him in close and dropped a kiss on his head.

"Neither do I, to be honest. Kyle was in on it. He's the reason the twins managed to keep quiet."

"God, I fucking love you, Aiden Montgomery-Ward. Is this our family?"

"It is. Every single crazy one of them."

Nora held baby Jane, and Kyle entertained the older children while they had a quiet moment as the cameras rolled. This was going to be some whacky update for *Manny SOS*.

"Love you, Cinderella," Carter said, remembering the first time he'd met Aiden. It seemed so long ago now.

"Love you, too, Manny Poppins," Aiden teased. "Now, this is the Hallmark life I always dreamed of."

ANDI LEE LIVES in the UK, close enough to Birmingham city to be considered a 'Brummie,' but far enough away to enjoy the Staffordshire countryside. She enjoys writing in many different genres as long as they contain a large dose of cute guys falling in love. She's a sucker for a happy ending.

When she's not writing, she enjoys making junk journals and also jewelry out of polymer clay and resin.

She has kept pet rats on and off for twenty years, and she fell in love with her first ferret when she found him on her way to work one day. Years later she happened to find another ferret on her thirty-first birthday. He was the best present she ever received. She is now owned by a small but fierce ferret called Oona.

MISCHIEF MAKER BY ANDI LEE

What to expect when your pet rat is expecting, or how to fall in love at a pet show.

Jamie Hewett rescues and breeds prize-winning fancy rats. While he's surrounded by supportive, animal-loving friends, his ex-boyfriend has never been one of them. One embarrassing breakup later, he definitely isn't looking for love again, but perhaps a rebound relationship might ease his broken heart.

Liam Donnelly's quirky dating life is the subject of a popular vlog, and his viewers have interesting ideas on where he might find romance. When they suggest he take Mabel, his new rat, to a pet show, he's up for the adventure.

Although they can't deny their growing interest in each other, neither Jamie nor Liam believes in love at first sight. They've both had bad luck with men, and Jamie isn't pleased that Liam makes a living as a serial dater. On top of that, others are conspiring to keep them apart, and Jamie is left holding the baby—or twenty-plus babies—when their fur children have no trouble making a connection. Will a YouTube ukulele serenade convince Liam that Jamie's love for him—and their unborn rat children—is for real?

"… a really intense, beautiful "romance" —LoveBytes

RISKY BUSINESS BY ANDI LEE

Veterinarian Dane Vincent is used to being unlucky in love. That's why his crush on new friend Ben is No Big Deal. He's more than happy to swoop to Ben's rescue when he brings a ferret into his practice. It's what friends do—and vets.

Ben Clifford came to Lockstone for a new job and a fresh start. He didn't expect to make friends, never mind a tightknit group of them. They're all wacky and wonderful, and he fits right in, something he's never done before. They even support him when he finds a ferret at work and decides to keep the cute little bundle of joy.

There's just one tiny problem. Ben's house doesn't allow pets.

Moving into Dane's spare room is meant to be temporary, but the more time he spends with him, the less he wants to leave. They connect on a level he's never experienced before, and slowly but surely, the feelings of friendship Ben has for Dane morph into something deeper.

The question is… does he have the courage to act on them?

" The author has taken two wonderful, endearing men and woven around them a fabulous story of self discovery "—LoveBytes